Move On Up

Nick Coventon

authorHOUSE®

AuthorHouse™ UK Ltd.
500 Avebury Boulevard
Central Milton Keynes, MK9 2BE
www.authorhouse.co.uk
Phone: 08001974150

First published by AuthorHouse 6/25/2007

ISBN: 978-1-4259-6990-5 (sc)

Printed in the United States of America
Bloomington, Indiana

This book is printed on acid-free paper.

Acknowledgements

Ady Croasdell for my musical education, Matt at the BMC J2/152 club for van info, the Resource desk at London Transport Museum, AFSHO Research for air base info, Angela Bear at the Air Force Historical Foundation, Dave Rimmer at New Century Soul, the Bank of England museum, Royal Mint museum, my mate Gerry for reading rough transcripts, Gina for the cut-throat, David Evans for help with my nut, my wife Rebecca for her begrudging help with those new fangled computer thingies and Barbara Lynn, Smokey Robinson, Barbara Lewis, Marvin Gaye, Martha Reeves, Otis Redding, Bettye Swann and all the other inspirational artists who have given me so much pleasure.

Authors Note: Not only have I written this novel and carried out my own research but I have also edited and proof read it.

So if there are any mistakes- TOUGH!

Love and happiness to:

Charlotte and Holly
Shaid and Rebecca.

Some of this story is autobiographical
It is up to the reader to decide which bits!

MOVE ON UP

NICK COVENTON

Chapter one

A single bead of sweat ran from the nape of his neck and down his spine. It was the only thing that would have given away his façade of cool, but his young body was covered by an electric blue, two tone tonic mohair suit different colours when viewed from different angles. The suit was a work of art. Three buttons, side vents 7 inches long, black silk lining, worn over a white button down cotton shirt and black inch wide tie. The teenage stylists outfit was finished off with a pair of beautifully soft, black leather slip on moccasins. Perfect dancing shoes which looked the bollocks. Hair short, in a French crop style.

Blurred faces around him were covered in sweat from their gyrations and drug intake, but he was an iceberg. Cool as you like. He moved effortlessly across the dance floor of The Scene club, in a world of his own, cocooned from a room full of people. People greeting and acknowledging him were but a distant echo on his periphery. He was in the centre of the universe. Speeding on Smith Kline Frenchs finest pharmaceuticals, letting the sounds of "Jam Up Twist" by Tommy Ridgely on the Atlantic label no. 2136 rush over him like a tidal wave. Why would he want to be anywhere else?

He was cool and slick and hip baby and he knew it. His attention to detail was spot on. From his hair, clothing and dance moves to his knowledge of record titles and label numbers. He was a Face and life was fucking great.

It wasn't just the Drinamyl, amphetamines nicknamed Purple Hearts making him feel this good which had been gladly supplied by Fat Tony and gladly bought and swallowed by 99% of Soho's subterranean night people. It was more, much more. It was a combination of the Sounds, the Look, the ambience and the location.

1

Many things that you couldn't just throw together and expect the magical effect. It was the RIGHT speed, the RIGHT track, the EXACT RIGHT look.

Everything all coming together at precisely the right time. One fleeting moment which could never be re-produced. There were many, many of these moments every weekend, but one was never the same as another.

Johnny caught a glimpse of his shadow projected on to the sweating wall beside the dance floor. Shit even that was cool man!

Good looking in a hard, street kind of way, dark blond hair, piercing hypnotising blue eyes, slightly flattened boxers nose(although he had never been in the ring) which added to his looks rather than detracted from them.

5ft 10, slim build, not an ounce of fat. Perfect Modernist shape. There *were* no fatties. All that speed and dancing.

He had been at the club since midnight, having previously spent a couple of hours at the Flamingo in Wardour Street watching a set by Georgie Fame, a keyboard playing R&B singer. Not bad for a white guy although he had just watched, not feeling inclined to dance. Perhaps the speed he had picked up in a coffee bar in Dean St. had not kicked in yet.

Johnny glanced down, peering through the gloom at his wristwatch. 3.00 am. The rest of the country safely tucked up in bed, oblivious to this secret world he lived in.

The disc jockey put on a Marvin Gaye song, beautiful Marvin, "Pride and Joy" label number TR54079. A great song but Johnny needed a breather so he left the floor, his place being taken instantly. The temporary gap he created being swallowed up by sweating bodies.

Johnny swaggered through the club to the men's toilet which was packed with pill takers. He dropped a couple more Purple Hearts himself. How many was that? Hard to keep count sometimes. Checking his look in the cracked toilet mirror, he smiled at what he saw and made his way out of the now heaving club.

Once outside in Ham Yard he casually leant against the wall, looking up at the summer night sky, and took in the air.

The Scene could be so hot it was claustrophobic at times and to call the air of Soho fresh, seemed to him ironic, considering the pollution of central London but he did gain some relief outside.

He also liked to spend some time outside surreptitiously checking out what some of the other Faces were wearing. The little courtyard outside the club was full of people he recognized.

Martin and Paul leaning against a wall chatting at a hundred miles an hour. Little Ian buzzing around from group to group, a real up and comer.

Roz, gorgeous Roz, one of two sisters who were always around, looking stylish and very cool.

"Hi Johnny," a voice beside him made him jump but he didn't show it. Keep cool. He turned to see Julie smiling up at him.

Oh fuck, he thought.

She had come onto him Wednesday at La Discotheque and he'd taken her back to the nurses' quarters where she lived. One of the perks of being a Face was the availability of willing females. She wasn't the best screw he'd ever had or the best looking but hey any port in a storm!

"Hey Julie, how's it going?" Johnny asked nonchalantly then flashed what he knew was a winning smile.

"I thought you were going to take me out Thursday night?" she said accusingly and very unimpressed.

Oh fuck, he thought again, was she mad? Thursday was Le Kilt, a top night. Not a night for taking some soppy bird out. She seems to think we're engaged or something just cos she opened her legs for me.

"Yeah, sorry baby, something came up," he replied automatically.

"But Debbie saw you at Le Kilt," she moaned.

She was really getting on Johnny's tits now.

"I know but that was after and I didn't think you would wait," he said, thinking on his feet.

He looked at his watch in an exaggerated manner and said "Hey look at the time baby, I've got to be somewhere, I'm meeting someone, I'll take you out next week," he lied

"When?" she insisted.

Now Johnny knew some guys who would have turned around to her and said "Listen you tart, we fucked, that was it, now fuck off!"

But that wasn't Johnny's style. Besides he never knew when he may be in another storm.

"Don't worry baby I'll call you," and with that he turned on his expensive heels and swaggered off.

"But I'm not on the phone," she wailed after him. But he was lost to the night.

He hadn't lied. Well, not about having to meet someone. He had to meet Steady Eddie.

Left out of Ham Yard, up Windmill St, second left into Beak Street, first right into Marshall Street. Number 16.

Johnny rang the top bell, the one above "French lessons" and waited. Nothing. Johnny rang again, this time holding his finger on the bell for longer. Again nothing.

Where the fuck was he?

Johnny stepped back off the pavement into the road and looked up to the top floor. Lights were on. Weird. Eddie was always about, one of the regulars on the scene, but he had not been seen by anyone for a week.

Disappointed he walked back down the street looking back over his shoulder just in case. Where was he?

Confused, Johnny walked away, lost in thought. Eddie was always about. That's why he was known as Steady Eddie. Regular. Like clockwork. Never missed a night.

Johnny walked and walked. To any observer, aimlessly. Almost directionless.

After ten or so minutes he found himself in St. James's Park and sat himself down on a bench.

He was coming down, he knew. He could feel it. He had noticed in recent weeks that his tolerance level to the amphetamines was rising. Not good. He had taken his first speed of the evening about ten and regularly topped up during the night. But it was wearing off now.

Johnny put his hand into his jacket pocket and felt the reassuring rustle of the wages pack containing several more "Hearts."

He considered taking a couple more but he wasn't going to dance anymore tonight and he didn't want to be chewing the inside of his mouth till 10 in the a.m. Not good.

For the umpteenth time that night he looked at his watch. 5 a.m. Time really does fly when you're having fun and especially when you're speeding.

Johnny's walks always ended up here. St. James's Park. He didn't know how or why. He just wandered and he always ended here.

It was a good place to think. Something most people he knew never even attempted. They just carried on. Not thinking about what was next.

Things were changing. He was looking at the next stage. How long had he been a Modernist? Forever it seemed. People were calling them "Mods" now, an abbreviation he didn't like. It seemed to sum up what was happening to his world. It was being watered down. Standards were dropping. It was still hard keeping up. Not with the "numbers" but with his rivals. You had to keep one step ahead. New styles, hard to find Soul records. Little touches. Details.

Johnny reached inside his jacket and retrieved his silver cigarette lighter and his pack of Gauloises. Even when there was no one to impress he still, by nature, flicked the bottom of pack which produced a cigarette and placed it into the corner of his mouth. James Bond style. Flicking the lighter, his face momentarily lit up, and he touched his French cigarette with the flame.

Taking a deep draw, he eased back against the bench and blew smoke into the night air. Sun would be up soon. He loved watching the sun come up. Always different colours and patterns. Original, like the life he led.

Although he loved watching the start of a new day it always left him feeling a little depressed, knowing a dawn of a new day made him that little bit older and a day nearer having to make a decision. And a day further from his life he knew and loved.

His whole lifestyle was about changing and finding something new. New styles, moves, records. That's why he loved it so much, but now he was scared of the massive change that he had to confront. "A change is gonna come" as Sam Cooke had said.

Johnny wanted this lifestyle to go on forever but he knew that was just not possible. People he knew had already fallen by the wayside. Burnt out by trying to keep on top on office boy or messenger's wages.

Drinking gallons of water before shopping at the weekend because its bloating effect stopped them feeling hungry, so allowing more cash to be spent on "The Life". People unable to stay young, all of a sudden feeling a hundred years old. Just like their parents. Settled down, house, married, sprog on the way. The normal life that terrified Johnny.

Where could he go from here? He still wanted the clothes, the night time existence, but he wanted more. He needed more. He wasn't going to get it on his earnings plus tips and fiddles.

Johnny had a few ideas. Most people he knew had big ideas, especially when speeding. Ideas of how to get the "Good Life" but they were full of shit and had no ambition other than the coming weekends highs. But he was different. Ambition burnt deep into his soul. Johnny wanted the high life. Whatever it took he would do to get it.

CHAPTER 2

The stolen silver S Type Jaguar 3.8 roared past the dark blue security van and swerved across its path, forcing the van driver to take avoiding action, yanking the steering wheel to the left. The van mounted the pavement, narrowly avoiding a pedestrian and ploughed into a shop front.

Three balaclava clad figures leapt from the Jag. Two of them brandishing sawn off shotguns, the third carried a sledgehammer. The fourth member of the gang, the driver, stayed in the car, his gloved fingers nervously tapping the steering wheel. He chewed gum and scanned the area for interference.

With one huge blow the sledgehammer was smashed through the van driver's side window shattering glass over the man inside, covering him in dozens of tiny cuts.

The door was yanked open and the driver pulled roughly from the van and thrown to the floor. The hooded man towering over him formed a terrifying sight and the words he shouted did nothing to calm the situation.

"KEYS," he screamed "OR I'LL BLOW YOUR FUCKING KNEECAPS OFF!"

The van driver's partner had also been grabbed from the van and was viciously punched in the face by another of the masked men, knocking out his front teeth and splitting his lip open. The taste of his own blood and his fear made him gag and he fell to his knees. His assailant sharply brought the butt of the shotgun down onto his exposed skull, splitting it wide open, rendering him unconscious. Witnessing this brutal attack on his colleague had the intended effect and persuaded the van driver to hand the keys over. Not that he needed any encouragement; he was already beginning to gasp for breath. He had fumbled into his uniform pocket and passed the keys over with a severely trembling hand to his impatient attacker.

"Lay flat on your face you cunt or I'll fucking do ya."

He did as he was told and the two thieves ran to the back of the van. Quickly slipping both keys into their respective locks, the robbers heard the satisfying sound of the tumblers falling into place and swung open the heavy door. Another key opened the inner doors which were flung open.

The third and final guard stood in the back of the van readying himself to defend the precious cargo but upon being confronted by the hooded armed men in front of him, he thought better of it and declared.

"Alright lads, I'm on your side, you'll get no trouble from me," and with that he allowed himself to be pulled from the back of the van saving himself from nothing more than a gloved slap across the face.

"On the floor," one thief growled.

"Right you are," the grateful man replied, and did as he was told.

With the guards nullified the masked men formed a chain and started lifting bags of cash from the van and loading them into the waiting getaway car. Once the van had been emptied of the cash bags, the thieves grabbed the stricken guards and tossed them into the back of the van and locked the door behind them.

The Jag boot was slammed and the robbers jumped back into the car, first gear was engaged and the car screeched away. The whole thing had lasted just under 4 minutes.

Another successful day at the office for the chaps.

As they sped through the streets of South London making good their escape, balaclavas were removed and sweat wiped from brows. Checking the roads behind them for any pursuant, they chewed gum, excitedly chattering amongst themselves and bursting into nervous laughter as gags were swapped. The only one not talking was the driver whose concentration was absolute. His eyes fixed to the road ahead, expertly changing gears and touching the brakes when necessary. Avoiding other road users with the skill of the professional race driver he used to be.

Once sure they had no company, the driver slowed to a more respectable pace and gently cruised the streets until they arrived at the change car, slowly driving past, checking that all was well and no one was about, especially Old Bill.

On their third trip past the parked car the men were satisfied all was okay and they glided up to the kerb. The driver reversed up to the rear of the change car, a non-descript Austin Wolseley. Nice family car. A space of about a yard was left between the car boots.

The thieves had removed their work gear, blue boiler suits, to reveal a nice line in understated casual wear although they still left their gloves on. Professional.

Quickly, but without rushing, the men exited the Jag, opened both car boots and began transferring the bags of cash. Once this was accomplished the thieves, leaving the boiler suits and balaclavas in the Jag but taking the shooters and hammer, climbed into the green change car.

The wheelman always got in last. He still had one last job to do. He unscrewed the petrol cap on the silver S type and stuffed a rolled up rag into the opening, leaving a few inches showing.

The driver lit his cigarette lighter and held the flame up to the cloth. The cloth lit instantly and the flame quickly made its way into the tank. The petrol ignited and a huge explosion filled the air, leaving the once majestic car a burning wreck. The acrid smell of burning rubber, leather seats and metal drifted down the deserted street. All evidence burning, rendered useless by the flames. The Wolseley already several streets away before the explosion attracted onlookers and 999 callers.

The Wolseley sedately made its way to the gangs lock up. One of a set of railway arches arrived at via a warren of grubby backstreets in Lewisham, South East London. The huge door was opened and the car rolled in, the door shutting quickly behind it.

Job done.

The bags of money were removed from the car and placed in a specially concealed strong box under the floor and covered with a heavy stove cooker. They would have a count up and share out their ill-gotten gains tomorrow.

The three men who hit the pavement during the raid were Frank Saunders, 28, 6ft, brown hair, brown eyes, handsome, a real ladies man. Loved Frank Sinatra. And "The Good Life."

Alfie Booth, 29, 5ft 10, black hair, blue eyes, happy-go-lucky, a permanent grin played around his lips. Always taking the piss and having a laugh, especially at the expense of:

Jimmy Sewell 32, the "old man" of the group, 5ft 10, balding fair hair, always saying he was going to retire. One more big coup, then down to Bournemouth and a nice cottage by the sea.

The others knew this was rubbish. They knew as sure as a bear shits in the woods that he could never retire, he would miss the buzz. That high they all felt after pulling off a good 'un.

The driver was Tommy Newman, much sought after for his fantastic driving skills which were once used on the race tracks of Britain and Europe. Unfortunately for Tommy he wasn't born with a silver spoon in his mouth like most of the other drivers. Snobby little rich kids who got all the breaks. No, he had had to do it the hard way using just his skill and determination. A skill which put all the other drivers in the shade. But in the world of motor racing it was money and who you knew that counted, not your skill. You had to buy your way in. His resentment burnt deep.

He was a loner by nature and by inclination. A legacy of his life alone behind the wheel. Although he came from the same tough background as the other men his life had taken a different path. Dedicating himself to his racing, suffering setback after setback, seeing others progress who were not fit to lick his racing boots until he finally had had enough and knowing Frankie Saunders from school days he began to apply his skills to screeching through the streets in high powered getaway cars. What was he supposed to do, drive a fucking taxi?

After a piece of business, he always went his own way, leaving the others to do his celebrating for him. They always tried to persuade him to join them, but he never did. Preferring his own company and besides he didn't drink. Too many careers had been destroyed by booze and old habits die hard. Although the others took the piss it was only in a light hearted way because he commanded the utmost respect for transferring them safely away from the scene of their crimes like no other driver in London could do and they didn't want to lose him. Other firms tried to poach him but he wasn't interested. He trusted his comrades.

His comrades were all career criminals from the shitty backstreets of South London. Streets which were replicated all over London and every other city and town in Britain. Streets which smelt of poverty and dejection, where if you were born in them you were condemned to a life of struggle. The only way out was through football, boxing or villainy. And it was a lot easier being a villain than a footballer. Unless you were a Bobby Moore. The chaps knew class when they saw it and the lad had class.

The gang had all been brought up in poverty. Abusive fathers, broken homes, alcoholic mothers, unemployment. Every piece of shit that could be thrown at them had been by the time any of them had reached the age of bunking off from secondary school.

Their lives had all led similar patterns. Truancy, petty theft, street gangs, fights. Then stealing cars, tearing around the streets until they ran out of petrol. Approved school, beatings, borstal. Making a stand, bigger crimes, prison. An apprenticeship of crime.

Each visit to Her Majesty's gleaned more knowledge and information. Small crimes brought small times. Two months, six months. But each period of incarceration gave them more insight into the lives they had chosen to lead.

The most important thing they learnt was that mistakes cost you your liberty. The only way to get your collar felt was by fucking up. Fucking up and trusting the wrong people. Their world was full of grasses and long before they met each other they all vowed to only work with people they could trust. Totally.

There is always a moment of fate that turns individuals into partnerships, whether it be Morcambe and Wise, Burke and Hare or Taylor and Burton and in the case of three South London villains it was no different.

It wasn't the northern club scene; foggy 19th century Edinburgh or a Hollywood movie set that brought these three men together. It was a smoky, non-descript snooker club in the South London borough of Wandsworth.

The three men had crossed paths briefly in the past. Prison and in the various pubs and clubs their kind frequented and they were all on nodding terms. And as was the way with these type of men they had all made discreet enquiries about each other. The feedback was good.

On this particular night the three men had all turned up independently of each other at "Frames" snooker hall in Wandsworth High St. An area which was off their usual manor of South East London.

Frank Saunders walked through the entrance, then up the stairs and through the double doors to the club. He was there to pick up racetrack winnings from a Clapham bookie who he felt had been avoiding him and this was one of the man's regular haunts.

Jimmy was there to meet a man who had an E-Type for sale and Alfie Booth was there spending the evening playing snooker with an old friend who lived in the nearby Putney area.

Jimmy was standing at the bar nursing a large scotch and Alfie was into his fifth frame of the night, leading 3-1, when the double doors swung open and Frank Saunders walked in.

As if a switch had been thrown by some invisible hand the atmosphere became electric with every head turning towards the new arrival. Frank Saunders was known. Saunders calmly made his way to the bar at the back of the hall, eyes following him all the way.

"Whisky," he snapped to the barman and nodded recognition to Jimmy Sewell, who nodded back. Gradually the hum of conversation returned to the room and the sound of snooker balls clicked again.

The two men at the bar struck up a casual conversation, which continued for some minutes until the entrance doors swung open again.

Two large men with re-arranged faces walked in. One held the door open and another smaller man walked in followed by a fourth, as large and ugly as the first two.

The smallest man of the group was Bert Thomas, the man Saunders had come to see. Someone, looking for brownie points with Thomas had slipped out of the club and raced round to a pub nearby where the bookie was drinking. A phone call was made and the extra muscle duly arrived to escort Thomas to the snooker hall.

The bookie knew of Saunders reputation for violence and as he had no intention of paying him what he owed he decided to bring along some company.

With his brutish companions and helped by a belly full of alcohol he was full of bravado as he made his way to confront the man who had sought him out.

With his minders flanking him he approached the man at the bar and stopped a few feet away.

"Looking for me Frank?" he said.

Saunders leaning casually against the bar, eased himself up to his full height and replied,

"You owe me money." All very matter of fact.

"Well we have a bit of a problem there me old son," said Thomas

"What's that then?" replied Saunders

"I ain't fucking paying ya," said Thomas, spitting as he said it.

All snooker matches now ceased and the double doors now became the exit for a couple of players who didn't want to know.

Alfie Booth's opponent suddenly became very thirsty and said to him.

"Fancy a pint Alf?"

"Yea," he replied as his mate made his way towards safety. But Booth stayed where he was.

"Come on, down the Nags Head," he called.

"You go, I'll have a pint here, I like the atmosphere," and with that his pal shot off.

Back at the bar Saunders turned to the man standing beside him.

"Best take off yourself mate, this is gonna get messy."

Jimmy stayed put "Nah, I think I'll stick around," he said.

"Nice one," countered Saunders with a grin of appreciation.

Turning back to the bookie he was confronted by one of the minders who had eased in front of his employer.

"Look Saunders," he growled, "you ain't getting no money so why don't ya fuck off to where you come from?"

Saunders leant forward "Out the way or I'll kick your teeth so far down your throat, you'll be eating your dinner with your arse."

"Nice one," said Alfie approvingly, and the group at the bar turned to frown into the darkened hall. As the men turned back to face the interlopers at the bar Saunders struck with a speed that surprised everyone in the place. His right fist smashed into the face of the man directly in front, spreading his nose all across his face, following it up with a knee to the bollocks and completely ruining the man's day by savagely kicking him in the right shin with his heavy brogue shoes snapping the bone like a dry twig.

The man fell to the floor screaming in pain and was kicked unconscious by Jimmy Sewell, keen to get involved.

The room exploded as it all kicked off. Bert Thomas's bottle completely went and he backed off leaving the rough stuff to the others. The second heavy took his stricken mates place as the other locals in the hall moved quickly to join in on the action. Five men in all rushed over to get stuck in, joining the two remaining heavies in seemingly favourable odds. Seeing the men at the bar being outnumbered, the other South London villain swung into action. Grabbing a snooker cue and the black ball he hurled the 7 pointer at the head of one of the pack, making contact with a hollow thud knocking him onto his arse, unconscious. He then snapped the cue in half, discarding the thin end, and waded into the pack who were not expecting an attack from their rear. Skulls were cracked with ferocity, Alfie putting the cue to a more violent purpose for which it had been intended.

Frankie and Jimmy charged into their attackers. Kicking, butting and generally inflicting damage on anything in their way. Seizing one unfortunate, Sewell grabbed him by the ears, locked his teeth onto the man's nose and clamped them together, twisting and shaking his head like an enraged shark. Jimmy Sewell pulled his head back with force, his teeth still shut tightly together. The mans nose separated from its rightful position, shooting a gush of blood across the floor and leaving a gaping hole in the middle of his face, causing him to scream in agony and pass out with shock and pain.

It was carnage; the bookies' minders were completely outclassed in the violence department and the local snooker playing toughs had never encountered such ferocity, being used to a bit of fisticuffs with other third rate 'erberts.'

The action had only taken a matter of minutes. As usual to the participants-especially those on the receiving end- it had seemed a lot longer. The three victors stood over their badly battered opponents. The only sounds were their heavy breathing and the groans and whimpering of those laying on the floor who had not been beaten into unconsciousness.

Looking around the carnage which had taken place, the three men grinned at each other, knowing that amongst all this mayhem they had created a friendship that would endure.

"How much did that slag owe you?" enquired Sewell.

"Twenty quid," Saunders replied.

"Twenty quid? All this for a score?"

"It's the principal involved. You can't let people take liberties. They'll think you're soft."

Jimmy Sewell and Alfie Booth looked at each other, then at Frank Saunders.

"Fuck me," the two men said in unison and all three burst out laughing.

Now, a mere four years later they would often look back and reminisce about that night, how they became a team.

Their rise had been spectacular and were now in a position of respect and authority in their illicit world. Their first coup, a mail van, had cemented them and from there they constantly grafted. That mail van in Bayswater lead to more mail vans, wage snatches, jewellers and ultimately the big one- crossing the pavement- banks. Any job was considered as long as the money was worth the risk.

They worked like a finely tuned engine. Close knit, mouths shut, no outsiders. EVER.

They watched, waited and listened. Picked up bits of information everywhere.

But they always did their own work. Some teams did jobs passed to them from another source in return for a flat fee or a cut, but they always passed. Some jobs seemed too good to be true. They were never tempted. Too good to be true jobs, sure things, normally ended tits up!

That was why they were out celebrating another result.

That evening they met up at the Duke of Argyll. 'The Duke' in Berwick St. W1. Their usual post match celebration starting point.

Saunders was there first, and apart from the barman, was the only person in the place. He was drinking a pint of lager when the other two men arrived together.

"What you 'aving?" asked Frank.

His pals requested pints which were duly poured.

The three thieves raised their glasses and clinked them together.

"A right result," said Jimmy, each man taking a long sip before they all burst out laughing.

They spent the next hour reliving the day's events with relish. Reliving the excitement, the buzz that only this activity could bring. Not once feeling remorse or regret about the victims of their violent attack. The guards stood between them and their prize, they had to be removed. Simple as that.

Each man had been speeding on amphetamines when they carried out the robbery. It was a necessary part of their equipment. Along with balaclavas and shooters.

When Jimmy put his hand into his jacket pocket and produced more speed the others eagerly accepted and swallowed several pills each washed down with more lager. It was going to be a long night.

CHAPTER 3

Monday morning, come down time. Fucking nightmare.

From being so high in a different universe, and then to come down so far. Reality.

It wasn't just the physical come down from the speed. It was the psychological aspect. He had been up for the whole weekend. 48 hours non stop. Dancing, posing, shopping, sharing his time with Smokey, Marvin, Otis, Cecil Gee. From feeling like a million dollars to nothing.

Monday morning 7 o'clock . Up for work. No choice. He had to work to pay for the life. He hated it.

Into the shower, dries himself off and selects his clothing for the day.

Working as a messenger for an import/export company in Holborn just about kept him going. Just about. Basic pay was shit, bumped up with a few fiddles and a bit of petty theft. It took all his imagination to stay on top. At least he could still wear the gear at work. Some people he knew were painters or bricklayers. How could they feel the same when they were at work covered in shit?

Johnny could go to work and still be Modernist. Toned down, not his best gear but still cool. The clothes he wore to work put his *bosses* in the sartorial shade let alone his colleagues.

Every day, one item of his clothing probably cost more than his boss's whole suit, shirt, tie etc.

Every day the clothes he wore stood him apart from the others. They were wary of him. Intimidated.

"Morning boy," his boss greeted him with practised indifference.

"Morning Mr.Clark," Johnny replied. "Prick" he wanted to say.

"Morning prickface," he really wanted to say. Boy? Who did he think he was? Didn't he know who he was dealing with?

"Take these down to Sotheby's and collect the transportation documents for the Lots Mr. Cavendish successfully bid on. Then go over to him at Ovington Square and drop them off for his signature."

His boss continued "Take the money from petty cash and take a taxi. Time is of the essence. Mr Cavendish wants everything done as quickly as possible."

Nice one thought Johnny, use my scooter and keep the dough. One of the perks. Plus Mrs Cavendish was a bit of alright and always flirted with him. Today might be his lucky day and she might drop her knickers.

Johnny smiled to himself at his carnal thoughts. Optimism was one of Johnny's strong points.

Taking two envelopes from his boss's secretary he swaggered through the front door of the company building and on to the street. He didn't know what was in the envelopes and he didn't care.

Johnny sauntered to the end of the street and turned right. Out of sight of the office.

Twenty yards up the next road was his scooter parked up on the pavement.

Lambretta TV175 series3. White with chrome side panels. Sleek, stylish lines, shining in the early morning sun. It was THE scooter to have. A Faces scooter.

Johnny put the key in and turned on the ignition. Sitting astride his machine he kicked her into life.

Shades on, clutch in, first gear, clutch out gradually and right hand pulled back on the accelerator. The scooter flew off its' stand, down the kerb and on his way.

He had been told not to drive off from his stand, weakened the springs or something, but he always did because it looked so cool.

He just had to replace the springs more than most, that's all.

Out of the end of Drury Lane, High Holborn, into Shaftesbury Avenue. Round the Circus. Neon wasn't the same in the sunshine. Piccadilly. Right into New Bond St. No.34-35.

Pulling up outside the fine art auctioneers Johnny eased his Lambretta back onto its stand.

He sauntered through the grand entrance and up to the reception desk.

"Allo darling, here to pick up Mr. Cavendish's docs."

The receptionist looked up, recognised Johnny and just about swooned.

She was 20-22 not bad looking, a bit like Audrey Hepburn. Only a bit. Well she did have black hair!

Johnny gave her his best smile and leaned against the counter.

He knew he made an impression, his blue eyes bore into hers, he was good looking and he knew it and he knew the effect he was having.

"Just a moment," she said, trying to appear casual. Her insides doing somersaults.

Johnny had seen the flush of red invade her cheeks and he instantly knew.

I'm in here, he thought.

He logged the look and took the documents requested.

"See you soon sweetheart," he finished.

Walking back into the sunlight, buoyed by the receptionist's desire, he put his sunglasses back on and climbed aboard his scooter, keyed it and kicked it into life and was away, heading south down New Bond St.

Right into Piccadilly.

Twice around Hyde Park Corner just for the pose.

He knew people clocked him, watched him go by. It felt good and his spirits rose. Down Knightsbridge. Brompton Road, past Harrods, great windows to watch yourself in. Left into Ovington Gardens and on into Ovington Square.

His journey had taken 15 minutes. The sun was out and he felt alive again. It was always sunny. Riding through London, capital of the world. No mirrors, no extras, nothing to take attention away from him. People watched as he cruised by. Knowing what he was. Not knowing what it was all about. Shades on.

No.14, he knew the address well, having visited it on many occasions to deliver documents for Mr.Cavendish and to flirt with his sexy wife. Cavendish was a multi millionaire, rich git!

Johnny knocked on the front door and took a step back, awaiting a response and anticipating another perk of the job. The eternal optimist.

The door opened and as he had hoped, it was by Mrs Cavendish. Trophy wife. Cor!

Five ft six or seven, blonde (dyed) tanned (St. Tropez) knocking on a bit (29-30) but still looking good. Especially in what she was wearing today. A tight white tennis dress, bare feet, her toenails expensively polished.

"Hello Mrs Cavendish, I'm delivering forms for your husband and need his signature."

"Hello Johnny, come in," she replied with a smile, turning to walk down the long hall.

Johnny followed her, watching her well shaped arse wiggle up one flight of stairs and into the kitchen. Kitchen on the first floor. Only for the seriously rich thought Johnny.

"My husband is at a meeting at the moment, he will be gone quite some time," she said.

"That's a shame, I need these signed."

It was only 10.30 in the morning but she had already had a few judging by her appearance. A bit flushed, bit giggly.

"Give them to me and I'll sign them," she offered.

Johnny opened the envelope and took three pieces of paper out and laid them on the large pine kitchen table.

"You need to sign here, here and here please Mrs Cavendish," indicated Johnny in the appropriate places, as he recognized the standard documents.

She wobbled over and stood beside him. So close he could smell her. Perfume and vodka. Johnny copped a sneaky peak down her top and was admiring the view when she spoke.

"Call me Laura," she said and patted herself down slowly "I don't seem to have a pen on me," she continued, looking Johnny directly in the eyes.

"I don't suppose you can give me one, can you?" she asked, wetting her lips with her tongue.

Johnny, never one to pass up on such a blatant come on, took a step forward and felt her breath on his face.

The moment of truth, thought Johnny, she hadn't backed off. She was obviously up for it.

"Course I can," he said with a smile, leaning forward and placed his lips on hers.

Her tongue slid into his mouth searching for his as he pressed his body against hers. His cock stiffened as he put his hand on her tit and squeezed gently.

She had her arms around his neck and she let out a groan as Johnny's left hand ran over her arse, his fingers clawing up the bottom of her dress.

Johnny's fingers moved under her tennis dress and expertly hooked into her knickers and slid them down her shapely, tanned thighs.

Laura's knickers fell to her ankles and she squealed with pleasure as Johnny slid a finger into her. She was soaking.

Mrs Cavendish frantically kissed, bit and licked Johnny's neck as she fumbled for his fly.

Fucking hell, thought Johnny, she's keen, as his cock grew. But at the back of his mind he was hoping she wouldn't fuck his trousers up.

Finally releasing his cock, she gasped as she wrapped her fingers around it and moaned, "You're so much bigger than my husband I've been dying for this for ages. I bet you know how to use it too," she said panting as she flicked her knickers away from her ankles.

"There's only one way to find out," Johnny said, fighting the desire to take off his trousers and fold them neatly over the back of a chair.

He cringed inside as his trousers fell to the floor, a crumpled heap at his ankles. The married woman slid down Johnny's body onto her knees and looked up at him as she opened her lips and licked his cock from his balls to its tip, slowly and deliberately.

These posh birds are a damn sight filthier than working class chicks, thought Johnny as the posh bird on her knees slurped hungrily on his working class knob.

Johnny groaned in ecstasy as she took the whole of his cock into her mouth and sucked.

Fucking hell, thought Johnny, I'm gonna drown her in a minute.

At that moment, as though she knew he was about to shoot his load into her mouth she stood up and undid the buttons on the front of her dress exposing her large firm tits.

Johnny instantly lowered his mouth to one of her nipples and sucked like a new born baby causing Mrs Cavendish to shudder with delight.

The millionaire's wife extricated her tit from Johnny's hungry mouth and laid herself back on the table, propped up on her elbows and begged for it.

"Fuck me, come on fuck me," she pleaded.

Being an obliging sort of fellow, Johnny positioned himself between her glistening, damp thighs and slid his cock deep into her.

Oh well, he thought as he pumped away, hope she knows where the iron is as he looked down at his trousers scrunched up around his ankles.

She was like a woman possessed, screaming and scratching, biting and crying. Her fingernails dug into his back under his white short sleeve button down shirt.

Hope she don't draw blood, it'll fuck me shirt right up, worried Johnny.

She reached yet another orgasm as he shot his load, and collapsed on top of her, the two of them panting and sweating from their exertions.

This was always an awkward moment Johnny found.

How to extricate oneself from a satisfied woman and bid a retreat without appearing too hasty. But once he'd come, he just wanted to get out. It was always the same.

However on this occasion he didn't need to fabricate an excuse. Fate handed him his exit card.

Now Johnny had been in some dodgy, frightening situations. Threatened with knives in Soho alleys, nearly forced off his scooter by psychotic lorry drivers. But nothing, absolutely nothing compared to the sound of a husbands key in the front door.

"What's that?" Johnny asked, easing himself slightly off his latest conquest.

"The front door," she replied helpfully. "It must be my husband."

"FUCKING HELL," Johnny whispered, "You said he was out all day," he added, panic gripping him as he leapt off the worried looking Mrs Cavendish.

Bending down, he pulled up his creased and crumpled trousers that were now covered in dust, fanny juice and spunk from his dripping cock.

Looking down he groaned, "Oh shit, this is getting worse."

As any form of underwear spoilt the line of his trousers he didn't wear pants so when he hastily pulled up his trousers and yanked up his zip his day just got worse. A searing pain coursed through his bollocks which were half in, half out. But the sound of steps walking up the hall caused him to focus his attention on getting the fuck out of there.

His irritation increased when the stupid bitch hissed, "Quick, quick, hide. My husband's home."

"Hide?..........hide where you stupid cow?" he hissed back, looking around the kitchen, "In the fucking oven?"

"Out the window, quick," she helped.

Johnny rushed to the window and observed that they were two floors up as all these houses had basements.

The sound of footsteps coming up the stairs convinced Johnny to forget about being cool and he fumbled with the lock to the sash window. Finally releasing it, he slid the window up.

The ominous footsteps got closer and as Johnny contemplated his next move Mrs Cavendish retrieved her discarded knickers and attempted to appear like she hadn't just been fucked on the kitchen table.

Johnny took a precautionary peek out of the window and said to himself.

"I am never going to fuck a married woman again. In fact I'm never going to fuck anything again. It's just too much agg."

He gingerly climbed on to the stone window sill, six inches wide and balanced himself, looking across the yawning gap between his present position and a rusting drainpipe which was his only route out.

His quick evaluation of his desperate situation told him that he had to jump from the window sill onto the drainpipe. Then shin down the pipe till he was level with the top of the high garden wall. Another leap, this time of about eight feet on to the wall and finally from the top of the wall to the street below. Piece of cake!

It was high. About forty foot up. The kitchen door opening was just the encouragement he needed and he leapt for the pipe.

Johnny just about reached the pipe and grabbed on for dear life. His desert boots dug into the brickwork and his hands wrapped around the rusting metal. His face pressed up against the pipe sweated profusely as his whole body shook with the effort of clinging on.

The window from where he had made his exit was still open and he heard Mr Cavendish's voice as he entered the room.

"Hello my dear," the voice said.

"Daaarling," the wife said with exaggerated fondness, "I thought you were going to be gone all day."

"Finished early my love." Then a pause. "You look ever so hot."

"Me? Oh yes darling, I've been exercising."

Johnny, outside on the drainpipe, raised his eyes heavenward. Silly cow, he thought.

"I thought you had a tennis lesson booked?"

His wife stammered her reply "I...I...err...well I didn't fancy it."

There was another pause before he replied "Well I bloody well fancy it. You look bloody sexy in that gear my dear....come here I want you right now."

The unfaithful wife simpered "Oh darling, are you going to be naughty with me?"

"You know what I like my dear." said Cavendish.

Then Johnny heard his most recent conquest, in her best little girl's voice say "Does my big man want me to put it in my mouth?"

Johnny nearly lost his grip as he heard the millionaires zip being undone.

"Oooh....you're SOOO big," he heard her say and then heard an array of slurping and sucking noises.

Fucking charming. Dirty slag, Johnny thought with moral indignation. Unable to listen to anymore he eyed up his next move.

"OH YES, OH YES," erupted Mr Cavendish. Johnny could stand it no longer and slid awkwardly down the pipe until he was level with the garden wall and throwing caution to the wind, leapt.

His desert boot clad feet missed the top of the wall by inches and his body hit the brickwork full on and started sliding down the face. In desperation his fingers stretched out and he felt his nails dig into the top course of bricks. Johnny's body hung full length against the moss covered bricks for seconds until he mustered all his strength and inch by green slimy inch clawed his way upwards.

It seemed to take forever, but he finally dragged his aching body on to the top of the wall and sat there for several minutes catching his breath.

Eventually he leapt the remaining twenty feet down to the pavement and turned to look ruefully at the window to the kitchen above.

Johnny looked down at himself and surveyed the damage. Desert boots fucked. Sta Prest trousers fucked. Shirt totally fucked, covered in blood and moss, collar all over the place.

What a state, he thought and quickly looked around to see if anyone could see the condition he was in.

Thankfully, it seemed nobody had seen his escape and leap from the top of the wall.

Burying his head in his chest, he scurried down the side street to the front of the house from where he had just escaped. Checking the square for witnesses to his shame he jumped onto his scooter, inserted the key and kick started it.

This time instead of cruising at a steady speed so he could be seen by the public, he throttled back and tore off around the square, going south, head down, hoping and praying no one he knew saw him.

He didn't head back to the office, but south across the river to the safety of his bed-sit at the Elephant. Feeling as self conscious as he could remember.

Arriving home in record time, Johnny dismounted before the engine had died, left the scooter in the backyard of the house, not in the shed and slammed the street door behind him. Then he bounded up the two flights of stairs and into his room. Sanctuary.

Johnny heaved a huge sigh of relief and collapsed on to his single bed. Staring up at the cracked ceiling he thought he'd have some explaining to do at work in the morning but he was too exhausted to think up anything plausible now and drifted off to sleep all the way through till Tuesday. Catching up.

The next morning Johnny woke feeling battered and bruised as if he'd come to after a long weekend of pilling and dancing and being attacked by sabre toothed tigers.

But it wasn't Monday but Tuesday and there were no prehistoric animals about.

If his body felt damaged then his ego felt a lot worse as he remembered yesterday's traumatic events.

His arse and back scratched by those expensive nails. Face and fingers bruised from his leap onto pipe-work and wall. He winced and gingerly felt his bollocks and was relieved that everything seemed to be in order despite their confrontation with his zipper. He'd have to have a wank in a while just to make sure.

And worst of all his clothes, which he had slept in. Something he never did but it didn't seem to matter just this once.

What a disaster, he didn't even get a tip.

7.00 a.m. into the communal shower on the landing below. Lukewarm as usual. Still, it felt good this morning as he pressed his face against the cold tiles, the water washing away his negative thoughts and the filth from his body.

Things have to change, he thought as he climbed out of the shower and dried himself down.

With his towel wrapped around his waist he padded back to his room as the rest of the house came to life.

Back in his room he discarded his towel and stood in front of his full length mirror and admired his naked form. Even without the clothes he looked good.

Johnny's attention shifted from the mirror and took in the room that was home.

Home, 1 single bed, wash basin. View of the gasworks from the cracked window. Still, it was cheap. Three of the four walls were taken up with clothes rails. Packed. One side casual. Sta Prest, Chinos, Fred Perry's, Knitted tops, crew necks, short sleeve button downs.

The other side contained suits. Half a dozen, beautiful colours and material. Mohair, two tone, checks, pin stripes. Smart shirts, tab collar (his favourite, the way it lifted the tie forward, cool), long sleeved button downs, ties.

Under this was his shoe racks. Black, brown, beige. Slip ons, lace ups, lattice top, Loafers. Mock croc. Beautiful.

Next to the bed his Dansette record player and record collection. The soundtrack to his life.

Stax, Motown, Atlantic,Volt. Smokey, Etta, The Impressions, The Showmen. Soul, jazz and Blues, with a little bit of Ska. Secret music, known only to a select few. No Hit Parade shit.

Johnny carefully selected a 45 and placed it on the turntable. The needle hit the vinyl.

"WHOO," Muddy Walters intro shout to Mannish Boy always made him jump even after the first couple of bars. He loved the old blues guys and this was his current pick me up fave. It was old now but what a song.

As the classic blues riff echoed round his room, he danced over to his casual rack.

"I'm a man, a hoochie coochie man."

"Yeah," sang Johnny, "I'm a natural born lover's man," mimicking the blues legend.

His spirits lifted, he selected a pale blue, short sleeved button down, black sta prest, and loafers topped off with a white cardigan. Back to the mirror to sort his hair, easily done and knew he was ready.

He gave himself a wry grin as he remembered yesterday's events. What a lark, he thought. All his shame and embarrassment forgotten. It had now become a good story to recount (without the un-cool bits of course).

Outside, on the scoot and away. As he rode he concocted his story for his non appearance back at the office the previous day. Once he had decided on his fabrication he settled down and enjoyed the journey. The sun shone and he wore his shades. He was cool. Back on top. You don't become a Face without being able to cope with a little adversity.

CHAPTER 4

The Wolseley change car had had its plates changed even though it was just a couple miles to the scrapyard where for a drink the owner Billy Milligan would reduce the car to a two foot square cube. No evidence.

Back at the lock-up the stolen money had been shared equally. Each man receiving a sum of £2000. Not bad considering the average wage was £960 a year and a two bedroom house would set you back about six grand.

The four thieves then went their separate ways in order to stash their loot and to go about their daily lives until the next job.

The driver Tommy Newman went to work at the garage he owned in New Cross, doing services and MOT's (legal)

Getting his hands covered in grease was a way of life and he loved it. This wasn't just a cover to explain his income. He loved cars and it broke his heart when he had to torch getaway cars. A necessary evil.

Jimmy Sewell opened up his antique shop, put on a sensible cardigan and waited for customers he didn't need.

Alfie Booth headed for the racetrack to increase or blow his earnings. He won enough to name his profession as "gambler."

Frank Saunders took an altogether different approach. First thing in the morning he drove his Jensen Healey 3000 to the car showroom he owned in Chelsea. He parked round the back yard and walked to the street entrance.

The huge plate glass windows that met the pavement reflected his approach. Dressed casually but smart in suede bomber jacket, black crew neck, cream chinos and desert boots he carried an expensive leather holdall.

If he had intended working today he would have been suited up but he had just visited to drop something off and pick something up.

Saunders opened the door and the dazzle off the highly polished paintwork and chrome on the E-Types, Astons and other top marques nearly blinded him.

"Morning Tony," he said to his showroom manager.

"Morning Mr Saunders," the showroom manager replied.

"I'm only here to leave the log book for that yellow E-Type and to pick up the grey DB5. Sort the keys out and get one of the lads to get my suitcase out of the Jensen and stick it in the Aston."

Tony sent one of the showroom lads out to the yard and retrieved the keys for the Aston Martin DB5 Convertible from the office.

"Going away Mr. Saunders?" he enquired as he handed the keys to his boss.

Saunders grunted in the affirmative and informed him that he would be gone for a couple of weeks.

With that Frank Saunders unlocked the car he had chosen for his journey and placed the holdall on the passenger seat. He ordered one of his staff to open the large, floor to ceiling glass doors and fired up the engine. The twin exhausts roared, first gear was engaged and Saunders gently drove out into the busy Chelsea traffic.

The businessman/thief patted the leather holdall lovingly, put on his sunglasses and began his journey.

The leather bag contained two casual t-shirts covering two hundred pounds in Sterling.

Money from the last job, to be spent on living the good life.

In his suede jacket pocket was his passport and ticket.

The DB5 made its' way through South West London down Chelsea Embankment across Battersea bridge, through Battersea, Vauxhall and onto the Old Kent Road. Down to Dover.

Passport control was always a bit dicey, carrying the money he was, but he had slipped the cash into the secret compartment he had had made in his suitcase and was waved through without a problem. Just a few admiring glances at the car from the Customs men.

Once on the continent the robber had a leisurely drive through Northern France to Paris.

Arriving in Paris he made his way to La Place Vendome and his favourite hotel, The Ritz. He followed the suitcase carrying bellboy to his room and tipped him generously with some of the francs he had changed at reception. Dirty Sterling for nice clean French Francs.

Once showered and refreshed in a change of clothing consisting of Van Heusen pale grey short sleeve button down, black slacks and black slip-ons he made his way to the classy boutiques of the Champs Elysses.

The continent had always had better clothing than England. Especially France and Italy.

Things were picking up in London. A few shops had sprung up around the West End which were good for casual stuff, like Cecil Gee.

Even the kids seemed to be catered for, with a little side street off Regent Street called Carnaby Street where shops had begun stocking more exciting gear so they didn't have to dress like their dads anymore.

Two hours later, his hands full with shopping bags stuffed with jumpers, cardigans, shirts and shoes, he headed back to The Ritz.

Another shower and into a lightweight grey summer suit, crisp white open necked shirt and lightweight black crocodile skin shoes all of which he had just purchased. He wouldn't dream of buying a suit off the peg in England but France was totally different.

The thief headed for a restaurant he knew on the left bank of the Seine and enjoyed a sumptuous meal of Lobster Thermidor washed down with Dom Perignon 53 champagne at a fortune a bottle. The best.

He sat alone at his table watching The Seine bubbling past. The lights of Paris twinkling, the way only Paris lights seemed to do.

The romance capital of the world.

And here I am on me Jack Jones, he thought with an ironic smile and took another sip of champagne.

Now Frank Saunders had a sixth sense. It was a top criminal's in-built sense of knowing that he was being watched. From years of Old Bill following him and carrying out surveillance, from constantly watching his back for the predators that inhabited his murky world.

He knew he was being watched now. Calling over a waiter he asked for the menu again, at the same time doing a quick reconnoitre. Nothing.

Ostensibly checking the desserts on offer, Saunders panned his gaze from right to left of the room.

There. He knew it.

But it wasn't his old adversary Mr Plod or a rival villain, but a tasty looking dark haired bird sitting at the bar, legs crossed, her skirt riding up her thigh.

The woman dangled her right shoe off the heel of her foot and blew a steady stream of smoke from her cigarette into the air.

She was watching him intently.

What's that about being on me own? thought Frank with a smile.

He returned her look and smiled. She held his gaze and gave a slight smile back.

She hadn't turned away in embarrassment as most people do when they've been caught looking at someone.

Frank smiled again, this time to himself and signalled the waiter again.

"Oui Monsieur?"

Saunders, in fluent French, told the waiter to ask the Mademoiselle if she would care to join him in a glass of champagne.

Sixty seconds later, Frank was standing as the waiter pulled out a chair and the woman was seated opposite.

Frank Saunders, despite his often brutal profession, could be charm personified and the two strangers had a very enjoyable evening full of laughter and flirting. Both knew where the evening would end and sure enough after paying the bill and leaving a nice tip Frank led his companion through the Parisienne streets back to room 194 of The Paris Ritz.

Once inside his room the two tore at each others clothes and made heated love for hours. Starting against the wall, then on the king size four poster bed, finally ending up on the floor.

Both having climaxed at the same time they lay panting in each others arms, with the taste of salt from the sweat on each others lips. Eventually they untwined their limbs and climbed back into bed.

In the morning, his internal alarm clock rang at 7.00 o'clock and he slipped out from under the covers, her soft breathing the only sound in the room.

Frank got dressed quickly and quietly, pulled the holdall from under the bed and counted out 100 Francs.

He didn't think she was a hooker, she hadn't quoted him a price or anything but he left the money just in case. He didn't want to rob anyone!

Frank left the room, carrying his holdall. The bags of shopping had already been placed in his car boot by the bellboy. He paid his bill and checked out.

The parking valet nervously drove the Aston round to the front of the hotel and opened the door for Mr.Saunders hoping for a tip, which duly arrived.

The thief climbed in and roared off through the streets of Paris, heading south. The South of France where for the next two weeks he would live "The Good Life." He loved the south of France with its' weather, beaches, restaurants, clubs and casinos, not to mention the women. Ooh La la!

This was his treat to himself after every successful blag. Taking a motor, an Aston, Jag, sometimes even a roller and heading for St.Tropez, or Nice or Cannes and the high life.

He could never understand other villains who blew all their dough at the bookies or the boozer, never venturing further South than Brighton and that was to visit the racetrack there.

This is why he did what he did, he thought as he gunned the car, top down, sun blazing, through the winding lanes of the French countryside

Unfortunately as Frank Saunders enjoyed himself in the French countryside, things in grimy London were not so good for his mates.

Every known villain in London had had a visit from Old Bill to "Help with enquiries" regarding the security van heist.

Anyone with form had been pulled in or visited.

The three available perpetrators of the crime had had their alibis already prepared and the police visit hadn't caused any of them any undue concern. They had expected the visits and were ready for all questions thrown at them.

It wasn't the Old Bill that was the concern; it was a visit the three gang members got from an altogether more worrying group.

One morning, while servicing a Mini, Tommy Newman watched the approach of three rather large men in suits.

Definitely not a return visit from London's finest. They were just an irritation. These unwelcome guests oozed menace and Tommy instantly felt uncomfortable.

He greeted the men nervously, wiping his greasy hands on an old cloth rag.

"Hello gents, what can I do you for?" he said.

One of the men, standing about six foot two and about the same across walked up to the mechanic as the other two men hung back.

This man obviously held some sort of seniority amongst the trio.

"Got somewhere we can talk in private?" he said with menace.

Tommy indicated to the office at the back of the garage and the three men followed him in.

Once inside Tommy asked his visitors what the purpose of their visit was. But deep down inside he knew. This was a shakedown from parasites who didn't have the brains to arrange their own blags. It had happened before. Some firm gets wind of a result and tries leaning on them. As soon as Frank Saunders was told the parasites always disappeared. No one fucked with Frank.

However, on this occasion things were altogether more serious when the leader said,

"Mr.Raven sends his regards and congratulations on the wages job."

Tommy Newman's heart skipped a beat and a cold fist gripped his stomach.

Eddie Raven- psychotic head of the top firm in London. Eddie Raven –gangster.

"What you talking about?" Newman managed to respond. The name Eddie Raven struck fear into the hardest of men and Tommy was not a heavy. He was a driver, a professional, a robber.

"Look, don't fuck us about. We know you and your little firm done it and Mr.Raven feels you might need our help."

"Doing what?"

"Getting your money cleaned," then a pause, "or making sure this garage, the antique shop and the showroom don't get any trouble. Know what I mean?"

Newman knew exactly what the goon meant. "We want your hard earned."

Newman needed to think, but the man who stood before him blocked out any chance of that. Eventually he replied.

"The money ain't about at the moment," was all he could come up with at such short notice.

"Well, Mr. Raven would like to know its' whereabouts," replied the thug sarcastically to snide giggles from his companions.

The man in charge continued.

"Look. You've had a good run for your money. The boss has left you and yours alone to carry out business without any interference from us but he feels that its time to let you know who runs London. Every time you pull off a caper Old Bill are all over the gaff. Shutting down spielers, strip clubs, gambling joints, trying to put the pressure on for information.

"Eddie is losing a lot of dough and he's got the right 'ump. He feels he ain't getting enough respect from some quarters.

"Everyone pays," he said looking directly at Tommy.

"It's now time you did. UNDERSTAND?" he shouted the last word for emphasis.

He picked up a monkey wrench from the desk and slowly tapped it in his left hand.

Tommy Newman was hypnotised by the rhythmic tapping and nearly did a shit when the gangster slammed it down on to the desk.

"You've got a week. When we return, you'd better have something for us."

The ex racing driver spluttered, "Look, I'll have to speak to the others. They may not be about. I'll need a bit of time."

The man laughed and said. "We know Saunders is swanning about in Frogland. That's you're problem.

"One week and don't fuck us about."

With that he hurled the heavy wrench over Tommy's shoulder and through the glass partition of the office, smashing it to pieces.

Then they were gone.

Newman slumped down into his office chair and reached for the phone.

CHAPTER 5

Johnny parked his Lambretta around the corner from work in its normal place and swaggered to the office entrance.

Strolling through reception he winked at Mary behind the desk, "Morning darling," he said.

The young receptionist smiled and replied "Morning Johnny. Mr Clark wants to see you straight away."

Any intention to do his first flirting of the day evaporated and he questioned her with.

"What for?" As casual as he could. Shit, he thought he'd have a bit of time to ease into the day. Double shit. What if Cavendish had found out about him shagging his wife? Bollocks.

Johnny headed down the corridor and even though he was concerned about his fate he still managed to check himself in the glass office partitions and the paintings hanging on the walls.

He looked good and this gave his confidence a boost.

Fuck 'em, he thought. I'm a Face.

Johnny knocked on the door bearing a brass name plate proclaiming the occupier to be Mr. Clark.

His boss.

"Come in," Johnny heard from inside and walked in.

"Sit down," ordered his boss, to which Johnny complied.

"We have had a telephone call from Mr. Cavendish," his boss said.

Fuck, fuck, fuck, thought Johnny. The silly bitch had told her old man.

Johnny started to try to explain how the wife was drunk and had come on to him. How she had stripped off and how he had had to exit from the window and that absolutely nothing had happened. He spluttered and stammered. Talking as fast as he did when he was on speed.

Mr.Clark looked up from the papers he had been studying, oblivious to Johnny's ramblings. He was always oblivious to his workforce.

"What are you gabbling about boy?" he said with an exasperated look on his face.

"It seems you have made quite an impression on Mr.Cavendish and his wife."

Johnny sat in his chair, confused. He knew he had made an impression on her but he wasn't too sure about her husband.

"Mr. Cavendish has insisted that in future, you and only you deliver any paperwork to him."

Now Johnny was really confused. And for the first time he questioned his intake of pharmaceuticals. All the speed must have scrambled his brain. He just couldn't work it out.

Why would Mr.Cavendish only want him? Mrs.Cavendish, yes. But Mr Cavendish?

Now his paranoia kicked in.

It was a trap, he thought. Old man Cavendish had found out about him shagging his wife and this was a way of getting him back to the house. She'd blabbed and he wanted revenge.

That was it, thought Johnny, his imagination running wild. He'd go round there to deliver something and there would be some heavies hiding some place ready to leap out and give him a right kicking. Or even kill him. Or worse- cut his dick off. Shit, shit, shit.

"Are you listening?" questioned Mr. Clark.

Johnny woke from his desperate imaginings, "Pardon sir?"

"I SAID," replied Mr.Clark with exaggerated effort, "Well done, keep up the good work. Now off you go. You could go far in this organisation."

No thanks, thought Johnny, as he climbed to his feet, pushing the chair away with the back of his legs.

Slowly walking down the corridor, he was so lost in thought he didn't look at his reflections. Arriving at the cubby hole he shared with the other messengers and post room boys he was confronted by Simpson. A tall gormless idiot who he normally avoided if he could.

"What the boss want?" he enquired.

"Don't be so fucking nosey," barked Johnny.

This would take some serious thought, he mused.

Before he had a chance to make sense of events and work out a plan of action he was summoned to the documentation room and given several envelopes.

"Take these to Export Control Office in Lower Thames Street. Get them stamped and bring them back. You'll probably have to hang about for a bit," ordered Mr.James, his immediate boss. So many bosses.

Nice one. Give me a chance to sort this mess out in me head, thought Johnny.

Off he set, taking just over 15 minutes to get to his destination, weaving in and out of the City traffic.

Once at the Export Control Office, he dropped off the documents and hurried out.

Johnny made his way to a little Italian café he knew in Aldgate, near the tube station.

Morrelli's made the best Cappuccino East of Soho and catered for cabbies, market boys, and usually a couple of teenage peacocks.

As he approached the café, he clocked the machines parked up on the pavement outside.

Three Lambrettas, and two Vespas. Three of the five scooters were adorned with an array of lights and mirrors and two were plain like his. He didn't understand why some Mods, even some Faces, put all that crap on their scoots. To him the whole point of choosing the scooter as their mode of transport was the clean lines and sleek look. Adding all that malarkey spoilt the whole effect and drew attention away from the rider, which couldn't be right.

Johnny pulled up outside and entered the café. The whoosh of the coffee machine made a welcoming sound.

The owner of Morrellis stood serving behind the counter and recognizing Johnny, smiled and started pouring the cappuccino before it was even requested. He always knew what his regulars had.

Johnny smiled and nodded at the owner, placed the correct money on the counter and picked up his drink.

Carrying his coffee to a vacant table he glanced around. At one table sat the obvious owners of the scooters. As soon as he had walked through the door he had felt their eyes on him, checking him out and he did the same to them. Surreptitiously. Not bad. Not as good as him but one of them had a very tasty suede jacket. Brown, with leather collar. Very nice. He walked past their table and they nodded a greeting which he returned. He knew they were admiring him.

Johnny had once looked up the word narcissistic in a dictionary and he loved what it said. "An exceptional interest in or admiration for oneself." He was definitely narcissistic.

On another table sat four older men in suits. Hard faced, huddled together, deep in conversation.

Plotting something by the looks of things.

Johnny sat down and slowly stirred his coffee and stared into the distance. Thinking. Pondering.

The teenagers mind drifted back through his past to the beginning.

*

The story so far. His dad had returned from the war, got mum pregnant again, hung about for a couple of years, got itchy feet and fucked off, leaving his mum to bring him and his older brother up on her own.

Things were tough. They were really skint. Never mind second hand clothes. Third or fourth hand more like. Real struggle. Mum out working her three jobs. She did her best but cleaning didn't pay too well.

The house was always cold. Clean but cold.

And always dark.

When Johnny was about 10 and his brother was 14, his mum met a fella. She was happy, but him and his brother hated him. Thought he was a right cunt.

So it was a bit of a blow when she told the two boys she was marrying him.

Reg moved in after the wedding and made their lives hell. Out on the piss most nights, he'd come back and depending on how much he'd lost at the bookies would slap the boys about. Sometimes the prick would take his belt to them.

When Johnny's brother was old enough he packed a bag and left to join the Marines leaving him to be the human punch bag. Still, the way he looked at it, all the time Reg was whacking him he wasn't knocking his mum about.

One afternoon after coming home from school, his mum and Reg were standing in the lounge waiting for him.

They told him that Reg's firm were relocating to Wales and they would all be moving there.

The boy was stunned. Wales? Fuck that!

Weighing up his options he decided that living on his own would be better than living with his mum and wanker Reg in the land of sheep shaggers.

So, just as his brother had done, he packed a bag and slipped out of the house one night. He was fourteen years old.

He headed for the bright lights and glamour of London's West End. He ended up sleeping in a builders skip in Beak St. Very glamorous.

He'd been to the West End with his brother a few times when they were younger, looking at the painted ladies in scanty clothing and getting chased away by big blokes. Johnny sort of knew his way around, although he didn't know what he was going to do or where he would stay, but he knew he couldn't live in Wales.

For the first few days he slept in doorways and alleys. The skip had been filled pretty quick.

When he'd left home he nicked some of Reg's money to tide him over, but it didn't last long and he was soon skint. And hungry. He didn't mind sleeping rough, it was summer so it wasn't too bad. But he was a growing lad and needed his grub.

After going hungry for a couple of days he tried stealing some fruit from a stall in Berwick St. market. Unfortunately the old boy who owned the stall was a bit quicker than he looked and caught him after he had only got a couple of yards and gave him a couple of slaps.

Johnny hadn't cried in years and if that cunt Reg couldn't make him cry, this old codger wasn't going to manage it. Although it was a close run thing. More out of guilt than pain.

The stall owner had been joined by the other market boys who were stopping him from doing a runner.

The fruit and veg man was called Alf and once Johnny had calmed down he asked him what he was up to and where he lived.

Johnny told him the truth! That his parents had been killed in a car crash and he was a homeless orphan. Well, it sounded better than running away from home!

Alf instantly took pity on him and let go of his arm.

"Wanna a cup of tea son?" the old boy asked with a gap toothed smile.

Alf turned out to be Johnny's guardian angel. Gave him a job helping on the stall and let him kip in his lock up.

Soon he was a regular face, with a small f, on the market and in the area. On friendly terms with the traders, hookers, porn shop workers, and with the night club people who were just finishing as Johnny's day on the market was just starting.

At night, he would wander the streets of Soho, past the clubs, through Theatreland and when he saw someone interesting would follow them around and try to imagine who they were, where they were going and what their story was.

It was a warm summer's evening. Johnny had been strolling his usual patch when his eyes were drawn to a man bowling down Shaftesbury Avenue.

A black man, dressed immaculately in a really sharp light grey single breasted suit, white shirt and tie and pointed black shoes.

Under his right armpit he carried some sort of case. Black leather. What was it? A gun?

The youngsters' imagination went into overdrive.

This needed investigating. Johnny followed, keeping up with the pace his quarry was setting. The man swayed from side to side, not like one of the West End winos, but in a deliberate, hypnotic manner. His hands in his jacket pockets, head buried between his shoulders. Not looking left or right.

The Negro turned left into Greek Street and the youngster did likewise. The man crossed over and quickly entered a doorway.

The doorway was the entrance to a club. Above the door flashed a red neon sign bearing the name "GERRYS". Under that a sign advertised "LIVE JAZZ."

The teenage runaway crossed the road, narrowly avoiding being run over by a black cab and receiving a volley of abuse from its driver.

He hadn't been in London long but he quickly came to the conclusion that black cab drivers were wankers. Thought they owned the road.

Johnny edged up to the door. Music drifted up the stairs of the basement jazz club. A sound like nothing he had ever heard before. Trumpet, drums, double bass. The collection of sounds grabbed hold of him, ran silky fingers up and down his spine. The music enveloped him like a beautiful warm blanket, draped over his shoulders after a lifetime of winter.

In a trance he crossed the threshold to the club, drawn towards the noise like an inhabitant of Hamlin following the pied piper.

"Oi, where the fuck you going?"

The dreamer was abruptly woken by a different sound.

The sound of the burly doorman who had been chatting up a couple of passing dollies and had not noticed the boy's approach.

Johnny turned and was confronted by the doorman, a man whose face hadn't ended up the way God intended. He put his arm across the entrance barring his progress.

"Too young," the gorilla barked, then continued eloquently. "Now fucking do one."

Johnny retreated to a doorway opposite to watch and listen. From his grubby vantage point he witnessed an array of wonderful people, men and women, black and white, dressed in beautiful clothes.

Colourful people who carried themselves with style and confidence.

He stood and watched the doorway of the club for a couple of hours and it was one o'clock when the doorman spoke to him for a second time.

"Oi, what you still doing here?" the man shouted across the street, "Ain't you got nuffink better to do?"

"Not really."

"Well wot d'ya want?"

He ambled over to the man, checking left and right for traffic as he crossed the road.

"Nothing," he said, "Just watching. Listening. Ain't no law against it is there?" He added insolently.

"Well, you'll get to hear it better inside" said the doorman, "Slip us a shilling and you can sneak in."

"aven't got a shilling," he replied walking up to the man.

Under the light the doorman got a better look at the boy's features. He looked even younger close up.

"Ow old are you son?" he said, with a gentleness that didn't fit his scarred and battered face.

"Seventeen," the boy lied.

"What you want here?" he asked the boy.

Nodding towards the club he replied.

"Whats this place all about?"

"Its'a fucking jazz club, what d'ya fink?"

"I've never heard that music before, it's great."

The big man looked at the young boy, suddenly feeling unusually compassionate.

"Oh for fucks sake," he said more to himself than anyone else,

"Go on then, in ya go, but keep ya fucking 'ead down. If anyone catches ya, tell em ya sneaked in when I was dealing with a piss 'ead. O.K ?"

"Yea, cheers," mumbled Johnny, already making his way in.

He made his way down two short flights of steps past the cloakroom and through another door.

The heat and sound hit him instantly. Standing transfixed by this attack on his senses, it took some seconds for his eyes to get accustomed to his new surroundings, the darkness.

The youngster felt the need to take a couple of deep breaths as he was draped in heat, sound and the ambience.

Johnny couldn't quite comprehend the scene before him. It was as though he had been transported to a totally different universe. A world he knew nothing about but instantly felt at home with.

His eyes were drawn to the stage where a three piece combo of drums, double bass and trumpet played a music which lifted him to a higher level.

People all around moved and swayed, slid and shook and for the first time in his young life Johnny began to dance. Watching his neighbours he copied their moves and even threw in a couple of his own, glancing around self consciously in case anyone had seen him.

The young boy's clothes and age should have excluded him from feeling comfortable, but aided by the smiles and warmth from the other dancers he felt at home, felt that he belonged for the first time in his life.

He had arrived at a place his subconscious knew existed. Hadn't known what or where it was or if he would ever find it. But he had, he was there, in the middle of a whole new world.

Johnny danced non-stop until kicking out time and as the club emptied and he walked back out onto the street he was amazed to see that dawn was breaking. The summer sun already permeated the streets of Soho and lifted him up yet again.

He didn't want this to end just in case it was a one off, but listening to his fellow Jazzers, reassured him that they would be there next week.

And so would he.

Back to the present and the young Face's coffee had gone cold with all his reminiscing, so he gave the café owner a nod, indicating another.

As the cappuccino was being prepared Johnny once again delved into the back catalogue of his life.

CHAPTER 6

The bell over the door jingled, and the young boy entered the gloomy shop and was greeted by a small Jewish man standing behind the counter. A tape measure draped around his neck.

"Good morning sir," the old tailor greeted, "What can I do for you?"

Johnny, unaccustomed to being in this environment blurted out, "A suit."

"Well you've come to the right place sir. That's what we make here." smiled the man.

"Any particular style sir?" he enquired.

"Sir," he liked that. He'd never been called sir before.

It had been six months since his re-birth at "GERRYS" and with the wonderful idea that was Hire Purchase and his new full time job as a messenger for an import/export agency he could afford his first ever made to measure suit. In fact it would be his first suit, full stop.

Since that night at the Jazz club all his money had gone on following this new lifestyle. Going to clubs and buying ever increasing amounts of stylish clothing until he now was in a position to acquire the suit of his dreams.

When the teenager had walked through the door to the tailors shop he knew exactly what he wanted. It was all registered in his mind, down to the finest detail, but now he had to explain it he was lost for words.

"Its alright, take your time," said the tailor gently, recognizing the boys nervousness.

"Would you like a cup of tea?"

"Yes please," replied his teenage customer, grateful for the chance to compose himself.

The old man went through a grey curtain at the back of the shop and Johnny wandered around touching and stroking the different cloths on their rolls.

He studied the framed photographs of film stars, singers and sporting heroes hanging high on the wall above him.

Photographs of the tailors clients, wearing his creations.

The old man, waiting for the kettle to boil on the gas stove pulled the curtain back a couple of inches and watched his latest client inspecting his shop.

He smiled as the water heated up. He had noticed that more young boys like this were frequenting his establishment and could feel there was something in the air.

A change was taking place.

Solomon Levinson had arrived in England as a refugee from Poland in 1939 just as the Nazis invaded. Landing in Dover by way of France with his wife Sofia, he made his way to London, the best place he thought to gain employment for his tailoring skills.

With his meagre savings smuggled out of his homeland he had rented a one room flat above a shop in Marshall Street, Soho, London W1. and sought out work. He was forty years old and at first he found it hard. Not speaking any English, starting a new life. A different culture but at least they were safe. As long as the Nazis' didn't invade England.

Sofia found it especially hard as they had had to leave her parents behind in Warsaw unable to get them out.

It took Solomon a couple of weeks until he found work in a tailors shop in Old Compton Street making officers uniforms, and what with the war there was great demand.

With the war won and his reputation growing, Solomon Levinson worked like a dog. He worked fifteen/sixteen hours a day, seven days a week until he had saved enough to put with his own savings from back home, to enable him to rent a small shop of his own with living space above. It was 1955.

The premises were in St.Annes Court. A small, dead end side street off of Dean Street.

It was not an ideal location as there was no passing trade but it was cheap and it was all he could afford. However, he was confident in his skills and was sure he would soon drum up business based on the reputation gained in his previous workplace.

The first six months were hard, business was slow and his savings were rapidly shrinking, despite him and his wife living a frugal, almost monastic lifestyle.

Solomon Levinson's luck changed that summer. July 6 to be precise, a Tuesday.

The bell above his door jingled, signifying a prospective customer.

The old tailors' heart sank when he looked up as the man standing in his shop was carrying rolls of different cloths under his arm. Obviously a salesman, he thought with disappointment.

"I'm not buying," he proclaimed in his heavily accented English.

"Good, cos I'm not selling," was the strangers' instant reply.

The shopkeeper studied his visitor. Tall and confident, wearing a lovely dark suit, the style of which he had not seen before and to his tradesman's eyes was the work of a highly skilled tailor.

He felt a little foolish for mistaking this wealthy looking man for a salesman.

"I want five suits made. All the same. From these materials," the man said.

For the next hour the tailor and his new customer went over his requirements. Measuring and taking notes, listening to the precise instructions of the man.

The cloth the man had brought with him was new to the tailor. Lightweight, in beautiful shades. Top quality.

The customer described exactly how he wanted his suits. They were in a style the tailor had never seen before, let alone made, but he was sure of his skill and knew he could make them to the exact requirements.

When Solomon had taken notes and done rough sketches he showed the man, who nodded approval.

The suits were more fitted, closer fitted, single breasted, two buttons. Lapels were to be thinner than was the current style. Trousers with just two pleats. Closer to the leg and narrow at the bottom. Turned up outside.

The jacket lining was to be made from bright, colourful silk the man had provided.

Once all details were taken, the tailor offered the man a cup of tea, which was declined.

"Here's my number," the man said, "Call me when you're ready for my first fitting. How much?"

The question surprised the old man. He had been so pre-occupied and excited by his new customer, the challenge ahead, and the chance to show his skills that the sudden and abrupt manner in which the question was asked caught him by surprise.

Scratching his head, the tailor looked perplexed.

"Er.... Well.....I've.....   These suits. The styles are new to me and....."

The tall man before him interrupted,

"Look, work out your price, then call me for a fitting. You can let me know then."

Then with ever such a slight hint of a threat, he continued "I'm sure you won't rip me off....Will you" It wasn't a question. It was a statement.

"No sir, not at all sir," the tailor blurted.

"Here, take this on account." The man put his hand into his trouser pocket and pulled out a big roll of cash. Peeling off a tenner, a generous amount in 1955, he thrust the money into the tailors hand.

"But I want the suits quick," he said. "Okay?"

"Yes sir, as soon as possible," replied Solomon.

"Quicker" the customer countered with a smile. With that he was gone.

The old Jewish tailor fell down into his chair exhausted but excited. He looked at the cash in his left hand and then picked up the piece of paper the man had written his number on from the counter and looked at it, then turned it over. The number was there, but no name.

The man had not written down his name and Solomon couldn't recall him mentioning it.

The tailor from Warsaw set to work immediately, using a pale cream cloth the customer had provided.

While he worked he wondered about the man. Who was he?

Was he one of the theatre people? They liked their clothes. An actor perhaps?

No, they were a soft looking lot.

Musician perhaps? No, not a musician, they were always broke.

Then he got it and the thought ran a chill down his spine.

A gangster. That was it. The man was a gangster. He had met the type before back in Warsaw before the war. Hard looking, confident and that wad of money. There must have been £200 there.

Only gangsters carried that sort of money.

The thought made him tremble.

What if the suits aren't ready on time?

Or if they're not to his liking?

The tailors' natural sense of the melodramatic conjured up all sorts of dire scenarios.

Perhaps the man would beat him up? Or kill him even? To come all this way. Having escaped the Nazis, just to be murdered in his adopted country. In his own shop.

Solomon Levinson clasped his hands together and rocked gently backwards and forwards, close to tears.

Eventually he pulled himself together and pushed all such dramatic thoughts from his head. And doubled his efforts.

The tailor worked like never before and day turned to night.

He woke, slumped over his machine, to the sound of his wife's shrill voice calling him from the top of the stairs.

The old tailor groaned as he straightened his aching back. After having been hunched over his machine for so long he was in agony.

The morning sun which never permeated St.Annes' Court due to the high buildings and narrow street was rising over Soho and he had to check his watch that hung on a chain, connected to his waistcoat, to get his bearings. The elegant old time piece informed him that it was 5.30 a.m.

Levinson's nimble fingers and work rate had already got him to the stage of the first fitting.

The call was made from the red public telephone box on the corner of Wardour Street and Brewer Street as the shop had no telephone.

The mystery man returned. Slight alterations were made. The man left.

Two days of hard slog later and the first suit was finished.

The tailor made another call and when the man returned, he gently helped him into the beautifully made suit.

The client purred with appreciation as the suit moulded itself to his body like a second skin.

Checking himself in the shop mirrors from every angle, he smiled broadly.

"Nice one Solly," he said. "Nice one. Perfect. Just what I wanted. Do the other four like this and you'll have more work than you can handle."

"From you sir?" the tailor enquired.

"Yea, from me. And from people I know. Now, how much do I owe you?"

The old man handed him the bill for the completed suit, which was immediately paid from another big roll of cash from the mans original jacket hanging over a chair. Along with an extravagant tip.

It was a long time since the old man had felt so appreciated. His wife no longer caring about anything since their flight from the Nazis and not knowing if her family were dead or alive.

But this mystery man had made him feel alive again. Worth something. After years of nothing.

From that day he worked like never before.

His newest customers four other suits were quickly finished and, as promised he was given a constant stream of work. Suits, jackets, trousers, shirts were all ordered and produced as requested.

The mans' friends and associates beat a steady path to his door and although they seemed to be a rather dubious looking bunch, they all paid him on the dot. All gave him a tip.

It made Solomon Levinson smile as he thought of himself as "The gangsters tailor."

Then, as he toiled over his machine, a man he recognized walked into his shop. His face was very famous, as he had appeared in many feature films and was known worldwide.

The movie star said that Solly had been recommended by a friend of his and ordered five shirts to be made to his dimensions and style. This was followed by a vast array of made to measure schmuter.

And, just as his first mystery client had been followed by an A-Z of London criminality, so his Movie Star customer was followed by faces from movies, theatre and the music world.

No matter how famous a client was, he always made a priority of his original visitor and his closest friends.

And now, Solomon Levinson, Polish Jewish refugee from war torn Europe, was seeing the beginning of another breed of customer.

Much younger, less affluent but no less particular about their sartorial needs. In fact, these young men were, if anything, fussier than the gangsters and movie stars he was used to dressing.

The tailor was jerked back to the present as the kettle boiled and considered the boy before him. He was definitely one of the new breed.

And once again casting his mind back, he recognized a similarity with his first customer.

Both had an arrogant feel about them. He suspected they came from the same hard background. Both knew what they wanted.

The only difference was the man had got where he wanted to be and the boy had an ambition to get there.

Carrying a tray, on which sat two cups of tea and a small jug of milk and a bowl of sugar, the tailor parted the curtain with his foot and walked back into the shop.

"Well sir, are you ready?" Solomon asked the boy.

Johnny was more than ready. He knew this tailor made suits for show-biz people, which was why he chose him. Show-biz people came here because they were fussy and Solomon Levinson could get the materials other places couldn't. Light weight mohairs, in two-tone. Material that looked one colour, then viewed from another angle looked totally different. Blue/black, red/green, gold/black, amazing.

For the next hour, just as the tailor and the gangster had designed a suit, so did the old man and the young man.

A deposit was left by the boy and two fittings and one week later the suit was ready.

Johnny returned nervously to the shop. Hoping that the tailors' version of the suit would match his.

He needn't have worried. Solomon Levinson apart from being highly skilled with his hands had an instinct for what his customers wanted. This instinct was what set him apart from most other tailors.

A box was produced from under the counter as soon as Johnny walked into the shop. He greeted the old man and the old man smiled back.

The lid was removed from the box and the crepe paper pulled to one side. The tailor gently lifted the jacket from its resting place.

Johnny's cheeks flushed red with pleasure and his stomach flipped. It was the most beautiful thing he had ever seen.

He slipped off the casual jacket he had worn to the shop and hesitated. Johnny was almost scared to touch the jacket held out to him by the tailor. The Jewish man stood behind him and slipped the jacket on. Perfect.

Into the changing room to remove his trousers and to put the new ones on.

He had brought with him a white shirt, black tie and shoes to get the full effect.

When he walked back into the front of the shop, the tailor was beaming with pride.

"Wonderful sir, you look wonderful."

Johnny felt wonderful. The suit was everything he had imagined and hoped. It didn't just fit like a glove. More like a second skin.

Silver/black two-tone tonic. Jacket had three buttons, centre vent eight inches long, slanted pockets, black silk lining. Trousers- no pleats, razor sharp permanent creases, 10 inch bottoms, turned up inside.

As he admired his image in the full length mirrors, Johnny knew he was on his way.

*

A burst of laughter from the Mods at the other table jogged him back to the present and he noticed his coffee had gone cold again.

"Fuck it," he thought as he stood and made his way out into the sunshine.

CHAPTER 7

Frank Saunders was back in the 'smoke' and he had the right 'ump.

After enjoying his sunshine break in the South of France, returning to drab old London and its problems always pissed him off. Returning on this occasion however had really pissed him off.

Having collected his many messages from the showroom he contacted the chaps and he had been filled in on what had occurred during his absence.

He arranged a meet, in their well rehearsed coded language, in a small café they knew in Aldgate. It was always better to meet off their manor, to avoid nosey local plod.

When he arrived, the others were already there, seated around a table drinking tea and smoking.

Saunders entered and ordered coffee from the Italian owner standing at his counter.

All heads in the place turned to see his arrival and conversation ceased momentarily.

Taking his coffee he gave the thrupence required to the owner and made his way to join his crew.

"Seems we've got a problem lads," Saunders started.

"What exactly happened when I was gone?"

The three other men all began talking at once and Saunders had to tell them to keep their voices down.

One at a time the robbers, starting with Jimmy told their leader about the visit from Eddie Ravens' goons.

About the threats and the "request" for donations.

Once they had all given their own account of events they all fell silent and looked at Saunders expectantly.

Frank Saunders had listened carefully and was running things through his head. Working out what they should do.

"The muscle were definitely Ravens boys?" he asked no one in particular.

"Definitely," replied Jimmy Sewell, "It was Fletcher and he had Lane and McGuire with him."

"Three of Ravens top boys," said Frank "Definitely his firm."

This was a very tricky situation. On one hand they couldn't just fold and give in to the threats. They weren't mugs.

On the other hand Eddie Raven had an army of thugs and although some of them were idiots, there were plenty of tasty geezers there.

Geezers who wouldn't think twice, in fact would love to blow Frank Saunders and his team away.

Now Frank and the chaps were not adverse to a bit of aggro and they would use shooters themselves if required but the simple fact was that they were out manned and out gunned.

Frank Saunders had never let anyone walk over him in his life and he wasn't about to start letting it happen now. Besides, he and the boss of London's underworld went back a long way.

All the way to borstal in fact.

A meet would have to be arranged.

Saunders stood up and walked to the back of the café where the pay phone was located, took out his small leather bound address book and dialled the number.

It rang twice before it was answered and then the rapid beeping told the caller that the money should be inserted.

The whirring stopped and before anyone at the end of the line spoke, "This is Frank Saunders. Get me Eddie Raven."

The phone answering lackey didn't reply but put the telephone down onto the desk and sought out his boss.

The most powerful man in London picked up the hand piece and spoke.

"Frankie son, how's fings?" the voice had smoked a thousand fags and drank a million whisky's. It was a deep growl of a voice. A voice that suggested it gargled with razor blades.

"We need to talk," Saunders replied simply.

"Sure, sure what's on your mind?" continued Raven feigning ignorance of the reason for the call.

"I think you know that already," answered Saunders again.

"Well, I tell you what," the rough voice said "I'm going over to The Admiral a bit later, checking out a young middleweight who looks a bit tasty. I'll be there about two."

"I'll be there," said Frank and put the phone down.

The Admiral was one of Eddie Ravens' boozers. This one in Bethnal Green had the added attraction of a boxing gym upstairs and was one of the favoured hang outs of his firm.

Frank re-joined his pals at the table and related the conversation.

"Right lets get over there then," enthused Jimmy Sewell, rising to his feet.

"Now 'old on lads," interrupted Saunders as they re-seated themselves.

"If we go over there mob handed it'll look like we're up for a right kick off and you can guarantee he'll have an army down there, proper tooled up."

Silence descended upon the table until Saunders spoke again.

"Nah, I'll go over there on me own and talk to him. See if we can come to some arrangement."

The lads instantly and noisily voiced their objections, drawing attention again from the other patrons.

"Quiet down boys," Frank hissed. "It'll be alright, go to the Duke and I'll see you there when I'm finished."

They didn't like it, but Frank was adamant.

"I'll sort it," he insisted.

The five men all stood, scrapping their chairs backwards across the lino covered floor and walked past the group of Mods sitting at another table.

Outside on the pavement the men huddled together lighting more cigarettes in silence.

They realised Frank was going into the lions den and were all worried about the outcome.

Saunders sensing the groups concern tried to put them at ease.

"Don't worry lads, we go back. I'm only going to have a chat with that psychotic paranoid maniac. Nothing to worry about. Now fuck off and I'll see you later."

The sense of doom was eased by Franks comment and they all had a chuckle.

With that he strolled over to the Aston, climbed in and headed east.

The chaps got in to Tommy's red Mk II Jaguar and headed west to Soho and the Duke.

The first thing anyone noticed on entering the gym above The Admiral was the smell of stale sweat.

The legacy of years of hard men working for a chance. The chance to get away from poverty and the squalor they had been born into.

The chance to get away from their dead end existence.

Many fell by the wayside. Dreams shattered by a right cross or a left hook to the chin.

These men unable to rely on intellect found their services sought after in a world that needed hardness and a man who could land a punch who wasn't too bothered about the Marquess of Queensbury.

Many who had managed to go beyond the smoky halls and fairground fighting booths and had created something of a career in the fight game often ended up back at the bottom of the heap, broke as when they had started.

Victims of crooked managers and promoters, who exploited their blood and sweat, promised them the world until certain faceless people, lurking in the shadows got a better price on the opponent and had "had a word."

There were loads of fighters who "Coulda been a contender."

However, such was the grinding poverty and hopelessness in Britain's slums, that there was an endless stream of men hoping that it would be their fists that could make them the new Henry Cooper. It only took one like 'Our 'Enery' to give them hope and to ignore the hundreds of broken dreams and bodies.

Frank Saunders looked around trying to spot the gang boss. Finally his eyes found him, leaning against a wall covered in faded boxing posters, talking to a lackey, hardly moving his lips. The lackey straining hard to catch the man's guarded words.

Saunders headed for the man.

The Man- Eddie Raven, pub owner, club owner, racehorse and restaurant owner. He owned many things but his favourite and most profitable thing he owned was people.

Fighters, hoods, hookers and pimps. Businessmen, bent briefs, cops and judges.

Eddie Raven stood in the boxing gym above an East End boozer, watching a couple of his fighters spar.

Surrounded by underlings who were ready and eager to cater for his every whim and order.

A tall thin man stood a few yards away from him. Waiting for his turn to approach his guvnor.

The man held a brief case full of protection money collected from West End clip joints "protected" by the Eddie Raven firm.

Frank Saunders made his way past the pugs, young and old, beating shit out of old leather punch bags, which swung back and forth with each heavy blow.

The gangster looked up to see Saunders making his way across the room and immediately broke off his current conversation and walked over to greet him, completely ignoring the waiting bag man.

"Frankie son. How the fuck ya doing?" he greeted, and offered an outstretched hand.

Putting his personal feelings of distaste to one side Frank shook the extended hand.

The two men stood opposite each other both shaking hands with deliberately firm grips.

Both men were over six foot and of similar build. Both had very short hair and it was striking how similar the two men were physically.

To the uninitiated they could have been mistaken for brothers but it only took a look in the men's eyes to see how different they were.

Saunders eyes were brown and despite his profession displayed a charm and warmth.

Ravens eyes were black and lifeless. Like the dead, unemotional eyes of a shark. The perfect killing machine.

"Not bad. You?" Saunders replied.

"Good, good. Come on lets talk," said Raven.

The boss of London's underworld put his arm around the robbers shoulder and led him to the office at the back of the gym.

Frank bristled at the huge paw of a hand resting on his shoulder, but he let it go. Diplomatic.

Once in the office, Eddie Raven shut the door behind them and offered Saunders a chair.

Frank sat down, unbuttoned his jacket and crossed his legs.

"Drink?" offered Raven holding up a bottle of scotch.

"Yeah, rocks," replied Saunders.

Two drinks were poured and the host sat behind his large oak desk.

The ice in the crystal tumblers melted and cracked as the 12 year malt cascaded over it.

"Now what can I do for you?" the gangster enquired.

"Apparently, while I've been on a little trip abroad my boys have had visits from some of your firm. Making threats, trying to get their hands on some of our hard earned. They've been saying you sent 'em. It's out of order. We don't have nothing to do with your rackets. We don't tread on anyone's toes. We keep ourselves to ourselves and graft."

Saunders paused, "What the fuck's going on?"

The atmosphere in the room was akin to that of a pre-fight weigh in. Two hard men face to face putting on a show.

Eddie Raven had listened to what had been said and calmly took a sip of his favoured tipple. Silence.

Eventually he spoke.

"Frank. It's like this. You're too good son. Too successful. You and your chaps are always pulling off coups. Never getting a tug."

"So?" countered Saunders, "What's the problem?"

Eddie Raven took another sip of his Chivas Regal, stood up and strolled over to the half-glass door to his office and looked out at the pain and effort of the fighters. Still with his back to Saunders he spoke.

"The Old Bill are getting the 'ump. I've 'ad visits from P.C. fucking plod to Chief fucking Inspectors. The top brass. I've 'ad me bookies and spielers raided and shut down. Me grot shops 'ave 'ad all the stock taken. It's costing me fucking bundles."

The volume ever so slightly increased.

Saunders had also stood. He didn't like sitting while someone stood and spoke to him. He didn't like someone speaking to him without facing him and he definitely didn't like people raising their voice to him. Even if it was only slightly and even if it was London's most dangerous man.

Hearing the chair scrape back, indicating Saunders rising London's guvnor turned to face him and continued.

"It's only right and proper that the cause of me being out of pocket should recompense me for my suffering."

Saunders placed his glass carefully and deliberately on the desk. Raven had had a wary eye on it since Frank had stood. Crystal whisky tumblers were heavy items and could do a lot of damage in the right, or more to the point, wrong hands.

"Look, we go back a long way. You do your thing and I do mine. You make your dough and I make mine.

"It's like any business. Peaks and troughs. Ups and downs. You're just having a trough that's all."

"Well I don't like 'aving fucking troughs. I'm a peak only man. That's why I've been on top so long.

"Look, Frankie. If you and your team don't toe the line and show respect, then every cunt in London will start taking the piss."

"So? You can deal with them in your usual diplomatic manner. A couple of acts of gratuitous violence and everyone will behave themselves thus maintaining the status quo."

"Don't take the piss Frank," sighed Raven, "I don't need a fuss at the moment. Old bill are getting arsey. And we need to keep a low profile. Blood on the streets is always bad for business."

Saunders couldn't put his finger on it. But something didn't ring true. The gangster in front of him had never put the squeeze on him before.

Their paths only crossed at social functions. The casino, nightclubs, boxing matches.

A handshake, a polite nod. Saunders and his team stuck to their side of the street and Raven stuck to his. Why the pressure now?

"What if we don't fancy coughing up?"

"Don't be fucking silly Frank. I know you and your chaps are tasty. But you wouldn't stand a fucking chance and you fucking know it."

The atmosphere was starting to heat up and voice levels were starting to rise with the odd expletive thrown in, it was always a sign.

There followed a lengthy, awkward silence with just the sound of leather gloves making contact with flesh from the gym outside.

Eventually Eddie Raven spoke again.

"There *is* a way to resolve this situation so everyone comes out smiling."

"Oh yeah?" said Frank guardedly. Knowing he would regret asking.

He heaved an inevitable sigh.

"What's that then?"

A hint of a smile took hold of the gangsters' lips as he sat down again.

"A piece of information has come my way. A very interesting piece of information.

"It concerns the transportation of a large sum of dosh. A *very* large sum of dosh." He paused for effect.

"The sum of £100,000 in used notes."

Saunders didn't bat an eye lid, so Raven continued.

"I have the departure point and time. I have the route, the destination and I know the strength of protection.

"What I don't have is a team to do the caper."

So that was it, thought Frank.

The robber asked, "What's that gotta do with us?" knowing full well what it had to do with them.

"It's simple Frank," replied Raven, playing the game to the full.

"You and your boys do the job! You're off the hook. Everyone will know you did the job for me. Everyone carries on behaving themselves. You get a nice little earner out of it."

Yeah and you get a nice big fucking earner out of it, thought Frank.

"Look, Eddie," said Frank, "You know we only do our own work. That way we have less chance of problems."

The London gangster leant back in his chair. Elbows on the arms, fingers entwined, his chin resting on his fingers.

"Frank, it seems to have escaped your notice, but you've already got a problem. A big fucking problem.

"Now that makes two of us. As I see it, you and your firm are causing me grief.

"You're costing me a lot of dough. Now you can either pay me what I feel is right or you can sort out this caper. Do the job and the problem is sorted."

"And if we don't?" enquired Saunders with resignation.

Eddie Raven stared at Frank Saunders with his dead eyes.

"You're fucked," was his simple reply.

Saunders didn't like it. He knew he had been out-manoeuvred. He was indeed fucked whatever way you looked at it.

There was no way he wanted to work for this parasite and wouldn't expect his team to. But there was no way his team could take on Eddie Ravens' firm.

One on one he fancied his chances against any of the mob, even the psycho sitting before him, but he couldn't take on the lot of them even with the chaps. Besides Ravens' mob were sneaky cunts and would more than likely wait in the dark somewhere and get them individually.

Frank eventually gave his answer.

"I'll have to put it to the chaps."

Raven smiled a self satisfied smile and Saunders gritted his teeth, before continuing.

"If we do it, we do it our way. Planning, supplying the gear, motors. Everything.

"No help from your end. We do it exactly how we choose to do it. That includes the aftermath. Understand?"

The boss of London smiled in agreement and said,

"Course Frank. Anything you say. It'll be your baby."

Both criminals stood and once again Eddie Raven held out his hand, which once again was reluctantly shook by Saunders.

"I'll speak to the chaps and let you know," said Frank.

The two men walked to the door, which was opened by Raven, who followed Saunders through and back into the gym.

Reaching into his dark blue pinstripe suit jacket, Eddie Raven produced an envelope.

"Ringside seats for the Cooper fight tomorrow at Wembley for you and your boys. Speak to your team and I'll wait for your call."

Raven paused, then said with a smirk.

"Let me know what you decide."

Then once again he shook Saunders hand. For show. Everyone took note.

"Not that you've got much choice," he said, loud enough to be heard by those present.

Saunders bristled at this last comment. He thought he had had the last word by telling him he would "let him know" but the gangster had taken this little victory away.

"I'll speak to the boys," said Saunders.

Back at the Duke of Argyll, W1, having recounted the afternoons events to the chaps, the silence was deafening.

As usual the place was empty, how the landlord made any dough was anybodies guess.

Despite being the only punters in, the South London thieves had filled the place with cigarette smoke from their continuous lighting up.

Lager was supped, as the chaps all tried to think of a way out of their predicament.

But as their nemesis Eddie Raven had said, they were FUCKED. With a capital F.U.C.K.E.D.

The simple fact was either do the job or pay up.

They all knew if they gave Raven any dough it would amount to paying protection money and it wouldn't be the last time. Besides Frankie would rather die.

If they carried out the tickle at least they would earn some dough and keep the mob off their backs for a while.

Even as this was decided, Frank Saunders was already planning to get one up on Eddie Fucking Raven.

There was never any way of knowing exactly how much dough was in a safe, a bank, or security van.

And there was no way Eddie Raven was going to get the full contents of their blag.

Sometimes, there would be more dough than expected. Sometimes less. On this occasion there would be less. A lot less.

So, as the afternoon crept into evening, having made up their minds about doing the job and with the aid of ever increasing amounts of alcohol, the gang of thieves settled down for a right session, recounting old coups, fuck ups and generally having a trip down memory lane.

The feeling was that with this Eddie Raven business, things were never going to be the same again.

Even Tommy Newman had a couple of halves.

CHAPTER 8

Friday night at last. What a week.

Johnny was knackered. He'd had a quiet week by his standards but the planning and anticipation of what he was getting into had frazzled his nut.

Work had been a pain and the week had really dragged. Buying a tasty Arrows short sleeve button down in Cecil Gees' in Shaftesbury Avenue had broken the week up a bit. Pale green. Lovely.

Hopefully if his plan worked out he would be able to fuck his job off and buy more than one shirt a week.

Now, as he strode arrogantly down Wardour Street, bolstered by a couple of Blues he was alive again. 9p.m. Nodding gently to the tune in his head, clicking his fingers groovy style, greeting and acknowledging the occasional face he encountered.

He smiled inwardly at the admiring looks he attracted. Inwardly, because it wasn't cool to appear like a grinning idiot. Straight, serious face at all times. Cool, nonchalant.

As he reached his first stop off point of the night, The Bastille coffee bar, who should hove into view but Steady Eddie, doing the walk, bowling towards him.

Like everything in their special world there was a certain way of doing things, including walking and Steady Eddie had it off to a T. Hands in Levis pockets, thumbs sticking out, slightly leaning forward, shoulders swaying.

Although it was night time Steady Eddie wore sunglasses. Cool.

"Hey Johnny baby, how's things?" he said upon seeing his old pal.

"Cool man, cool," replied the fellow Face. The two friends checked the others threads.

Steady dressed casually cool. White Levis', des boots, blue and white hooped long sleeved Frenchy top. Shades.

Johnny as was his custom for nights out was suited and booted.

Black shiny mohair suit. Three buttons. Red silk lining.

Immaculate, crisp white button down, black inch wide tie. Patent leather chisel toed, Cuban heeled shoes.

Finished off with a white silk handkerchief triangling out of his breast pocket.

"Where ya been man, we thought Steady Eddie was Deady Eddie?"

"Not me baby," replied Eddie, "I've been Stateside, checking out some great Soul acts. Brilliant. I've been making moves, connecting. Gonna bring some of these guys and chicks over here. Put on some sort of Soul review. It'll be massive. Huge.

"Gonna set up my own record label too, like that black dude in Detroit. That Motown guy. Wow. Gonna clean up."

Johnny felt a twinge of jealousy. Steady Eddie was a mover and a shaker. Going places. Always up to some sort of entrepreneurial shit. How the fuck did he get *this* deal started?

Johnny consoled himself with the fact that he too would soon be moving up. That was why he came to be standing outside the Soho coffee bar.

To meet another of his twilight buddies. Chucky Wilson.

Chucky was a few years older than Johnny. Black. Played Modern Jazz trumpet. He was the dude Johnny had followed to "Gerry's Jazz Club" a hundred years ago. They had become firm friends.

Chucky Wilson played in various Modern Jazz combos' around the capital. But with the trend for the kids to frequent record only playing venues, started by the Flamingo in Wardour Street and copied by many other previous live band establishments, demand for his mercurial talents was dwindling. Making a living was getting harder and therefore he was in need of an alternative form of income. Blowing his horn didn't pay the bills anymore.

"Nice to see ya man," said Steady, "Gotta go. People to see. Deals to make."

With that, Steady Eddie was gone. Swaggering off down Wardour Street and into the night.

Johnny followed him with his eyes till he was swallowed up by the Soho twilight. And once again smiled inwardly.

He liked Eddie. He had ambition. Drive.

And so have I, thought Johnny.

Seeing Eddie had given him a boost for his own little business enterprise.

Steady Eddie wasn't the only Face who was going to make it.

Competition was an integral part of any Modernists make up.

The need, the desire to better yourself and to be better than those around you.

On a day to day, or night to night basis, this intense need to be better than the others was called "Topping up" and applied to just about everything from records, clothes, dance moves and haircuts. But on a greater level it applied to getting the good stuff, living the dream, attaining "The Good Life". James bond. The clothes, the cars, the birds.

Steady Eddie was on his way. He had a head start but Johnny was gonna be there soon.

Johnny entered the coffee bar, checked out the room, and sauntered over to the table where his black buddy was seated.

"Hi man," greeted the musician.

"Hey baby, howzit going?" replied Johnny, as he sat down at the table, exchanging skin as he did so.

"Any news?" asked the white boy.

The jazz man leant back on his bench seat, smiled and cool as you like, flicked a cigarette into the corner of his mouth.

His large Negro lips overwhelmed the cigarette as he lit up.

Johnny mirrored his friends' moves and both inhaled deeply before letting the smoke exit via their noses.

"Well?" The Face asked testily as Chucky's dramatic pause went on a bit too long and got boring.

Chucky leant forward, elbows on the Formica table top and beckoned his younger friend closer in a conspiratorial way.

Johnny once again mirrored his friend as Chucky looked over both shoulders to check for eavesdroppers.

"I've spoken to my cousin and he's well up for it."

Chucky Wilson's Cousin Louis originally from Alabama U. S of A. was a staff sergeant in Uncle Sams Air Force stationed at the USAF base at Ruislip just outside London and had until now supplied the boys with perfectly innocent, hard to get soul and R and B 45's, and impossible to get Levis 'jeans.

Johnny's record collection, thanks to Cousin Louie, was the envy of many record collecting Faces and a great source of his ability in the "Topping up" stakes.

Apart from the 45s' from his homeland and Levis' from the camp PX stores he was also able, in his position in the camp to supply another, much sought after commodity.

Top grade, 100% kosher, amphetamines. Speed, uppers, dubes. Whatever you wanted to call them.

Whenever Uncle Sam gave Cousin Louie a weekend pass he, like a lot of his black comrades would spend their time in the West End. Drinking, dancing, screwing and fighting. The white airforce men spent their time in London as well, but didn't frequent the same places. Rednecks can't dance.

The most popular place for these black G.I.s to dance was at the "Roaring Twenties" in Carnaby Street.

The club was also a haunt for some of the hardiest and most dedicated of Soho's Modernists.

You had to be made of stern stuff because most nights the place would kick off mid record and would end up resembling a Wild West saloon, with knives being pulled and faces slashed as punishment for some minor transgression. As quickly as the fights started, they would end. The participants being bundled out of the door and into the street, by a combination of the doormen and pissed off G.I.s, there to dance not fight.

Being a lot younger and a lot whiter than 99% of the clientele, Johnny always felt a bit wary upon entering the club. Not that he would ever show it. He was too cool to let anyone see he was shitting himself.

He always made sure he was accompanied by Chucky whenever he visited the "Twenties" in search of some decent gear. Rather than hunt down Fat Tony or one of the other small time dealers for their artificial energy Johnny was visiting the place more and more for his speed, especially as the stuff hitting the streets these days was getting worse and worse.

It was his need for better chemicals, and his subsequent visit to the Carnaby Street club which had given him the idea for his little business venture.

One night in the "Twenties" to the sound of Prince Busters' "Al Capone" Johnny, Chucky and Louie hatched a plan.

Now most plans devised whilst under the influence of chemicals were forgotten as soon as the speed wore off.

Johnny hadn't forgotten. He'd been dreaming of an idea like this for a long time. Each avenue of an idea had ended in a dead end. When the topic of Louie and his access to humongous amounts of factory manufactured uppers was dropped into a conversation one evening, Johnny's antennae was instantly alerted. The subject had been a throw away remark, which he had expertly caught. And since that evening he had pushed and pushed Chucky to convince Louie to get on-side.

Now he sat opposite Chucky to listen to Cousin Louie's verdict.

"Is he definitely gonna do it?" asked Johnny, trying to suppress the rising feeling of excitement in his body.

"Definitely," replied Chucky, "Apparently he's well in debt. They play a lot of poker on the base, and he's shit. Loses ALL the time.

"He needs money, big money and he needs it fast," grinned Chucky.

"And he can get as much as we want?" asked Johnny.

Chucky nodded.

"For as long as we want?" he continued.

"Yup." Chucky smiled once more and leant back in his seat.

"As long as he's stationed at that base, in charge of stores, which he says will be at least three years. Maybe more.

"See, apparently there is a Lieutenant Colonel who's in charge of supplies but he's always too busy playing golf. So he delegates everything to some Major.

"Anyway, this Major is having a sordid affair with the Colonels wife who is pissed off with her husband playing golf all the time."

Johnny looked at his watch and stifled a yawn to playfully encourage Chucky to get a move on.

Chucky tutted and continued, refusing to be hurried. Typical West Indian.

"So the Major is too busy, so he delegates to a Captain who is also too busy on the account of his liaison with a Corporal. A bloke."

"Fuck me," said Johnny "It's like Peyton Place."

Chucky rolled his eyes and continued.

"The two lieutenants next in line are total fuck ups so they leave everything to Louie who has really got his shit together. So you see my friend, Cousin Louie is in charge of all PX, uniform, leisurewear and.......
medical supplies.

"The medical team fill out requisition forms for all their needs.

"Bandages, plasters, splints and ......amphetamines.

"Amphetamines for aircrew on night ops. Can't have pilots falling asleep at the wheel, or whatever they use to drive those big motherfuckers.

"Louie simply forges signatures or amounts required on the forms."

Johnny listened intently.

"Apparently airmen have been using the stuff since during the second world war. To stay awake for all the bombing missions.

"They still use it today, although it's hush, hush.

"They also use it as treatment for stress, anxiety, that sort of thing, which is pretty common apparently."

Both night creatures had stubbed out their cigarettes and lit fresh ones. The nervous energy between the two was tangible.

Chucky hadn't finished and beckoned his pal forward once more.

"Louie sends the order forms off to the suppliers. Of which there are half a dozen. Usually these suppliers are rotated, a different one every few weeks. All Louie has to do is send the order for supplies to EACH supplier every other week. The companies supplying stuff ain't gonna complain about the increase in their profits. They send their invoices to USAF in the States.

"They get so many invoices from all over the world, the clerks just authorize payment. They haven't the time to check on every request for payment.

"It's perfect, man," Chucky finished.

The black jazz man had started off cool and calm, but by the time he had finished he was talking 16 to the dozen. Without speed.

Johnny was also finding it hard to contain his excitement, but just about managed to keep cool. On the outside at least.

This is it, he thought, this is the chance I've been waiting for.

There was big money in drugs. He had seen Fat Tony's brand new Jag.

In fact the Soho drug dealer had been one of his nocturnal targets to follow and had ended up following him on his scooter to a large three storey house in upmarket Hampstead, complete with twelve foot high iron gates.

The teenager had turned away from the house that night, not thinking that one day he would be in the same business.

But now, listening to the news Chucky was giving him, Johnny felt a real adrenaline rush.

Although he was pissed off with the way the scene was going, standards being lowered with every new recruit to the Mod cause, it did mean that there would be loads of potential new customers to supply.

Johnny knew he would be moving on soon, a thought that saddened him, but he was getting older and the media had cottoned onto his world. Things were changing for the worse.

As soon as articles started appearing in papers and magazines he knew it was the beginning of the end.

They'd be making T.V. programmes about them next, he thought.

But now he was presented with an opportunity to move on up again. A defining moment. Like leaving home, like getting caught stealing from old Alf's Berwick Street stall and like following Chucky and discovering "Gerry's Jazz Club", and "The Life."

He still wanted the clothes and would always love the music but if this deal came off he could have more clothes. Better clothes. Could travel Stateside like Steady Eddie and get the really obscure 45's.

Shit, Johnny thought, I could even open my own club. A dream he had had for a while now. Really exclusive. No wankers allowed. Only the coolest of the cool.

He even had a name for this imaginary Modernist nirvana….. "ALCATRAZ."

"You alright man?" questioned Chucky, waking him from his dreaming.

"Yeah, yeah, I was just thinking," replied his friend who drifted off again into fantasy land.

He could trade in his scooter for an E-Type or an Aston, like James Bonds one.

Move out of his one room shithole into a swanky West End bachelor pad.

Chucky was talking again and it brought Johnny back to the present.

"The beauty of it is baby, is we don't need any front money. Louie gets the gear, gives it to us we knock it out and then give him his cut."

Johnny carried on with the master plan.

"We can sell the stuff ourselves in the West End where we have a solid rep and we can get a couple of decent Mod kids to sell it a bit further out, in the suburbs. There's loads of pubs and clubs springing up all over the place catering for all the new Mods. You only have to look in Melody Maker, they're all in there.

"Fat Tony's gear is getting worse .I'm sure it's not proper."

Chucky broke in "I've heard he gets it made up himself 'cos he can't get the prescription stuff. Apparently he's got some factory set up in Essex producing the stuff. Fuck knows' what's in it."

"Fucking rat poison," spat Johnny

A couple of dolly birds the boy knew walked past their table and gave him a smile and a wave. The two would-be drug dealers clammed up and Johnny gave them a bored nod of acknowledgement.

The two girls stopped and wiggled up to the table.

"Hi Johnny, long time no see," said the blonde.

"Hello Diane, how are you baby?" replied the Soho Face, "Looking good darling."

"You're looking pretty sharp yourself," responded blondie.

"Yea, I know," said Johnny with his usual arrogance.

"Big head," laughed Philippa the brunette.

"You okay Pippa?" said Johnny.

"Not bad," she replied, licking her top lip seductively.

Realising she was no longer the focus of Johnny's attention, Diane tried a different approach.

"You still seeing Lucy?" she asked cattily.

Johnny slowly turned his head to face the jealous Diane.

"Not really," he replied icily.

"That didn't last long, did it?" she asked. Meouw.

"She lasted longer than you Di," he responded with a flourish.

Diane glared daggers at Chucky as he burst out laughing at Johnny's put down.

"Bastard," she hissed at the cocky boy and turned on her three inch stiletto heel and stormed out of the place.

Johnny gave a half smile to Philippa, winked and said.

"Fancy meeting up later Pip?"

"What for?" she asked coyly.

"Mad, passionate sex," he replied staring directly into her hazel eyes.

"I'm celebrating," he added, looking at his pal across the table and then back at the girl.

"Yeah, alright then," the girl spluttered.

"Well, I'll see you at the "Whisky", bout two. Okay?"

"Sure, I'll be there Johnny," said Pippa, nearly wetting herself with excitement.

"Off you go then," he said dismissively.

The brunette nodded and walked away, before stopping and hesitantly approaching the table once more.

"Er.....Johnny?" she said

"What?" responded the King of Soho, leaning back in his seat.

"You won't tell Diane, will you?" she asked.

The teenage Lothario winked at Chucky before turning to the girl.

"What do you take me for baby?" he asked incredulously, palms outstretched.

The answer was enough for the naïve girl, who smiled and bounced off.

"You dirty bastard," said Chucky in barely contained admiration, "I don't know how you do it."

"Good looks, charm and charisma," replied Johnny with a laugh.

"Where you gonna do the dirty deed? My place again I suppose?"

Johnny often used Chucky's place for various reasons.

1. It was closer, his conquests didn't have time to change their minds.

2. A flat in Soho, albeit an attic flat was cooler than a bedsit at the Elephant.
3. Johnny never let anyone know where he lived in case of reprisals.
4. He wouldn't have to change his sheets in the morning!

"Nah, I ain't gonna meet her," said Johnny.

"But you just arranged to see her at the "Whisky" I thought you were gonna dick her," said Chucky.

"Knowing I can is sometimes enough man," replied Johnny the stud, "And I know I can with Pippa. Besides she's probably shit anyway."

"Thank god for that," exclaimed Chucky, "I won't have to change my sheets tomorrow."

Both boys smiled.

"Anyway," Johnny continued, getting back to business, "I know a couple of young Mods we can use to help shift the gear. We won't have to pay them much. They'll do it just to be associated with us and for the rep they'll get.

"They'll jump at the chance to become minor Faces. And they're not wankers, they know the score. Half decent clothes, good music knowledge."

Just then someone put sixpence in the jukebox, the machine mechanically and noisily picked out the selected disc and the arm lowered onto the vinyl and the sound of Arthur Alexander's "You better move on" hit Johnny right between the eyes.

"London American Recordings 45-HLD 9523" knew Johnny instantly, having owned a copy for a while.

"You better move on," it was an omen. A sign, thought Johnny, as he drifted off into another world again.

The dreamer was jogged back to the real world when Chucky proclaimed,

"Shit, we've got a problem man," he said as he cast his eyes towards the figure that had just entered the coffee bar.

The man who now stood at the counter was Dickie Morgan, Fat Tony's minder and muscle.

Five feet eleven, boat race covered in scars, thick as shit. He came with a reputation for being a bit tasty. And a bit nasty.

Chucky averted his gaze and whispered across the table to his pal.

"If Fatty finds out we're moving in on his patch he'll have Morgan give us a right kicking."

"Don't worry about that prick man, I've already got it sorted."

"But look at him. He looks a right nutter. All those scars on his face," replied Chucky.

"Yeah, but who put those scars there, eh? That's who you should worry about. Dickie Morgan's alright for knocking kids around, giving 16 and 17 year olds a slap just 'cos Tony thinks they're out of order but I bet he ain't so tough when he comes up against his own size." Johnny paused, "And I've sorted out two blokes his size to take care of any rough stuff."

Dickie Morgan ordered a cup of tea and had taken a seat across the room from the two friends.

"Who?" asked Chucky, sceptically.

"Mickey and Stevie Franklin."

"You're joking?" hissed Chucky, "They're psychos'. How d'ya get them on our side?"

"I was in Eddy Grimsteads scooter shop over in Barking, buying some new springs for my stand for the millionth time and they were in there. I happened to have a copy of Maxine Browns' new LP which I had just bought in Imhoffs. I had thrown the bag and was carrying the album under my arm, casual like, just for the pose.

"Anyway, Mickey Franklin comes up to me and bold as brass comes out with "You're name's Johnny innit, bit of a Face ain't ya?"

"Now, you know me Chucky, normally if someone just comes up to me and starts talking like that I'd blank 'em. But I recognized them from one night in the Thomas a Becket on the Old Kent Road. I was in there to meet a bird I'd pulled at work and they were drinking at the bar when a group of geezers at the other end of the bar started getting leary, dropping glasses, hassling anyone who walked past them. Anyway the Franklin boys looked over at the noisy group and Stevie said in a voice which was designed to be heard, "WANKERS.""

Chucky listened intently as Johnny continued.

"Now this comment was like a red rag to a bull and these idiots charged over to the brothers.

"They were definitely not off the manor cos the Franklins have a bit of a rep locally.

"Well, the barman, recognizing imminent aggro slipped around the back and the other punters remembered appointments they had. I was fucked cos I was sitting at a table as far away from the door as I could be and to get out I would have had to walk past the group at the bar and that would have been a) dangerous, and b) very uncool.

"So, acting casual and unperturbed I settled back into my chair, lit a Gauloises and waited for the ensuing commotion, although I was ready to duck under the table if the action got too close."

Johnny was obviously enjoying telling the story.

"The group got over to where Stevie and Mickey stood.

"What d'ya say, cunt?" the leader of the group said.

"Obviously being men of few words the two brothers grabbed the Light Ale bottles from the bar and simultaneously smashed them on the edge of the bar."

The story continued. Mickey, with great force shoved the lethal jagged edge of the bottle straight into the exposed, vulnerable flesh of the first mans face. The blokes flesh just opened up as the bottle found its target, blood spurted out like a fountain. The man screamed and instinctively clasped his hand to his cheek, the blood squirting between his fingers all over his attacker, who had drawn the bottle back and once again plunged the weapon into the man. Fortunately the mans action in grabbing his ripped up face saved his eye, as the second attack with the bottle would have hit it, but instead sliced into the back of his hand.

Stevie had also caused considerable damage and pain to his opponent, sticking his broken bottle into the man's forehead, opening up a huge ragged flap, just under his hair line.

"Look, I've scalped him," laughed Stevie and let out an Apache like whoop.

The victims didn't see the humour at all. The two cut men grabbing their injuries, trying to stem the flow of blood, ran past their attackers, howling in pain.

The men's two companions had had it away on their toes as soon as the first piece of glass came into contact with the first piece of flesh.

Johnny finished the story.

"Then cool as you like, instead of fleeing the scene in case of Old Bill, they both leant against the bar once more and Mickey shouted out to the barman whose nervous face had peered around the door to the bar to see if all was clear.

"Two more Light Ales please mate!"

Chucky was shaking his head in disbelief as the tale was concluded.

"Both of them were covered in claret as the Light Ales were supplied. Then they both looked over to me. Apart from the barman I was the only other person in there.

"Alright mate?" Mickey said.

"Not bad." I said, "The live entertainments pretty good in here, what d'ya do for an encore?"

"For a moment," Johnny confided in his pal, "I thought I'd overstepped the mark. Have to say something clever, you know what I'm like. Anyway, they both didn't say anything and I thought "Shit". But suddenly they both burst out laughing and I breathed a huge sigh of relief."

Chucky was laughing at the story as Johnny remembered the last bit.

"Just then, who walks in the place? But Debbie, the bird I'd arranged to meet. She sees me talking to these two nutty looking blokes covered in blood. Chairs and tables all over the place, broken glass on the floor.

"Ello Deb" I say, "what you having?"

"She looks at me, then at the Franklin boys, then back at me, turns round without saying a word and walks out. She hasn't spoken to me since."

Chucky was cracking up with laughter.

"So anyway there I was in Grimsteads and Stevie says, "Who's that?" pointing to my Maxine Brown album.

"I told him that Maxine had the most beautiful voice, a Soul goddess. That mere mortals should feel privileged to share the same planet as her. That she could take you to a higher place. That her voice was like honey dripping over your soul.

"And do you know what he said?"

"What?" asked Chucky.

"He said, "Never mind about all that. Is she any good?"

Chucky let rip with another laugh as Johnny smiled and shook his head.

"What did you do then?" enquired Wilson, convulsed with mirth.

"I told him to buy a copy and listen for himself.

"Gave him the number and where to buy it cos it was quite obscure. Normally I wouldn't be so helpful but I felt like I was doing missionary work, introducing a savage to such beauty."

Johnny smiled again and continued.

"I didn't think any more of it. I didn't think he'd bother buying the L.P. He was probably into The Who and all that crash, bang, wallop music. Each to their own.

"Anyway, the following week, I was in the Becket again to meet a fella who was interested in buying something I'd nicked from the warehouse at work, when in walk the Franklins.

"Stevie makes a bee line for me when he sees me and totally takes me by surprise with what he says."

"Go on," says Chucky.

Johnny replies "He says. "That Maxine Brown bird is fucking brilliant mate.

"Bought that L.P. Fucking nice one."

"I was totally stunned. To see this shaven headed nut case, who I had witnessed sticking a bottle in another persons face be so obviously moved by the voice of an angel really freaked me out."

"Then he said, "Got any other stuff like that?" So I introduced both of them, Stevie more than Mickey, to the delights of Doris Troy. Aretha Franklin, Brenda Holloway, Marvin and Smokey.

"Now they think I'm the dogs' bollocks and they would do anything for me.

"So as you can see, Dickie "the prickie" Morgan is no problem."

"Like it," approved Chucky.

Johnny wanted "The Good Life" with all the trimmings. He wanted his own club, where he had his own table, slightly raised, over-looking the dance floor, where his staff would serve him the finest Champagne. An exclusive club for the coolest of the cool. Playing only the best in Soul and Blues with a little bit of Ska. Strict dress code, no mugs allowed.

The teenage dreamer already had a name for this Modernist utopia.— "ALCATRAZ" after the prison. The walls would be adorned with wanted posters of Al Capone, Lucky Luciano, and other top gangsters.

Chucky wanted to make records.

A career in music, not just blowing his guts out for the short end money. If things took off with this deal he could finance himself, hire a studio, backing musicians. All the made up tunes he had in his head could be put down on vinyl and sell a million copies.

Both young men had a desperate need for this business to succeed. Both men needed this to work so they could run even further from their past. As if money and possessions would throw a cover over their background of poverty and insignificance.

So there it was. Louie would supply them with the gear. Johnny and Chucky would sell in the West End. The Franklin boys would pair up with the two young Mods Pete and Phil who Johnny had sorted. Stevie and Mick would transport them on their scooters to sell the stuff in the suburbs and to provide protection if Fatty got the 'ump.

The two friends shook hands on the deal, got up and walked back out onto the street.

Soho was really kicking into life. Darkness had enveloped the sky and the neon signs of the nightclubs, coffee bars and amusement arcades flashed on and off. Green, red, blue. Music blared from doorways; the excited chattering of night people was a constant hum. The occasional screech of laughter interrupted the rhythm and beat of the streets. Taxis' honked jaywalkers out of the way and scooters pop popped up and down.

"I'll see you later man," said Chucky "I'm off to jam."

"Yeah," replied Johnny dreamily as he looked up to the sky.

Chucky looked at Johnny, smiled and slowly shook his head.

He's off again, thought the jazz man knowing that look. He knew he wouldn't be getting much out of Johnny when he slipped into his private world, so he lit another cigarette, gently slapped his friend on the back and headed off into the night.

Johnny just stood there, taking in the sights and sounds of the most exciting and coolest city in the world.

The young Modernist with a dream did a complete 360, absorbing the atmosphere like a sponge, feeding on his surroundings.

He loved London, or more precisely the West End. The people walking by consisted of cool Mods, actors, dancers, pimps, gangsters, whores. Men dressed as women, women dressed as men. Musicians, dealers, cut-throats and chancers.

It was like the back lot of MGM studios or something and it was like this every night, a public display of a private world.

Johnny gobbled down a couple of Blues, adrenaline already pumping through his body and headed for The Scene. He needed to dance.

Walking in to Ham Yard he was greeted by a couple of guys he knew. Faces. Only faces at The Scene.

"Howzit going man?" greeted one of the dudes.

"Cool man, cool," he responded feeling better than he had ever done.

"Looking good Johnny," admired the other Face, who was looking very sharp himself in a black and white dogtooth jacket, black strides, white shirt, black tie and black waistcoat.

"I'll see you inside," said the centre of everyone's attention as he swaggered off into the heat of the club.

Once inside, another couple of people he knew came and greeted him and he launched into some speed induced conversation which lasted a good twenty minutes, the content of which would instantly be forgotten.

Suddenly, half way through a new subject of discussion there occurred a Soho night time phenomenon.

Mid sentence, the D.J put on "What's easy for two is so hard for one" by Mary Wells, and a giant unseen hand dragged Johnny away from his companions and onto the dance floor.

Some records just had to be danced to. It couldn't be explained, and the "straights" of the world would never be able to understand it. But when the opening bars of particular 45s filled the room, it was like a religious experience. A calling.

No, it wasn't a hand that dragged him and made him dance. It was the angel of soul, gently lifting him onto the dance floor.

The most important conversation, argument or dodgy deal was instantly curtailed, as the need, the desire to move your body to a certain song overwhelmed you. Filled your heart, soul and mind with a pleasure so intense you felt like you would explode.

Johnny didn't believe in God but when for instance "Hello Stranger" by Barbara Lewis was put on he knew there was a heaven.

CHAPTER 9

The sound of a lone trumpet drifted across the Soho night. 4 a.m.
Chucky Wilson, Jazz man. Modern. Smooth.

Chucky had joined in with other Jazz musos' at Gerrys Jazz Club for a three hour jam. Paying gigs were thin on the ground lately but he loved to play and there was always a chance there might be someone in the crowd who could give him a leg up.

After blowing up a storm at Gerrys he declined the invitations to party, dance, get high or get laid at some swanky pad in Knightsbridge.

Tonight, he just slowly walked back to his little attic flat in Beak St.

The streets of Soho had been empty. A few drunks staggered about looking in bins for dregs. A couple of hookers tottered back from their last punters of the night. Subterranean Soho was still going strong in the basement clubs which would empty at 7 or 8 in the morning. The underground world of the Modernist. Unless you *knew*, you would never *know*.

Once home, Chucky sat on his chair positioned next to the window which stretched from floor to ceiling put his feet up on another chair and played.

The tune that floated across the rooftops was slow and mournful but man was it cool!

One of his latest compositions. A tune that would only ever exist in his head. Chucky never wrote anything down.

Alone with his trumpet and his talent, he slid into a trance as he played, improvising sounds into his own creations until he sat back in his chair and fell into a deep sleep, his instrument lovingly cradled in his arms.

CHAPTER 10

Frank Saunders picked up the phone in his Chelsea car showroom and dialled the number.

With every slow painful turn of the dial he wanted to slam the receiver down but eventually he completed the number and a voice said hello.

"Get me Raven," he ordered bluntly. "It's Saunders."

After a long pause, which Saunders knew was deliberately done to keep him waiting, Raven picked up the phone.

"Allo," the voice barked.

"It's me," said Saunders, "We're in."

"Nice one Frankie," replied Raven.

"Now just carry on as normal and I'll be in touch a bit nearer the time when it's a goer."

"When?" demanded Saunders.

"Soon enough," and the phone went dead.

CHAPTER 11

Monday morning again, back to work for Johnny. The usual aches and pains he felt after a weekend of being "blocked."

He had stayed at The Scene until six o'clock Sunday morning then made his way by scooter to Portobello Road market for a full English in a café used by the traders there.

Normally after a night of speeding he didn't have much of an appetite but he fancied eating for once.

Money spent on grub was money not spent on clothes or records or living the life, but Johnny was feeling up-beat and optimistic about Chucky and their business venture which if all went to plan would kick off the following weekend.

The week at work really dragged but his mind was firmly set on the weekend. More than usual.

He stayed in at night. Monday, Tuesday and Wednesday laying on his bed listening to his record collection and dreaming of his life that lay ahead. The clothes he would buy, the car he would have, even though he couldn't drive, trips abroad.

Thursday night, showered and dressed casually in a tasty blue and white stripped button down, tucked into white Levis with a brown leather belt. Brown suede, leather soled desert boots and a beautifully soft brown suede bomber jacket finished off the outfit.

He wasn't going dancing tonight. Tonight he was going to head up West, ride around a bit, pose. Have a coffee, ride some more. Then at the arranged time, head off to Liverpool Street Station to meet up with Cousin Louie to collect the first batch of merchandise.

Johnny was on edge as he headed across the water from the poverty of South London to the affluence and endless opportunity of the West End. Bright lights. Big city. Glamour and style.

Cruising across Waterloo Bridge, the Face slipped on his shades as the evening sunshine reflected off the Thames. The sound of "Money(That's what I want)" by Barrett Strong ran through his head and he smiled.

After hanging around the West End for a while continuously checking his watch he headed off for his rendezvous.

Twenty minutes later he arrived outside the train station to see Louie dressed in civvies leaning against a lamppost by the taxi rank.

Johnny tooted his hooter as he glided up to the American serviceman clutching a battered leather holdall.

"Alright Lou?" greeted Johnny as the scooter stopped at the kerb and he planted his feet on the road either side of his machine.

"Hey, Johnny my man, how ya doing, grooving?" said Cousin Louie.

"Moving and a grooving man, jump on."

Louie got on and Johnny slipped the scooter into first and took off, nipping around an arriving taxi, who's driver suggested he indulged in self love.

Louie leant back in pillion. One hand holding the spare wheel rack, the other clutching the bag of valuable cargo, clamped between his legs.

"You got the stuff then, Lou?" asked Johnny over his shoulder feeling safe to talk now they were on the move.

"It's all here man," said Louie, "Ten thousand of the little babies."

"WHOOOO…….. YEA," hollered Johnny as he went through a red light, causing a number 52 bus to break sharply. Johnny received another volley of abuse from another pissed off driver.

Arriving at Chucky's Soho residence, Louie climbed off shakily and said, "You're one crazy motherfucker boy. I'll take the goddamn bus back."

"You got here didn't ya?" laughed the boy, as he pressed the bell to Chucky's flat.

Chucky buzzed them up and the two arrivals took two stairs at a time until they reached the attic flat. The door was open and they rushed in, slamming it behind them, panting for breath.

The cousins embraced and Chucky and Johnny slapped palms.

Louie made his way over to the small wooden table that was pushed up against a wall, and placed the holdall in the middle.

Turning back to the others his left hand, palm outstretched pointed to the valuable cargo.

"There you are guys, all there. Don't take 'em all at once," he said.

The boys' came to join Louie at the table and Johnny opened the bag.

"Fucking hell," he exclaimed "We're gonna make a fortune."

Chucky looked on in amazement, before reaching under the table to retrieve a brown paper carrier bag. Putting a hand inside, he pulled out a bunch of wage envelopes.

"Let's get to work then," he said throwing the envelopes onto the table. "It's gonna be a long night."

Louie laughed and proclaimed "For you guys maybe, I've done my bit, I'm off."

"What about helping fill the envelopes?" complained Chucky.

"No chance man," said Louie "I'll see you guys later. Don't wait up."

Before the two Modernists could say a thing, Louie had bid a hasty exit, running down the stairs as quick as he had run up them.

Johnny and Chucky looked at each other, then at the table with the holdall and envelopes, then back at each other.

"Git," Johnny said as they both shrugged their shoulders, resigned to the fact they wouldn't be going out that night.

Six hours later, the boys with backs aching like bastards had finished their toil. The pills had been placed into the envelopes in quantities of two, three, five, ten and twenty.

The final pill had been placed in their brown, windowed envelopes and the boys leant back in their chairs and stretched their arms to the ceiling, both letting out loud groans.

Only then did something dawn on Johnny.

"Chuck," he said, "We haven't even tried 'em."

Both boys looked at the huge pile of envelopes and burst into laughter.

"Well, we can't try any now, we'll be pacing the floor all fucking day. Look," he said pointing to the window. "The suns just coming up." Said Chucky.

"Nah, I'm gonna get me ead down," replied Johnny "We'll try em this evening."

With that, he manoeuvred his way over to the single bed in the corner of the room and stretched himself out on to it.

"Hey man," protested Chucky, "I get the bed."

But Johnny was already pushing out the Zeds. Chucky shook his head and plonked himself down in the threadbare armchair and was soon fast asleep himself.

CHAPTER 12

The Face, the Jazzman and the four Mods stood on the corner of Greek Street and Soho Square in all their Friday night finery. Swapping speed induced stories of the evening's events. The night had been a resounding success for all concerned and the chemicals racing through their bodies caused them to all tell of their experiences at the same time, gabbling over each others words talking 16 to the dozen, a hundred miles an hour. Each pill popper fought against the others conversation, oblivious to the others and what was being said by them. Five minutes later and they would all be unable to recall what they had said and what had been said to them.

All pills had been sold. The only problem had been encountered by the young Mod Peter and his minder Mickey Franklin at a Mod hangout called The Station in Woolwich, South East London.

As soon as the two Mods had pulled up outside the club on Mickey's stolen Vespa GS160 they had felt bad vibes, receiving dodgy looks from the local Mods hanging around outside.

Peter jumped off the scooter but didn't stray from Mickey's side as he pulled it up onto its stand. The young Mod felt distinctly uneasy at the looks they were getting but the older harder boy didn't seem bothered in the least by the intimidating atmosphere.

Most clubs and pubs on the scene outside the West End, be it North, South, East or West were very insular and were places where everyone knew everyone else and anyone from outside the manor was treated with veiled hostility. The small groups of South London Mods huddling together outside The Station turned to cast suspicious eyes over the arrival of the unfamiliar scooter carrying its unfamiliar passengers. They watched as the scooter pulled up alongside the row of other machines, chrome and paintwork gleaming in the South London moonlight.

The two outsiders dismounted and headed to the entrance of the club. Peter sticking to Mickey's side like a Siamese twin, thinking perhaps this drug dealing business wasn't such a good idea after all.

The two of them paid the three shillings entrance fee and entered the dark, sweaty club. Mickey first, bowling into the place like he owned it, his younger better dressed companion following.

"Mickey's Monkey" by Smokey Robinson was being played by the disc jockey as the two would-be drug dealers headed to a dark corner of the club, away from the bar and the dance floor.

"Take a seat," instructed Mickey Franklin indicating a table, flanked by two unmatching wooden chairs.

"I'll get us a drink," said the young tough, "What you having?"

"Just a coke," replied Peter nervously, worried that his minder would leave him for too long. He just wanted to sell their gear and get the hell out of there.

Mickey Franklin barged his way to the bar and snapped his fingers at the barman.

"Pint of bitter and a coke," he ordered.

The barman was going to ignore the man and his rudely delivered requirement but one look at the features of the voices owner made him decide to pour the drinks.

"One and six," said the barman as he handed over the drinks. The money was chucked on to the varnish free bar top and the drinks snatched from his grasp.

"And thank you too," said the barman sarcastically thinking he had said it quietly and to himself.

The customer stopped in his tracks and turned to face the rapidly whitening barman.

"What d'ya fucking say?" he growled.

"Nothing," replied the barman who was just about to crap in his pants.

"Good, keep it that way YOU MUG!" said Mickey who turned and made his way over to the table, where Peter sat squirming impatiently.

Mickey Franklin necked half the contents of his glass, wiped his mouth with the back of his hand and said.

"Right Pete, you stay here, I'll go and drum up a bit of business."

Peter nodded okay, as Mickey headed off to discretely inform the clubbers of the purpose of their visit. Or as discretely as someone who looked like him could.

Ten minutes later he returned to the table. No takers. Not one.

Peter hadn't taken his eyes off his companion as he made his way unsuccessfully around the club.

"What the fuck's the matter with this lot then?" Mickey said as he slumped down in the seat next to Peter and reached for his beer.

"I told 'em what we got. Top quality, best prices, all that old bollocks and they all blanked me!"

At that moment Mickey and Peter turned and looked up at two figures approaching the table. Peter stayed seated but Mickey stood, sensing that the visitors to their table hadn't come up to offer them a drink.

The first figure standing in front of them was a skinny runt of a Mod, with bad skin and dodgy gnashers. The other Mod was bigger and stood behind the first boy.

Peter leant back nervously and pressed himself against the back of the chair when the first boy started talking.

"This is my patch," he said angrily, "We sell the gear in this club and all the others round here, so if you don't want any trouble you'd better fuck off."

Peter let out a small squeak of fear from the back of his throat and slid the chair back further against the wall. Mickey meanwhile took control of the situation.

The skinny Mod flinched ever so slightly as the Franklin brother put an arm around his shoulder and raised his voice above "Green Onions" by Booker T and the MGs.

"We need to talk me old mate. Outside. Got a bit of business to put your way."

The boy looked suspiciously through slitty eyes at the dangerous looking boy with his arm around him. His huge shovel of a hand resting on his shoulder.

"Come on then, I'll give you 2 minutes to do your talking, but no funny business."

With that he turned and beckoning his mate with a flick of his head made his way to the door.

"Stay here," Mickey growled to Peter who thought it was a great idea and who didn't really have the look of someone who was going anywhere in a hurry. That is unless the bogs had a window he could climb out of.

"Green Onions" came to an end and was replaced on the turntable by the falsetto sound of Smokey Robinson and the Miracles singing "Shop Around" but the patrons of the club, their curiosity getting the better of them, filed out after the newcomer and their regular supplier.

The D.J., his head looking down to cue up the next 45 was well pissed off when he looked up to see the dance floor empty except for three young Mod girls who were the only ones giving dancing attention to Smokey. Oblivious to the goings on at the other side of the room, the girls shook and shimmied around the floor.

The runty Mod walked out first and was followed by his minder, with Mickey Franklin next. Once outside the two drug dealers turned to see what this stranger had to say for himself.

SMACK!

Mickey Franklins right fist landed on the chin of the dealers minder, knocking him flat on his arse beside a gleaming Lambretta LI 150 whose owner had just dismounted. The scooter rider winced as the already unconscious figure fell, narrowly missing his pride and joy. He winced again as did all the others present as Franklin followed up his right cross with a repeated and completely unnecessary barrage of kicks to the stricken boys head. Girls watching screamed and the guys muttered a few "fucking hells" but did not intervene.

Feeling enough was enough Mickey quickly spun around, fully expecting the runt to have had it away on his toes. But no, there before him was the teenage drug dealer holding a flick knife with a six inch blade pointed in his direction shining menacingly as he approached his mates slayer cautiously.

Having fought hard for his lucrative patch it appeared that he wasn't prepared to give it up easily.

The slums of Woolwich and Plumstead bred a hard type of animal.

Slowly, step by step the boy approached Franklin, slashing his weapon from side to side, but was slightly perturbed to see his intended victim smile in the moonlight. Not the look he expected that's for sure!

Mickey Franklin didn't back up an inch and as his aggressor got closer and closer he timed his move to perfection.

As the blade in front of him slashed to one side, Franklin's blood covered Loafer swung up and connected with the knife boys bollocks.

It doesn't matter if you are carrying a knife, a gun or a fucking bazooka one perfectly aimed kick in the nuts and its goodnight Vienna.

The boy dropped his weapon and sank to his knees, crying out in anguish, howling in pain as he clutched his rapidly swelling testicles in both hands. The knife had clattered tinnily to the ground as the male members of the watching crowd winced in empathy, some of them going so far as to cover their own nuts.

After a gasp from the crowd the scene was totally silent. All eyes on the newcomer with a skill for inflicting pain watched him look around on the floor until his eyes rested on the dropped knife. Bending over to retrieve it from the gutter you could hear a pin drop. Grabbing the now former drug dealer's hair, he lifted his head a couple of inches from the ground. The boy groaned.

"This *may* have been your patch and you *may* have been the main man, but not anymore," Mickey growled into his face, "Understand?"

The boy groaned again which Mickey took for him agreeing to the new situation.

Turning to face the group crowding around the entrance to the club, Mickey spoke again.

"From now on everyone buys their gear from me and my mate. Don't worry. Its pukka gear. This wanker is history."

As if to emphasise his point, he quickly slashed the blade across the face of the boy whose head he was holding.

Another scream from the boy filled the silence, accompanied by a few more "oohs" from the assembled Mods.

The razor sharp blade sliced the boy's cheek wide open and Franklin let go of his hair, his head thumping heavily on the kerb.

The slashed boy forgot about the pain in his bollocks and ignored the pain of his head whacking on the kerb to clutch his hands to his cheek, trying to hold his face together.

"Right," said the teenage psychopath cheerfully, "Anyone want any gear, go and see my mate inside. He'll sort you out."

With that the crowd obediently filed back into the club and comically formed an orderly queue to the table where Peter sat, eager to get their nights supply of leapers.

Peter looked at the line of Mods in amazement as Mickey sauntered over to him.

"Fucking hell Mick," Peter said out of the corner of his mouth, "Shall we put a bleeding sign up?"

Mickey, not being too blessed in the brains department didn't recognize irony when he heard it and thought it was a great idea replying.

"Yeah, nice one Pete, what shall we make it out of?"

Peter stopped serving pills for a moment and looked around at Mickey to see if he was being funny, but the serious look on his face told him that his companion was all for the idea.

"GET YOUR ILLEGAL DRUGS HERE," thought Peter with a smile on his face, visualising the sign.

"Never mind Mick, give us a hand here."

The three young Mod girls still spun and twisted their way around the dance floor, oblivious to the drama having taken place.

Nothing could stop them dancing to James Brown, Jackie Wilson and Etta James and would soon be joined by the Mods who were buying their gear at the far side of the room.

Peter and Mickey, now back on the safer ground of Soho finally finished their tale and the group nodded their heads in appreciation.

Two a.m. on a Soho corner. Heads bobbing, gum being chewed, excited chatter filled the air.

The streets hummed with activity. Scooters glided by. Shouts of recognition and greeting could be heard. Taxis chugged by looking for fares. Music blared out of basement dives and the sound of bells and ringing from amusement arcades signified mugs throwing money into the machines.

Doorways were inhabited by "working girls" offering yokel tourists and theatre goers a "good time."

If they were lucky and were tempted by an 'honest' hooker they would part with their two quid and get a knee trembler up one of the warren of alleys that made up a large part of Soho.

If they were unlucky and a little bit too pissed, they'd pay their money over to the hooker, follow her up a darkened alley and get whacked over the nut by the girls pimp. The punter would then be relieved of his money, watch and any other valuables he had.

The victim of the perfect crime. Probably married, the man would be too embarrassed and ashamed to report the crime to the police for fear of his wife finding out. The girl and her pimp would get away scot free. Free to move on to the next unsuspecting punter. The victim would just have to put it down to experience.

The youthful gang of drug dealers started to get anxious feelings having been stood in one place for too long. Amphetamines always caused feelings of paranoia and the boys started to nervously look around them searching for danger and trouble lurking in the shadows.

Was that a plain-clothes copper over there, knowing what they were up to? Or was he part of a gang waiting for them to split up and rip them off of their ill gotten gains?

"Time to make a move guys," said Chucky, voicing the thoughts of the little group.

"Yea man," agreed Johnny, "Time to blow."

Glancing around him he was relieved to see the man who had been lurking across the street had disappeared and quickly weighed out the lads with their wages.

The boys all shook hands and headed off to taste the delights that Soho offered.

The Franklin boys headed off to the Marquee in Wardour Street to see a band called The Who, a group of white kids who played 100mph R and B which seemed to appeal to the new type of Mod on the scene. A lot of the newer, harder Mods preferred the excitement and aggression of these sort of bands as opposed to the sweet soul music of the purists.

The original stylists of the Modernist scene hated these new groups, who ripped off genuine Modernist heroes like Arthur Alexander and Martha Reeves.

The world of the true Modernist was a world of originality. That was the whole point. If you copied someone's style of collar, length of lapel or side vent, or did a shit cover version of a 45 by some black goddess from the deep south of the U.S. then you had missed the point. "Create, don't copy" was the mantra the real Faces lived by.

The two younger Mods had more of an idea and they headed off to the "Whisky A Go-Go" to take in some sweet sounds and to move a little.

Peter and Tony had kept a few leapers back for themselves. Johnny knew they would but there was plenty to go round so he wasn't bothered. Their money would be going on clothes from Carnaby Street and records from Stans Record Shack.

Johnny bade Chucky goodbye. The Jazzman was headed off to "Gerrys" to jam. "Gerrys" was one of the few places catering for live Modern Jazz these days. Chucky feared that it too would soon go the way of other venues, just playing records or putting on guitar groups, so he intended to make the most of it while he could.

Besides, he needed to blow the shitty feeling of becoming a drug dealer out of his system.

Johnny wandered north along Frith Street oblivious to the night time cacophony of the most exciting city in the world.

The boy about town stepped in to a doorway not frequented by a "lady of the night" to drop a handful of U.S. airforce supplied amphetamines before heading to the Scene to dance the night away. Johnny too had mixed feelings about the evening. On one hand the money was great, but on the other he did feel as though he had somehow crossed a line. A line which separated his beautiful world from another; a colder, harder place.

Standing in the doorway, across the road from a green neon light advertising "Adult Books and Cine films," Johnny cupped his hand and emptied the contents of one of the little brown envelopes he had retrieved from inside his immaculate mohair jacket. He smiled with anticipation at the sight of the pills in the palm of his hand and with the practised ease of an experienced drug consumer he threw the five little purple heart shaped pills to the back of his throat. No liquid was needed to help the speed on its way as his trained throat took one large gulp and swallowed the lot, slightly scraping the sides on the way down.

Johnny was still speeding from his earlier intake but knew he would be needing a top up around about now, the shadowed doorway protecting him from prying eyes.

Once the uppers had disappeared and were working their way through his system he removed a pack of Sobranie cigarettes from inside his jacket. He had started to smoke Sobranie after watching a French film recently and one of the characters smoked them. They were cool because they were all different colours and anyone seeing him smoke them, would realise they were unusual and as far as he knew he was the only one using them. Mind you, everyone would probably be smoking them in a week's time. Still, first is first.

Johnny sparked up his fag and his handsome, older than his years face was illuminated for a second. He knew anyone observing him would be impressed by his Cool. Everything he did, he tried to imagine what he looked like, what effect he was giving. He pictured himself as if his actions were scenes from a film.

"Hi Johnny." A voice from behind him made him jump and he spun around. Uncool.

"Long time, no see handsome," the honey covered voice purred.

Johnny instantly realized where he had inadvertently ended up.

"Hey Misty howzit going baby?" responded Johnny, leaving the cigarette dangling casually from the corner of his mouth trying to regain his momentary loss of composure.

"You're looking good Johnny," she said seductively.

"You too baby. Good enough to eat."

Misty pouted "You feeling hungry Mr Ace Face?"

He smiled.

Misty. Wow, what a babe. Light brown skin. Long straight black hair. Shiny. Beautiful big brown eyes with the longest eye lashes ever. No need for mascara. In fact hardly any make up at all. No need. Just lipstick.

Standing there before him, one hand on her hip, the other slowly stroking her throat, she was a vision of beauty. Slim. Tiny waist, which flowed perfectly into her womanly hips.

Her legs, long and perfect clad in a simple black skirt which daringly finished five inches above her knees.

Her tits. Man her tits, tumbling out of her top like an eruption from Vesuvius.

It was all Johnny could do to stop *himself* erupting like Vesuvius and keep his cool.

A feat he managed on the outside, but inside he was jelly.

This vision leant forward and placed a pair of bright red lips against his cheek, leaving a smudge which she gently removed with her thumb, moistened by an unnecessarily deliberate and slow licking with her tongue.

"Misty baby, you really are looking good," he proclaimed again to a deeply appreciative audience. Misty wasn't really part of his scene so he could afford this display of boyish enthusiasm.

"Why, thank you kind sir," exclaimed Misty in her best "Gone with the wind" Deep South accent.

But she wasn't from the Deep South. Well not the deep south of the U.S.A. And not from the deep south of London either, Brixton or Balham but from some far flung place south of the equator. A place of palm trees, white sands and turquoise blue seas.

A place where the days eeeeeezed by and the sun warmed your body to the core.

A land where clothing was minimal and the sand ran through your shoeless toes.

A tropical paradise she had decided to swap for grimy, sooty London.

What the fuck was that all about?

"You know what Misty?" Johnny asked cockily, having regained his usual confidence.

"You have got the best legs in London," he said, his eyes starting at her feet and raising up to where her skirt began.

Mistys' dark skin hid the blushes that crept across her cheeks, but she gave it away by lowering her eyes, avoiding his blue eyed gaze.

She was used to compliments. Being as beautiful as she was, it was like water off a ducks back, but when it came from someone she fancied as much as Johnny she reverted to the schoolgirl she was. That is if she went to school.

"Although," he continued with a frown, "There is something wrong with them."

Johnny had discovered in his short career as a ladies man that no matter how beautiful a woman was, they were all insecure and could easily be brought down a peg or two. To even the playing field so to speak.

The comment smacked the young girl straight between the eyes and she felt instantly desperate.

"What? What?" she said hurriedly, "What's wrong with my legs?" looking down at them, searching for imperfections.

"Well," sighed Johnny heavily, enjoying Misty's discomfort, pausing for effect.

"They," another pause, "Have never been wrapped around my back."

Forgetting his cool for once he burst out laughing at his wind up and the look on his friends face.

"Bastard, bastard," she said in her heavy husky accent, but laughing along with him as she hit him playfully on the chest, which along with Johnny's uninhibited laughter was another unusual occurrence.

Anyone else in the world touching an item of his clothing with such force, as Misty had done to his jacket and he would have been mortified and recoiled in horror as if he had just been shot. But it didn't bother him at all, in fact it didn't even register that she had creased his lapel. Any form of physical contact with her gave him a buzz.

"That could always be arranged," she said licking her lips.

When she laughed her husky, infectious laugh, Johnny fell in love with her a little bit more.

Misty had everything he wanted in a woman. Stunning good looks and a fantastic figure of course were important but she had a sense of humour and fun. She was gentle and sweet but she wasn't stupid. She could give as good as she got and was nobodies fool.

She could be stylish and sophisticated one minute and childlike and needy the next.

Misty was sixteen, beautiful and unfortunately for Johnny, a hooker. Not a three quid Soho hustler, but a hooker none the less. Her clients paid top dollar for her company and included judges, top businessmen, film stars and top names from the London underworld.

Johnny forgot sometimes. Times like now. The two beautiful young nightlifers stood in the semi dark doorway, their features intermittently lit by the flashing neon from across the street, surrounded by grime and the litter which slowly tumbled past in the warm summer breeze.

Wrapped up in a dirty, corrupt and dangerous world. A world where money was God. A God which the two of them had been seduced by and coerced in to praying to at it's alter.

She was a hooker and he had become a drug dealer. The only paths they felt they could chose to get them as far away as possible from the horrors of their past. Unable to rely on an education or good families to help them get on.

No one noticed the two doorway inhabitants, cocooned in a world of their own.

The outside world rushed by, not stopping for breath, everyone trying to get somewhere and it seemed as soon as they got there they were in a rush to get someplace else.

But the two teenagers stood still in mutual silence and let all the shit of their world slip off them like raindrops running from their heads and down their bodies to their feet and away into the gutter, down the drain and into the bowels of the earth where it belonged.

Johnny and Misty locked eyes and flew to a better place. In reality it was just a brief few seconds when their souls locked but to the two of them it seemed like beautiful eternity.

Then suddenly it was broken. A taxi hooter barked out angrily at a pedestrian's transgression and the two youngsters were startled roughly from their trance like state.

"Fucking taxis," muttered Johnny to himself as he turned to stare at the guilty cabbie. Johnny hated taxis.

The boy turned back to Misty who had her head tilted to one side and the two dreamers smiled gently at each other.

Johnny felt a faint flush of embarrassment climb up his face and it was his turn to lower his eyes to the floor.

In an instant he had flicked a switch, the barriers were erected once more and he slipped back into cool mode.

A Face once more.

"Well, it's been nice talking baby," he grooved, cool style, "Gotta hit the streets."

Misty smiled knowingly and once again leant forward and brushed her lips against his cheek and said,

"Bye honey, Behave yourself. Take care." And she meant it.

Johnny slowly wiped his own cheek clean this time and smiled back at her, winked and turned on his made to measure heels. Off to dance the shit out of his system.

CHAPTER 13

Johnny held his thumb against the bell to Chucky's flat. It was 10 o'clock Saturday morning and Johnny hadn't slept a wink. No change there.

After bumping into Misty he had headed for The Scene and despite the success of their first night in the drug trade and despite the large amounts of speed he had consumed, he felt strangely deflated.

Was it seeing Misty or was it something to do with becoming a dealer? Had he really crossed the line? Although everyone on the club scene took speed, you had to; the dealers were always despised and looked at as parasites. Being a Face and held in such high esteem amongst his peers, he believed would protect him from any ill feeling. But now he wasn't sure. A couple of times during the evening he had been given some funny looks from people he knew and an occasional frosty reception. Or was he being paranoid? Speed could make you like that.

Johnny felt he needed to be around people he knew just to make sure everything was o.k.

So, he ended up at The Scene and all his fears disappeared. If Otis, Smokey and Barbara Lynn couldn't lift his spirits, then nobody could.

He had stayed at The Scene until 5 a.m slipping and sliding, doing the Hully Gully, The Block and all the other dances he knew.

At five he got exititise- meaning head for the exit. He always knew when it was time to leave, as if a switch in his head had been flicked. As usual he would look up, see the exit and make a bee line for it, not pausing to say goodbye to anyone and then go wander the streets.

Johnny walked out of the club on to Ham Yard and then on to Berwick Street and looked up at the sky, flanked by buildings. Dawn was breaking, the sun was coming up but after the heat of The Scene he felt a slight shiver invade his body. Leaving the top button of his jacket done up, he pulled the bottom open and stuck his hands in his trouser pockets with just the thumbs sticking out, bent his head into the breeze and did the walk.

Instead of ending up on his usual bench in St.James's Park, something guided him in a different direction, smoking as he walked.

Ten minutes of walking and smoking and he found himself in a large Victorian square, flanked on all sides by five storey millionaires houses not unlike the Cavendish residence.

The thought of Mrs.Cavendish made him smile and decided he'd have to pop in and see her some time. The traumatic experience of his last encounter with her handily forgotten for the moment.

Johnny stood still listening to the faint rustle of the leaves on the trees in the private garden in the middle of the square. The only sound.

What was he doing here? he wondered, and where was he exactly? He was pretty sure he hadn't been in this place before so what had drawn him here?

The quiet scene was broken by the deep rumble of the twin exhausts on a motor car.

The boy looked to his left from where the noise was coming from and saw the maker of the wonderfully expensive sound. Aston Martin DB5, silver grey. The car used by James Bond 007 in the film Goldfinger.

A real hero.

The car drove around the far side of the garden and pulled up to the kerb outside a twin columned building on the left hand side of the square.

The building wasn't that much different from the other properties in the affluent square and it hadn't registered with Johnny that it wasn't a domestic property.

The inquisitive teenager, keeping close to the houses on his side, edged closer to the property outside which sat the car.

Peering through the shadows and the golden rays of the awaking sun, he could make out a brass plate attached to one of the large white columns flanking the entrance. As he got closer, stepping ever so slowly along the pavement the engraving became clear- The London Gaming Club and Casino.

The Aston sat in the road, its engine ticking over causing the body to slightly shake. A man climbed out. Johnny craned his neck to see who the man was and was greatly disappointed to see the man wore a uniform, obviously the casino parking valet.

His feeling of anti climax was short lived however as his attention was drawn away from the nobody to a somebody. A figure exited the building; or rather two figures exited the building and slowly walked down the marble steps.

The figures, a man and woman their arms linked, smiling and laughing. The woman was stunning. Blond, big tits, slim waist, dressed in a short black cocktail dress exposing a fine pair of legs. She wore diamond earrings, a diamond necklace and oozed class.

But it was the man who really drew his attention. The man was something else. Immaculately dressed in a dark blue mohair suit, white shirt and black tie. Sharp. Saville Row, Johnny surmised.

The man was obviously the owner of the car. What style, thought the teenager in awe standing transfixed at the little scene in front of him. Something was trying to burrow its way into his thought process but he couldn't grasp it. As the man in the suit waited for the valet to give him the keys, it dawned on Johnny who the man was.

It was *himself* in five years time. Or what he wanted to be. The clothes, the dolly bird, the brilliant car. Walking out of a London casino. It was exactly what he aspired to be. He didn't know the man and didn't know what he did for a living, how he attained his obvious wealth but Johnny knew he wanted to be him.

This man was the reason the ambitious Face had set up the deal with Chucky and Cousin Louie and why instead of selling the gear himself in dribs and drabs he had got the others involved. Reading somewhere that no one makes money on their own. Employing people multiplied profit. The Capitalist way. The Mod way.

Now he stood there watching a man who hadn't been prepared to settle for second best. Something about him told Johnny he wasn't born into money. He sensed that he came from the same streets as him and had earned every single penny the hard way. This was a man who had gone for it. And fucking well got it by the looks of him.

He imagined if he were close enough, the mans aftershave would smell classy and expensive.

The stylish figure opened the passenger door for his female companion then made his way around the car to the drivers side, the door already having been opened by the scurrying valet eager to please and anticipating a healthy tip for his troubles. The uniformed man was not disappointed when the man, as if by magic produced a note of some denomination and pressed it into his outstretched palm. Looking down casually the valet went into head nodding ecstasy. Obviously a good tipper, thought Johnny. And why wouldn't he be? He had the dough and he had the style.

The man eased into the driver's seat, the leather seeming to mould to his body like a second skin. Natural. Perfect fit. Belonged there, like a cock slipping into a fanny. The car fitted him as perfectly as his suit.

First gear was engaged and the still running engine lowered a tone and eased away effortlessly from the kerb, throbbing its way around the one way square towards where Johnny stepped back into the protection of the shadows.

As the car passed where the boy stood the driver instinctively turned his head and man and boy locked eyes for a second. Johnny watched the cars red tail lights head off into the distance.

Although he didn't know it, had just come face to face with Frank Saunders for the first time.

Now standing outside Chucky's flat going over what he had just seen, he was even more determined to succeed in his new business. Fuck what anyone thought.

Johnny could hear the bell ringing continuously in Chucky's place above, as his thumb started to ache.

Normally, calling around to Chucky unexpectedly, he would have rang the bell a couple of times, three at the most, and if having received no reply would have just fucked off. However, such was his eagerness to have Chucky contact Louie for more gear he pressed the bell for a full five minutes.

Fucking spades, all they do is sleep, thought Johnny, as upstairs the trumpet player responded to the ringing, thinking at first it was in his head.

Climbing groggily from his bed, he stuck his hand down the front of his shorts and readjusted himself.

"Who the fuck is that?" he muttered as he staggered to the window.

Slipping into a Jamaican accent he sometimes used for effect, he slid up the sash window and leant out.

"Wha da fuck ya wan, huh?" he shouted to the empty street.

Johnny took his finger off the bell and stepped back so his friend could see who was at his door.

"Chucky, you lazy black bastard," he shouted up to the top floor window, "Open ya bleeding door, its freezing out here."

The Jazz mans eyes tried focusing on the figure of his pal in the street below.

"What time d'ya call this man?" he called out sleepily, recognizing his friend.

"It's well late man," Johnny lied, "Its gone one." and although Chucky wouldn't have been able to see it, he pulled his shirt sleeve over his wrist watch to conceal the truth.

Chucky, like most musicians and indeed like most West Indians was pretty casual when it came to time keeping, and didn't own a watch or a clock.

Chucky sucked his lips in, Jamaican style and disappeared back inside, sliding the window shut once more.

A few seconds later and the street door was partially opened and before Johnny could enter heard the barefooted steps of his friend making their way back up to his pad.

As he entered he was treated to the sight of Chucky's boxer short clad arse disappearing up the stairs. Johnny called out after him.

"Chuck, we've got to contact Louie and order more gear. Twice the amount and quick."

Chucky stopped on the first landing, turned and rubbing his eyes, clucked again.

"You wake me up at this time to tell me that?"

Chucky dropped the Jamaican accent with people he knew!

This time Johnny put his hands behind his back to hide his watch once more.

"You sure you got the right time, or are ya bullshitting me again?"

"Would I bullshit you man?" Johnny said, trying to look sincere, "You're my favourite immigrant."

With that Chucky shook his head and muttered some Jamaican insults under his breath. To the white boy it sounded something to do with a blood clot or something.

Chucky once more turned and headed up the creaking wooden steps, followed by a buzzing Johnny.

Once inside Chucky's pad Johnny pounced again.

"Phone Louie. Tell him we need more stuff and we need it now if not sooner. He said he could get as much as we wanted. Come on let's go to the phone box and give him a call."

Johnny was jabbering excitedly, full of enthusiasm and ideas and full of adrenaline after dropping a couple more pills to take the edge off his come down.

"Calm down man," said Chucky, splashing his face with cold water, the only type he had, from the dirty basin in the corner of his hovel.

"What's the rush man?"

Johnny sighed exaggeratedly and spoke to his pal as if addressing a retard.

"The rush, my lazy Negro friend, is last night we proved there was a market out there for our stuff and if we don't exploit it some other fucker will. The stuff we knocked out last night beat the shit out of Fat Tony's gear. He's history. But we've got to strike now, while the iron is hot. We've got to let the kids know we're reliable and can supply constantly otherwise Fatty will blackmail 'em. Tell 'em if they don't buy from him he'll stop supplying. We'll be frozen out. They won't come near us if we only do it now and again."

Chucky raised his head from the basin grabbed a dirty looking towel and dried the droplets of water on his dark skin.

He gave his friend a doleful look and said, "What d'ya want man, Ya wanna take over the world?"

Johnny looked over to him and with deadly sincerity said, "Yeah. Why not?"

Chucky had thought this drug business would just be a handy little side line. After initially joining Johnny in their excitement when the idea first came up and making all sorts of ambitious plans, his natural laid back persona had taken over and thought it would just be something to make a bit of cash out of from time to time. Nothing serious or big time.

But now looking into his friends blue eyes he could see the hunger of someone determined to get what he wanted. The trouble was Chucky didn't have the same ambition or drive. He only wanted a quid more than he could spend.

Johnny badgered, harried and coerced Chucky who finally bowed to the inevitable and threw on a pair of Levis and a white Fred Perry top, slipped into his shoes and followed Johnny down to the phone box on the corner of his street.

After finally getting through to Louie who was sleeping off the affects of a late night poker game and being berated for phoning at such an early hour, Chucky passed the phone to Johnny. Swearing at him as he handed the receiver over.

"One o'clock! You fucking bullshitter."

Johnny grinned and told Louie that he wanted another consignment.

Louie explained that although the gear was in the supply room he didn't have a pass out of the base until the following weekend.

"Fuck that," said Johnny to this piece of information, "I'll come up there and pick it up myself on my scooter."

Louie reluctantly gave Johnny directions who then slammed the phone down, slapped Chucky on the back, said goodbye and headed off to where he had parked his Lambretta in Wardour Street.

Ten minutes later Chucky was back in bed knocking out the zeds and Johnny was tearing the arse off his scooter, heading out of town.

CHAPTER 14

After Johnny had got another batch of speed from Louie and arranged for the same larger amount to be delivered every week business really took off and the following weeks were like heaven for him.

Money poured in and he spent it as quickly as it was made.

He still had his dream of the club of his own but felt that for the first few weeks he would just go a bit mental seeing as this was the first time in his life that he had had any real money.

The first week, after sorting out Louie's share and paying the lads for selling the suburbs gear Johnny and Chucky cleared two hundred quid. TWO HUNDRED SMACKERS! EACH! The second week it increased to three hundred. This was at a time when the average wage was only twenty pounds a week, a new Mini cost five hundred and a two bedroom house would set you back six grand.

Johnny went and had suits made. Shoes made. Shirts. Bought dozens of records. He was out every night. He didn't bother going back to work and telling them he was leaving. He didn't even bother picking up his last pay packet. What was the point? Six pounds and three shillings. Fuck off! Although he was tempted to go and tell his boss where he could stick his job he couldn't be arsed.

At last he was really living "The Life."

The clothes, the music, the night life. So what if he got a few snide comments and looks of disdain from people he had previously thought of as friends? Jealousy, that's all.

Anyway, he was moving on. He knew. He could feel that this was his time.

Being a supplier of top grade amphetamines brought him into contact with the upper echelons of London society. One night in the Flamingo he had been approached by a right posh bird who asked him if he wanted to go to a party in Chelsea that Saturday and could he bring plenty of "stuff" along?

Johnny had gone to the party, sold all his pills to the chinless wonders at exorbitant prices and got his cock sucked by a posh tart called Samantha. Nice work if you can get it.

After that night he spent more of his nights further West in Kensington and Chelsea and less on his old stamping ground of Soho. The wealth and the confidence of the people he was meeting had had a strong effect on him. No one seemed to have jobs. Everyone just partied all night and slept during the day, only getting up to go shopping down the Kings Road and Sloane Street.

Johnny was in great demand on this new scene, not only for his little bag of chemicals but because the toffs found him dangerous and exciting, thinking he was some sort of gangster. A belief he did nothing to discourage. In fact he played the role to the hilt.

The boy from the streets was also in great demand among the "Olivias" and "Harriets" who were drawn to his tough good looks and cheeky charm, eager to bed a bit of working class rough.

Johnny thought he was pretty unshockable but was amazed at how sexually liberated these supposedly *upper* class birds were. Sex to them was like anything else that they wanted. If they saw something they liked in a shop they bought it. If they saw a bloke they liked, they had to have him.

He was constantly accosted at parties and clubs by these posh birds who were blatant in letting him know what they wanted. At first Johnny felt uncomfortable at this role reversal. He had always thought that blokes should do the pulling but after the fifth or sixth time of being propositioned and ending up in bed humping away he just came to accept it. It saved him from coming out with the old chat up lines.

*

She was fucking gorgeous and she was heading in his direction.

Johnny was stood in the opulent drawing room of an Eton Square townhouse at a swinging party held by a minor royal. Amongst the guest list were a couple of very well known film stars, a famous photographer and a couple of members of the group of the moment, the up and coming Rolling Stones. It gave him an immense buzz and a feeling of really having made it to get as much or even more attention as any of the celebrities present.

The girl walked past a couple of famous faces, ignoring them to stand in front of him.

This chick was stunning. Blond hair and freckles, she had the tanned skin of a permanent traveller and her blue eyes sparkled.

She wore not a trace of make up which was unusual as the fashion seemed to be to plaster it on, especially around the eyes. Black like Cleopatra.

The girl wore a simple, short, flower print dress with thin straps over her delicate shoulders. Her legs were long and slim and her tits were tiny. She was barefoot.

"Hello," she said to Johnny, looking directly in his eyes, a slight smile lifting the corners of her mouth.

"Hello," he replied, totally ignoring the toff who was boring him to death with some shit about horses and tried to stop his knees from buckling.

Wow, he thought as the beautiful creature just stood there in front of him sipping champagne from a crystal flute. Saying nothing.

Johnny started to feel slightly uncomfortable at the silence and broke it with.

"Alright darling. Howzit going? I'm Johnny."

Very casual. Nice and cool.

Again the two of them just looked at each other and the toff, instantly erased from his mind, realised he was superfluous and wandered off to bore someone else.

Johnny's mind reacted with another Wow when she spoke again.

"My names Sarah," she said, not dropping her eyes from his, "I want you to make love to me," and took his hand in hers.

Mr. Cool was momentarily stunned and just about stopped his mouth from dropping open like a retard.

Wow, he thought again, Fucking double wow.

"What here?" he said, gesturing to the piece of expensive Persian carpet beneath them.

Sarah burst out laughing at his joke and he breathed a sigh of relief at not having blown it.

"No not here silly. My flat is just around the corner and these people are such terrible bores. Let's go and have some fun."

Johnny looked at her as he let her well educated voice sink in to his soul and figured she must have only been about nineteen but had a confidence in herself which seemed to make her a lot older. A lot older than all the nineteen year old girls he knew from his usual scene.

Working class insecurity against upper class confidence.

Johnny didn't need asking twice and replied as coolly as he could, trying not to grab her, sling her over his shoulder and run with her out of the door to her place.

"Sure, why not?"

Sarah squeezed his hand tight, turned and led him across the crowded room, stopping several times to kiss friends goodbye on both cheeks. Men *and* women. She made no attempt to include him in the brief conversations she had and didn't even introduce him to any of them.

Johnny was pissed off no end at being made to stand there like some sort of tosser and would normally have shook his hand free from hers and told her to go fuck herself. But Sarah wasn't a normal bird and he wanted her more than any other girl he had met in his life, although Misty momentarily flashed into his mind before he closed his eyes and shook his head and she disappeared.

Johnny just stood there and waited till she had finished before leading him out of the room, down the stairs and out of the front door, still barefoot.

As soon as she had turned the key in her own front door and pushed it open the two eager lovers were all over each other. Tongues entwined, ripping at each others clothes, grabbing, squeezing and scratching each others young bodies. Licking and biting each others bare skin, naked on the hallway floor, the front door still wide open. Johnny climbed on top of Sarah and was about to enter her soaking wetness when she took him by surprise and flipped him over and climbed on to him, pinning his arms above his head. Her legs straddling him. She sat up, back straight and smiled a remarkably sexy smile and placed a gentle soft kiss on his lips before continuing on to his neck and shoulders. He closed his eyes and let out an ecstatic moan as Sarah kissed and licked her way down his chest, sucking each of his nipples in turn, which drove him crazy.

Johnny's head was spinning and it wasn't the reefer he'd smoked or the champagne he had drunk. It was the girl. It was the girl who had reached his cock, gently squeezing his balls in the palm of her hand as she licked his cock from its base, up his shaft to its tip, slowly pulling back his foreskin, licking his helmet as she slid his cock into her warm wet mouth.

"Fucking hell," groaned Johnny as her mouth slid up and down his rock hard cock, noisily sucking and slurping, her eyes shut tight enjoying the pleasure she was giving.

He had to use all his powers of restraint to stop himself exploding into her mouth, although he was sure she wouldn't mind and was half relieved when she took his cock out of her mouth, looking up at him and gently kissed his helmet again.

Johnny propped himself up on his elbows to watch her as she kissed his cock looking at him through her fringe, smiling.

Sarah slowly moved up his body and placed her legs either side of his hips again. Gently easing herself up, she felt for his hard cock and positioned herself over it rubbing her entrance with its tip before sliding down, impaling herself on him.

The beauty cried out with pleasure and continued to slide herself up and down his cock, increasing the speed and force of her plunging downwards.

He grabbed her perfect arse and joined in with her rhythm, retracting his cock slightly as her arse went back then thrusting his hips forward to meet hers. The temperature reached boiling point as the two lovers reached an earth shattering crescendo. Sarah climaxed violently, screaming with pleasure, Johnny shouted her name and shot his load into her repeatedly before the two sweat covered bodies collapsed, hearts pounding, panting hard trying to get their breath.

CHAPTER 15

"DO FUCKING WHAT?" roared London gang boss Eddie Raven into the profusely sweating face of his West End drug peddler known just as Fat Tony.

"Someone else is selling speed in the clubs and the kids are all buying from them," repeated the fat man in front of him by way of explanation for the sudden and dramatic fall in one area of Eddie Ravens profits.

"WHAT THE FUCK YOU TALKING ABOUT YOU FAT RETARD?" screamed Raven into the dealers' face who was shaking visibly.

Once a fortnight the boss of London's underworld summoned all his firm to his West End office above 'La Discotheque' one of the top Mod clubs at the bottom end of Wardour Street. The firm all attended with the purpose of handing over profits from the previous couple of weeks of illicit trade.

Money from clip joints, strip clubs, spielers and illegal gambling joints as well as "protection" money from the many pubs and clubs in the West End and beyond.

Fat Tony was there to hand over profits from selling amphetamines to the speed crazy kids of London's booming club scene.

"SOHO IS MINE," Raven bellowed. "The West End is mine. London is mine. No one farts in this town without my say so and you're telling me some cunt is trying to move in on one of my earners?"

The men standing in the office remained silent at this rant from their boss. They knew better than to speak when he was in this sort of mood. The bassy thump-thump of a record being played in the club below could be heard and could have been easily mistaken for the terrified heart of Fat Tony about to burst through his chest.

Along with Eddie Raven and Fat Tony in the windowless office, although he wished he wasn't, was Dickie Morgan, the two-bit hard man who was Tony's minder. In reality he couldn't knock the skin off a rice pudding, but was a big, ugly looking lump who looked the part and that was all that was needed when dealing with the young kids his boss was selling gear to.

Also in the room leaning against the walls, keeping well back but enjoying the fact that someone else was on the receiving end of a bollocking were Bill "Bronco" Lane, Mick "Mad dog" McGuire and Charlie Fletcher who didn't have a nickname because he was so hard. All part of Ravens inner circle, trusted lieutenants and tough as fuck.

"It's like we're lepers or something," blurted out Fat Tony, mopping his leaking brow with a hankie he had withdrawn from his crumpled jacket.

"No one wants our gear anymore," he continued, "One kid said they were getting better stuff from someone else, and cheaper too."

This latest statement produced silence from Eddie Raven who just gave the man in front of him a contemptuous and withering look which did nothing to ease Fat Tony's fragile state of mind.

The silence continued for what seemed like hours to everyone in the room.

It had crossed the gang leaders mind that the fat slob might be pulling a fast one. Had sold the gear and was keeping the money for himself but looking at the gibbering wreck in front of him he knew the man didn't have the imagination or the guts to pull such a stroke.

To Fat Tony, the silence was worse than the screaming and wished someone would say something to break the stifling atmosphere.

Eddie Raven brushed past the shaking drug dealer and looked around the room at his entourage, going from one blank face to another to see if any of them had a germ of an idea who the interloping liberty taker might be. Nothing.

Finally with an exasperated sigh he finally broke the silence.

"Well?" he asked "Any ideas?" taking his seat again.

"About what boss?" Bill Lane eventually replied awkward.

"About who's gonna be the next England manager," Raven said sarcastically, which led to the three hard men looking at each other in bewilderment.

"I don't know much about football boss," Lane replied nervously at which Raven raised his eyes to the heavens and shouted.

"For fucks sake you div."

Again silence. Eventually, the boss looking from blank face to blank face saw that Dickie Morgan looked like he had something on his mind. Eddie Raven stood once more and walked around the table until he stood directly in front of the tough guy who was looking extremely awkward.

"You got something to say?" questioned Raven.

Morgan looked down at the floor, too scared to look his real boss in the eye as he shifted his weight from foot to foot.

"I think I might know who it may be," he eventually volunteered.

"WHO?" shouted Eddie Raven in the frightened mans face.

"That bloke from Ipswich," he replied nervously.

Eddie straightened his back and pulled back his shoulders. A quizzical look on his face, he looked at the other men who all shrugged their shoulders and shook their heads.

"Ipswich?" said Raven, turning back to look at Morgan, "Who the fuck is the bloke from Ipswich? I don't know anyone from Ipswich."

"Alf Ramsey," replied Dickie, "he won the league with Ipswich, I reckon he'll be the next England manager."

The men in the room all tried to stifle nervous giggles as Morgan looked up from the floor to see what his boss's reaction was.

His boss took a deep breath, filling his lungs with air, then nutted him. His forehead coming into crunching contact with Morgan's nose who screamed in pain as blood splattered over his white shirt, before sinking to the floor.

The giggling stopped.

"You taking the piss?" said Eddie Raven calmly, towering over his victim.

The guvnor turned away from the whimpering shape on the floor and walked back behind his desk and stood, palms outstretched on the desktop before he spoke quietly, the calm after the storm.

"Who's at it?" he said, a smear of blood on his forehead.

Fat Tony had literally shit himself, the smell permeating the small room.

"We don't know boss, honest," the fat man stammered, "We ain't seen anyone. One night all the kids are round us like flies around a cows arse, the next night, nothing. All we know is the pill 'eads ain't buying our stuff. We grabbed one kid and he said they were getting better stuff from some kid who's a bit of a Face but he wouldn't tell us who.

"I know the stuff we sell 'em ain't pukka gear but these druggies swallow anything, even fucking cough medicine if there's no alternative. The trouble is someone has given them an alternative."

Fat Tony was speaking 100 miles an hour as if he'd dropped a dozen pills himself but it wasn't drugs, but terror which caused his speech to be so hurried.

Eddie Raven eased himself back into his leather swivel chair, his arms folded.

"This kid you spoke to? Why didn't you lean on him to get him to give you a name?"

Fat Tony looked back to his pal lying rolled up in a ball sobbing quietly and shuffled up to the desk.

"We tried Mr Raven, we gave him a couple of slaps, but he didn't know the blokes name so we let him go."

Eddie Raven sat quietly for a few seconds. Thinking.

"Right. Everyone on this. It shouldn't be too hard. Go to the pubs and clubs, put yourselves about a bit. All you gotta do is grab a couple of these Mods when they're speeding off their nuts, give 'em a couple of digs and they'll cough." Then looking at Fat Tony and his so called minder laying on the floor, continued.

"These two idiots couldn't scare their grannies. You" He said, pointing at Fat Tony, "Get the fuck out of my sight and take this prick with you."

The fat man stooped over his pal and wheezing with the effort dragged him to his feet, blood still running from his busted nose.

"And if I see you again," he said as the two men reached the door, turning as he spoke, "You'll get more than a broken hooter."

The door was opened by Bronco Lane and the two men stumbled out to the accompaniment of an increase in volume from the club below and a record by Brenda Holloway, ironically titled "Every little bit hurts."

The door was shut again and the remaining men approached the desk behind which sat their boss.

"Okay you lot, get the boys out there, give 'em the S.P. and sort this out."

With that the gangster waved a dismissive hand and instructed them to "Fuck off."

Bronco and Mad dog filed out of the office leaving Charlie Fletcher, Eddie Ravens closest ally alone with his boss.

"Shut the door Chas," the boss instructed. After the door was closed Eddie gestured to a chair and Charlie Fletcher sat down.

Two whiskeys were poured and the men both leant back in their chairs.

"Well?" said Eddie Raven loosening his thin black silk tie and brushing imaginary dust from his trousers, "What do you reckon?"

"You know who it could be?" said Fletcher after a pause and a deep breath.

"Who?"

"Frank Saunders."

Eddie Raven stood up and thought for a second before dismissing the idea.

"Nah fuck off, pills ain't his scene."

"Yea, I know. Not until now. Maybe he's trying to get back at you for putting the muscle on. Maybe he's having a pop. He knows the pill scene is a part of your business. A big part. Maybe he's got the 'ump about this job you're getting him to do.

"Could be he's having a pop at you. You know what a lairy cunt he can be."

Raven was lost in thought as he reached across the desk, opened the lid to his cigar box and removed an expensive Cuban.

The cigar remained unlit in his mouth as Raven contemplated the suggestion Fletcher had put to him and the more he thought about it the more it became a possibility.

"Remember a couple of years ago when that wages van from the pharmaceutical company in Middlesex got done?" he said.

Fletchers face lit up and he took up the thread. "Yeah, no one got done for it but it had Saunders written all over it."

Raven continued excitedly, "Old Bill said the blaggers must have had inside information. If it was Saunders and he did have a man on the inside then he might still be there."

"And he's supplying Saunders with the pills and Saunders has got a few of these Mod kids to knock 'em out in the clubs" finished off Charlie triumphantly, much to his bosses displeasure at having his thunder stolen.

"Right," said Raven after downing the contents of his whisky glass. "Grab one of the kids from a club; find out who's knocking out the gear to 'em. Whoever it is we'll get the fuckers to cough their guts about Saunders then we'll sort out some suitable punishment for that flash South London cunt."

"Sure thing boss," replied Fletcher with a grin, we'll get it sorted" and with that he stood, reached out and picked up his glass from the desk and emptied the contents in one. The whisky burnt his throat as it went down and gave him an instant lift. He hated Frank Saunders almost as much as his boss did and he was looking forward to the opportunity to sort him out. He doubted that Saunders would stoop so low as to supply drugs but putting the thought into Eddie Ravens paranoid mind might just tip him over the edge into finishing him off for good.

It was another warm night and Charlie Fletcher felt engulfed in the heat and noise of Soho's teaming streets as soon as he exited from the cold, damp stairway which led from Eddie Ravens office. He shut the street door behind him and as was his habit looked left and right before stepping out on to the street and headed off on his mission.

Fletcher turned left and headed up Wardour Street, across the bus and taxi busy Shaftesbury Avenue and into the Roundhouse pub.

"Time gentlemen please," shouted out the barman as he rang the bell for the last time and the punters started drifting out on to the street.

"It's shut mate," said one of the leaving drinkers to Fletcher, who ignored him and carried on to the bar.

"Evening George," the gangster said and saw the guvnors face drop as he was recognised. The Roundhouse was on the list of Eddie Ravens "protected" establishments.

George Jarvis greeted Fletcher politely.

What does he fucking want? he thought to himself, I've paid this weeks "insurance". Probably after free drinks like the other parasites who work for that bastard.

"Whisky," barked Fletcher, as he lit the cigarette he had placed in his mouth.

The man behind the "jump" reached up to retrieve a tumbler from the shelf above the bar, turned to the optics behind him and filled the glass with a generous three shots of Teachers before turning back to face Eddie Ravens hound.

"Busy?" enquired Fletcher, the whisky warming his insides as he took a gulp.

"So-so," replied Jarvis, drying a pint glass with a chequered tea towel.

Charlie Fletcher smiled knowingly, having received the expected down beat reply. No one ever seemed to have had a fantastically busy night of money making whenever he asked one of their protected businesses.

"Yeah, yeah," he said contemptuously and took another slug of Teachers before stubbing out his fag on the highly polished bar top, deliberately ignoring the ash tray handily placed next to him by the pub owner.

"Any of the boys been in?" asked Fletcher without looking at the man behind the bar.

"I've not seen anyone tonight," he replied, "My wife may know, I've been run off my feet."

As soon as he said it he snapped his mouth shut and just stood frozen like a rabbit in the headlights, blinking nervously.

Charlie Fletcher eased up from the bar on which he had been leaning his not inconsiderable weight and fixed George Jarvis with an icy stare.

The two men stood barely three feet apart in the now quiet and empty boozer. Total silence.

Jarvis expected the worst. It didn't pay to lie to any of these animals but breathed a huge and audible sigh of relief as he turned and scurried to the door leading to the upstairs living quarters.

"Mary," he shouted, turning nervously to Fletcher and smiling weakly to show how helpful he was being.

Mary Jarvis clomped down the stairs and into the bar and couldn't disguise the contempt she felt upon seeing who was standing in her pub.

The bee-hive haired blonde stood there with her tits trying to escape from her low cut top and her hands on her hips.

"Evening MISTER Fletcher," she said sarcastically, emphasising the Mister, "How can we help?"

"Mister Fletcher wants to know if any of his friends have been in this evening," said George hurriedly before the thug had a chance to react to his wife's derisory tone.

The brassy blond run her tongue around the inside of her mouth as if trying to rid herself of a bad taste.

"Yeah, Lane and McGuire were in poncing free drinks as usual," she said deliberately looking at the glass in Fletchers calloused hand.

"Left a message for you," she continued, looking the hardman in the face. "Said they would be at Ronnie Scott's place on Frith Street."

With that, as if she was unable to stand another second in the mans company she turned and made her way back upstairs, her generous arse swinging from side to side like a pendulum.

"Your wife's a gobby cow George," laughed Fletcher, "She's gonna get you in trouble one of these days."

George Jarvis looked down at the floor and mumbled something about giving her a slap to keep her in her place.

Once again Charlie Fletcher laughed and said. "Give her a slap? Don't make me laugh. She'd beat the shit out of you," and finished the contents of his glass.

The pub landlord said nothing because he knew it was true.

With a casual flick of his wrist, Fletcher tossed his glass over the bar onto the floor causing it to shatter into a hundred pieces.

"Thanks for the drink," he said and headed for the door.

Behind the bar George Jarvis sighed and ignored the broken glass, electing to choose another from the rack, in which he poured himself a large one. Downing it in one he poured another. He was going to get pissed.

*

"Mad dog" McGuire and Bill Lane stood across the road from Ronnie Scott's 47 Frith Street, watching the procession of stylish youngsters enter the noisy night spot, done up to the nines in suits and ties.

"Smart little fuckers ain't they?" observed Lane.

"Yeah," agreed McGuire, "Beats me where they get the dough from. Some of 'em look like they only just left school."

The two men waited until a particularly young looking Mod walked down the road on his own and approached the entrance. As he was about to enter the club the two men scurried across the street to intercept him.

Lane grabbed the boy by an immaculate jacketed arm and pulled him back.

The boy spun around with a look of total disdain on his young features. A look that said how dare someone touch such a precious item of his clothing.

The disdainful look however turned to one of grave concern upon clapping his eyes on the hard, serious looking faces that glared down at him.

"We want a word with you son," snarled Mad Dog and the boy nearly ruined his trousers.

"What? What?" the terrified boy spluttered, "I ain't done nuffink."

"Got your evenings pills yet?" asked Lane menacingly.

The boy had obviously consumed some because his pupils were as big as saucers and his jaw was still moving at a rapid rate, not realising he had swallowed his chewing gum with fright.

"Pills? What pills?" he breathed in a panic, starting to hyperventilate, unable to catch his breath, "I don't do drugs, not me. You must want someone else."

"Look," sighed Bronco Lane impatiently, "Don't fuck us about. We ain't Old Bill, so you don't have to worry about being nicked."

On receiving this piece of information the young Mod visible relaxed, but if he thought he was out of danger he was very much mistaken as Lane switched his grip from the boys arm to his young smooth skinned throat, squeezed tightly and lifted the boy up until he stood on his black Penny Loafer tip toes.

"But you DO have to worry about this," he snarled. His face barely an inch from the boys, his aftershave making his eyes sting and the smell of whisky and fags breathing into his face made him feel like throwing up.

"You tell us where you lot *have* been getting your pills lately and I'll let ya go. If you don't, you'll get some of this."

The boys eyes widened in horror as he held the man's wrist with both hands trying to stop him from choking him to death. In the man's other hand was a lethal looking cut throat razor which he had produced like a magician pulling a rabbit out of a hat.

The Soho hard man slowly, hypnotically waved the blade in front of the boys face. The cold, shiny metal barely a fraction of an inch from the boys face. He hadn't even started shaving properly yet.

The youngster suddenly became very cooperative and hurriedly spilled his guts to the two nutters.

"It used to be Fat Tony," he stammered hurriedly in a squeaky voice caused by the mans huge hand squeezing his wind pipe.

"But a couple of weeks ago, another guy started selling much better stuff, so everyone buys from him now," he continued quickly.

"Who? What's his name?" badgered Lane.

"I don't know," the boy squeaked, "I don't know. HONEST," he squeaked louder. "No one knows anyone's names on the scene. Not really. He's a Face. A Top bloke. Immaculate dresser. Stylish. A Face. You know. Someone who's known but not by their name."

Bronco Lane, still holding the boy pinned up against the wall by his throat turned his head and gave his partner McGuire a questioning look.

McGuire lit himself a cigarette and shrugged his huge shoulders before offering a smoke to Lane.

Lane extracted a Woodbine from the pack and bent forward to light it from McGuire's extended lighter.

"What d'ya fink?" said Mad Dog blowing out smoke through his mouth and nostrils.

"Dunno," said Lane, "Sounds like he's telling the truth. I don't fancy schlepping around every club in Soho trying to find him though."

"We could take the kid wiv us," suggested McGuire. "He knows what he looks like and he's more likely to know where he'll be at a certain time. These kids bounce from one club to another all fucking night."

Bill Lane took another drag on his cigarette and pondered on what to do until his train of thought was disturbed by a squeaking behind him.

"Sorry to disturb you," said the boy in a high pitched whine, "But I am still here you know."

Lane turned to face the boy again and McGuire peered over his shoulder to look at him.

"Ere, he ain't 'alf going a funny colour." he said.

Lane let the boy's throat go and the young Mod dropped to his haunches, coughing, spitting and choking for air. Although he was in a state of great distress the teenage peacock made sure he hadn't dropped to his knees and ruined his trousers and when he spat he made sure he didn't spit on himself. Indeed, although he was seriously perturbed, there was still enough cockiness in him to aim direct hits of saliva on Broncos shoes.

Luckily for the lad, Lane hadn't noticed as he was once again talking to his partner.

"That might look a bit suspicious," said Lane at his mate's suggestion, "If we're seen dragging him around the streets we'll look like a right couple of pervo's."

"True, very true," agreed McGuire.

The Mod seeing the two men in deep conversation saw his chance to escape and made a dash for it. Unfortunately for the boy Bronco Lane was quicker than his bulk suggested and before he had got a couple of paces he was in a crushing head lock, once again having the air squeezed out of him.

"For fucks sake, not again," he said, the squeaking voice having returned.

The young boy struggled, twisted and kicked until he realised it was no good. Then just as he thought he wouldn't see another Soho sunrise, a light came on in his head and just about managed to convey the piece of information which might get him off the hook.

"I DO know who the spade is though."

"Spade? What spade?" said McGuire, before Lane could remove his cigarette and say the same.

"His mate. Plays trumpet. Black dude," the boy in the know said triumphantly as Lane relaxed the grip around his neck.

Bill Lane turned the boy around to face them and said, "Go on."

"Well as far as I can make out," he said before pausing and smiling.

"Got a fag?" he said cockily savouring the two men's feeling of expectation.

McGuire grabbed a Woodbine from his pack and shoved it in the boy's mouth and lit it.

The cockiness now fully restored the Mod inhaled, then let the smoke slowly drift out of his mouth and nose like he had seen Steve Mcqueen do it and then spoke again.

"The Face and the spade seem to be partners. The Face sells gear in the younger more Mod clubs and the spade sells them in the older jazzy type places. They've also got a few of the other kids working for them selling stuff out of town in the suburbs like."

The boy leant casually against the wall, after checking it wasn't dirty and took another drag on his fag.

"Well what's his fucking name then you little prick and where can we find him?"

The boy finished his cigarette and casually flicked it into the gutter, the burning end glowing bright.

"His name," the boy proclaimed dramatically, "Is Chucky Wilson and he plays jazz trumpet at "Gerrys Jazz" on Greek Street.

"In fact," he continued, looking at his watch which said one a.m. "He'll be on stage there now. You'll catch part of his set if you get a move on. He's very good."

"Right," said Lane. "Let's get over there. And you," he said turning back to the young Mod, "If you're lying we'll be back to find ya and we won't be so gentle next time."

The two men turned and headed off in the direction of Greek Street only a very short distance away.

"I can't wait to see the bosses face when he hears he's got a nigger for competition," said McGuire and the two men laughed as they walked off to "Gerrys Jazz."

The young Mod stood at the entrance to Ronnie Scott's and watched them walk away until they were a safe distance up the street.

"WANKERS," he screamed and dived in to the club.

The two gangsters turned to see the boys foot disappear inside the entrance, looked at each other and laughed before carrying on their way to Greek Street and Chucky Wilson.

Charlie Fletcher wasn't far behind and reached Ronnie Scott's barely five minutes after the other two had left.

The doorman to the night spot had left the shadows of the doorway and retaken his spot just outside. He had witnessed the events that had just taken place but knew the two members of Eddie Ravens firm and experience told him not to get involved but had watched and listened. It paid to know what was going on in Soho.

As Charlie Fletcher approached, the man at the door knew something heavy was going down. Charlie Fletcher was big time.

"Alright Bert?" said Fletcher as he stopped beside the doorman and looked up and down the street, scanning the area.

"Evening Mr Fletcher." Respect paid.

"Seen any of my lot?" said Fletcher from the corner of his mouth his lips hardly moving.

"McGuire and Bill Lane. About five minutes ago. They've gone to Greek Street. "Gerrys Jazz.""

"Cheers," said Fletcher and walked off without saying goodbye.

Someone's in the shit, the doorman thought to himself as he welcomed a couple more kids into the club with a surly growl.

Eddie Raven's instructions had been quite specific. Find out who was dealing on his manor. Find them and take them to the office above the dirty book shop he owned in Berwick Street then give him a call.

It only took a couple of minutes for the two hoods to get to the venue in Greek Street where Chucky Wilson was plying his trade.

The doorman gave a nod of recognition to the two men as they strolled up to the entrance and stepped to one side to let them in.

The heavies walked straight past the little cubby hole where a girl with back combed hair sat collecting the 1/6 entrance fee. The bored looking girl glanced up to see the doorman shaking his head so she went back to filing her nails.

The sound of the Jazz combo on stage got louder as they made their way down the short flight of stairs and if they had been wearing hats they would have been blown off as they opened the double doors to the dance floor and stage area.

The heat of the confined space hit them between the eyes as they stood there, getting used to the darkness. Once accustomed to their new surroundings their eyes were drawn to the focal point of the room. A small, raised platform at the opposite side of the room which made up the stage area. Barely twelve feet by eight feet and just two feet high it wasn't exactly the Albert Hall but its' occupants performed with every bit of the intensity and dedication as the performers at that illustrious venue.

The be-suited trio on stage were playing an improvised be-bop sound akin to the New York groove of Dizzy Gillespie and Miles Davies, a sound that was totally alien to the uneducated ears of the two Neanderthals standing at the back.

The musicians, who played with their eyes closed as if in a trance, nodded their heads up and down to the groove, oblivious to the audience before them.

Nathaniel Edwards. Drums. Black. New Yorker.

On double bass was Alex Budd. White. Hailing from Chicago.

Centre stage and out front was the horn playing Chucky Wilson. Originally from Jamaica, then Peckham, now a full time inhabitant of Soho.

The man the two gangsters had come to see.

If any of the gyrating hep cats on the dance floor hadn't been so consumed by the music and so fucked up on speed they would have instantly noticed the two strangers in their midst sticking out like a couple of sore dicks. It wasn't just the clothes they wore or their ages. It was nothing to do with physical characteristics. The two men could have been wearing suits identical to the Brooks brother's suits worn by the jazz types and they would still have stood out as outsiders. The Modern Jazz enthusiasts had a feel, a way about them. An aura which dovetailed with the vibe of the place, the music, the feel of togetherness.

The two strangers gave off no such sweet feelings, but a totally different aura was attached to them.

The joint was jumping and the two incongruous figures were ignored by the ecstatic, sweating jazz aficionados.

"Fucking freaks," grumbled McGuire wiping his forehead and running a finger around the neck of his shirt trying to get some air in to cool himself in the unrelenting heat.

His companion nodded in agreement, an unlit cigarette hanging from his bottom lip, mouth open in amazement at the scene before him.

A be-bop kid taking a break from flinging himself about walked past still moving his body in time to the rhythm.

The boy's movement jolted Lane out of his non comprehending state and he grabbed the boy by the shoulder and spun him around.

"What's up daddio?" the boy complained.

"The coon playing the trumpet?" Lane asked the boy, "What's his name? And I ain't your daddio."

The boy looked at the two men in disgust, jazz didn't see skin colour.

"That's no coon man," said the boy contemptuously, his head still bopping, "That's Chucky Wilson man."

Bill Lane released his steely grip on the boys shoulder and shoved him on his way before turning to McGuire and shouted above the loudness of the music.

"Go and find Fletcher. Tell him we've found one of them. Ask him what he wants us to do. I'll keep an eye on our boy."

As McGuire slipped out of the club, he bumped into Fletcher making his way in.

"Charlie, we've found one of 'em," he informed Fletcher, "What's the plan?"

Charlie Fletcher replied instantly, the plan already worked out in his head.

"Go back to the office, ask the boss for a set of keys for one of the motors. Bring it back here. Park down the street a bit, with the lights off but leave the engine running. Where's Bronco?"

"He's inside," replied McGuire, gesturing to "Gerrys" with his head, "He's keeping an eye on the spade."

Fletcher raised his eyebrows and looked at McGuire, "Spade eh? That'll please the boss no end."

"That's what we thought," said McGuire with a chuckle. "He's the trumpet player."

Fletcher raised his eyebrows again.

"All right then, fuck off and get the motor. Get the Zephyr it's got a nice big boot."

McGuire turned and scurried off back to the office above La Discoteque and Fletcher headed into the club.

As he entered the club he too was hit by the heat and sound but unlike the other two gang members it didn't make him feel uncomfortable and what sounded like a load of disjointed noise to the others he recognized and appreciated as Modern Jazz as he had a collection of albums by Miles Davis, Charlie Parker, Dizzy Gillespie and other practitioners of the art.

Bill Lane turned around, saw Fletcher standing there and sidled up to him.

"You were quick," he said.

"I was in the neighbourhood," replied Fletcher laconically.

"Is that our man?" he said with a nod of the head in the direction of the stage.

"Yup, that's him with the trumpet."

"Pity," he replied again, "He's pretty good."

Lane frowned and said "What we gonna do then?"

"Mad Dog's gone to pick up a motor. We'll wait until the band take a break and we'll get him outside for a chat. Tell him we got a job for him or a record contract or some other shit. We'll whack him over the nut, sling him in the motor and drive round to Berwick Street. When we get him upstairs in to the office give the boss a bell, then it's up to him."

Lane nodded his approval as Charlie Fletcher added,

"Till then I'm gonna enjoy the music so shut up."

McGuire took no time at all to get back to the office, so keen was he to tell his boss the news and to get in his good books.

The street door to the stairway that led to the rooms above La Discotheque squeaked as McGuire opened it hurriedly and he was already on the first landing when it closed behind him, taking the stairs two at a time.

Out of breath at the top, McGuire, forgetting protocol burst through the door to the office on the left of the landing to be greeted by the sight of his boss with his trousers round his ankles.

McGuires mouth dropped open as he watched his guvnor banging some blond bird ferociously from behind. The tarts dress was pulled up over her waist exposing the tops of her black stockings and the suspenders holding them up.

The girl's jumper and bra had been slung aside, the jumper having landed over the telephone, her bra over the desk lamp. Her large bare tits made squeaking noises as they rubbed back and forth across the polished table top.

Both participants in this carnal scene were so engrossed in their activity that neither seemed to notice the interloper.

McGuire was mesmerised by the scene in front of him and started to get a hard on as the girl reached her climax. Eddie Raven pummelled into her faster and faster like an out of control piston and the girl screamed with orgasmic pleasure, gripping the edge of the desk so hard she broke a couple of highly polished red nails.

The gangland boss gave a couple of animal like grunts and then an open mouthed moan followed by a long "yessssss" as he shot his load into the shuddering girl.

After the noise and fury of the final few seconds, the silence that followed unnerved McGuire even more, as his boss, cock still in the prostrate girl straightened his back, pulled back his shoulders and lifted his head in a noble manner. McGuire wasn't sure whether he should sneak out or give a round of applause.

Mad Dog didn't move and after what seemed like an age his boss stunned him by turning his head to face him and asked.

"Well? Any news for me, or what?"

It seemed as though Eddie Raven had been aware of his employee's presence all along. A situation which didn't appear to bother him at all, as he made no attempt to withdraw from the girl.

The girl just laid there on the desk, a satisfied smile spread across her lips, her eyes closed.

"Get on with it you moron," barked Raven, "For fucks sake."

"Er…. Right," stuttered Mad Dog, "We found one of 'em. Over at 'Gerrys Jazz.' Chas sent me to pick up the Zephyr. We're gonna take him to Berwick Street."

"Right," said Raven with a grim smile, "Take the Zephyr 6, the keys are in the desk," and pointed to drawer.

Mcguire hesitated before awkwardly making his way across the room past the semi naked couple and around to the back of the desk.

The hard man opened the stiff top drawer, the noise waking up the girl spread across the desk from her post coital slumber.

Turning her head to face him, she opened her heavily made up eyes, smiled and said, "Hello."

The greeting shocked him so much that he dropped the keys noisily onto the floor, bent down to pick them up and smacked his head on the open drawer.

Seeing stars, he retrieved the keys, stood up and replied, "Evening Miss." It was the only thing that seemed appropriate to say and he quickly made his way to extricate himself from the bizarre situation.

As he reached the door, McGuire turned to listen to his boss once more.

"Get over to Berwick Street. I'll finish up here and see you there. We'll work on him and find out who he's working for."

"Right boss," said McGuire as he opened the door and hurried out, happy to get away.

Once again he took the stairs two at a time and was on the next landing down before he heard his boss shout.

"SHUT THE FUCKING DOOR."

The embarrassed hood shut his eyes, puffed his cheeks out and made his way back up the stairs to the door. Averting his eyes, he reached in grabbed the door knob and gently closed the door.

Back at 'Gerrys' the Jazz trio had just finished their second set of the night 2 p.m. One set left to do.

The pilled up jazz fans exploded into applause and the three musicians took their bows and left the stage.

Charlie Fletcher, after applauding, moved quickly as the trio made their way to the closet that was laughingly called the dressing room.

Moving through the crowd, pushing people out of his way, he intercepted Chucky Wilson before he could disappear for a piss and a joint.

"Ere mate," he shouted above the Charlie Parker record the D.J had put on the turntable.

Chucky turned and looked the man up and down. He didn't look like a fan.

"Wha ya wan man?" enquired the trumpet player in his affected Jamaican patois.

"You was really good up there," the stranger said and leant forward so his mouth was close to Chucky's ear.

"I've got a proposition for ya," he shouted.

"Wha sorta proposition?" Chucky asked.

"Look," shouted Fletcher again, exaggerating the difficulty he had in hearing and being heard, "It's too loud in here. How 'bout a bit of fresh air? Let's go outside. It'll only take a minute."

Then putting his hand on Chucky's shoulder he added, "You look like you could do with cooling down a bit," indicating the sweat on Chucky's forehead and down his cheeks. Hard work blowing a horn!

"Yea o.k. maan," agreed Wilson, "it do get haht under dem light. I give ya five minute."

Chucky Wilson led the way and Charlie Fletcher smiled to himself as he followed him out.

The two men had to stop several times as Chucky received congratulatory hand shakes and back slaps from members of the appreciative crowd.

"Maan, ya don realise 'ow 'ot it is in dere 'till ya get some fresh air in ya lungs," exclaimed Chucky as he tumbled loose legged out on to the street.

The Jazz man turned and with his back to the road faced Charlie Fletcher as the gangster made his way out of the entrance to the club.

Fletcher held out a packet of cigarettes with one slightly extended to the trumpet player after taking one for himself.

Chucky declined and fished out a large joint from the inner pocket of his sharp jacket and leant forward to accept the light which Fletcher extended to his spliff.

A flame flicked up from the end of Chucky's reefer then settled down as the paper burnt back quickly when Chucky toked.

As Wilson had his head bent forward to light up, Fletcher looked over the trumpeters left shoulder and signalled to McGuire with a flick of his head to get in position behind their quarry.

"Now, what dis all about maan?" said Chucky as he took a heavy drag on his reefer, breathing out a huge cloud of smoke from his mouth and nose as he spoke.

The cannabis hit home and his eyes glazed over as the drug draped itself around his brain, cloaking him in a comforting fog.

It was the last good feeling Chucky Wilson would ever have.

*

Chucky came to with a throbbing pain in his head and the realisation that he was in deep shit.

His blurred eyesight began to focus and despite the table lamp turned towards him, was able to make out that he was in a small dark office and that he was sat tied to a wooden chair.

Blood trickled from his broad nose into his mouth and he turned his head to his left and spat it out onto the floor.

"Urgh, dirty git," said a disembodied voice from behind him followed by raucous laughter from others and he realised he was not alone in the room.

Turning his head around as far as it would go, he called out into the darkness.

"What ya want wi' me man?" he shouted to no one in particular.

The laughter stopped and a single voice stabbed through the claustrophobic darkness of the room.

"What we want, my chocolate coloured friend," the voice said menacingly, "Is to know who you are working for?"

"Wha' ya talking about? Me don't work for no one," Chucky replied confused, "me jus' play de trumpet."

Not realising there was someone in front of him added surprise to the pain as a fist was smashed into his face.

Wilson screamed in pain as the fist shot out of the shadows and landed with expert precision in the middle of his face.

More blood sprayed from his already damaged nose and mouth causing him to choke and gag as it ran down the back of his throat.

"Fucking hell man," was all Chucky could mumble his chin slumped to his chest as the pain threatened his consciousness.

Through the fog which enveloped his head, a muffled voice spoke,

"Who you selling the pills for?" growled the voice, "It's Saunders ain't it?"

Chucky now realised why he was there but knew he was unable to give his tormentors the information they seemed determined to get.

"Saunders? I don't know no Saunders," he said wearily, losing the Jamaican accent, knowing he was not going to be believed.

Chucky was right, they didn't believe him and the voice in front of him screamed.

"LIES. LIES," and once more his face was used as a punch bag, splattering his features across his face until he passed out once more.

Ten minutes later and having regained consciousness again Chucky told his assailants the whole story. About Cousin Louie, the Franklin brothers, about the two young Mods. And about Johnny.

Chucky relaxed a little for the first time in what seemed ages and the sound of "Its alright" by the Impressions drifting up into the room from a club down the street seemed to be relaying a message to him.

"Can I go now?" asked Wilson hopefully.

A sudden movement from behind startled him as his head was locked in a vice like grip. A figure in front of him moved out from behind the light displaying himself for the first time.

The man's stone like features and cold emotionless eyes told him that The Impressions were being ironic. Eddie Raven leant forward. So close Chucky could feel his breath as he spoke.

"Fucking nigger," hissed his voice, "You should have stuck to playing the trumpet."

Chucky Wilson tried to move his head but it was held too tightly by the huge man behind him.

Unable to move his head, his eyes darted wildly from side to side as they took in the cut throat razor which was in the hand of the man in front of him.

It took all the strength of the man behind to hold the trumpeters head still as terror racked Chucky's body.

Wilson's eyes bulged until they almost popped as Raven got closer to his face with the razor sharp weapon of choice for Soho's nutters.

High pitched whimpering noises emanated from the back of Chucky's throat as he spoilt his pinstripe trousers with an uncontrollable flow of terror induced piss and shit.

Eddie Raven quickly grabbed forward and took hold of Chucky's shaking bottom lip.

"Fucking nigger lips. Lets see what we can do about them eh?"

The gangster slowly leant the blade down beside Chucky's lip as sweat mingled with his blood.

The gangster holding the lip in his left hand and the cut throat in his right moved in a sudden blur. The lip was pulled forward and with an expert move born of many previous attacks the blade sliced through the soft flesh, separating it from the jazz mans face.

A huge eruption of blood shot out like a geyser smothering Eddie Raven who stood shoulders back victoriously, the blade in one hand, the severed lip in the other.

The pain Chucky had experienced up till now was like a soft tickling from a loved one compared to the atomic bomb that went off in his head, as cold metal connected with flesh. Thankfully the pain was brief as its severity caused him to pass out.

This time there would be no waking up for Chucky.

The silence in the room was broken by Fletcher who said.

"So Saunders ain't involved then?"

Raven looked up from his butchery which had almost brought him to orgasm.

"Nah, that's bollocks. Saunders is involved. We'll have to find the other kid. This Johnny character. He'll know."

CHAPTER 16

Johnny was blissfully unaware of the trouble brewing in London as he sunned himself hundreds of miles away on the beaches of Casablanca, North Africa.

Sarah had suggested the two of them take a holiday, the first one he had ever had. That's if you don't count a damp weekend in Margate or hop picking in Kent when he was five!

Johnny had heard of Casablanca from the movie in which Bogart played a right cool fucker, but he didn't realise it was a holiday destination before he met Sarah. The Moorish town in North Africa was just one of the many new things she had introduced him to. In fact Sarah had opened up a whole new world to Johnny.

A world of Art and museums, a world of travel and different foods.

A world of sophistication, a million miles away from the place he had started. A place he was running away from as fast as he could.

Sarah had a relative, an uncle or something high up in the Passport Office in Petty France in Victoria who pulled a few strings to get him his first ever passport in record time and just as things in London were taking a turn for the worse, the two love birds flew out of the country from London airport.

The following week had been a totally fantastic experience and a real eye opener for Johnny, who realised that there was more to life than Soho and its full-on lifestyle. It made Johnny even more determined to move on up so this sort of trip could be a regular occurrence.

One warm, still evening, as Johnny sat at a table in a rooftop restaurant overlooking the old desert town he realised that the scene in London as he knew and loved it would be over soon and would be replaced by a watered down version. A version he wanted no part of except to supply the artificial energy needed.

Johnny shifted his gaze from the Moorish rooftops to Sarah sitting opposite him. A gentle breeze slowly moved the wisps of hair hanging by her cheeks and he felt relaxed for the first time since he came kicking and screaming in to this shitty world.

The two lovers sat in contented silence, communicating with their eyes.

Johnny took a deep breath and smiled at Sarah who smiled back, a smile which reinforced Johnny's intention to embrace everything Sarah exposed him to. Although he did draw the line at the Ballet. And Beethoven would never replace Otis or Smokey that's for damn sure! Johnny's love for soul music was too strong to ever be replaced. Once Soul was in your soul there was no going back. It could never be exorcised and Johnny didn't want it to be.

The more Johnny had relaxed the more he realised how hard it was back in London.

The life he led there was a life of constant pressure. The pressure to keep one step ahead in the style stakes. The pressure to be the first to discover unheard classics by little known artists. Developing new hairstyles or dance moves and getting made to measure clothes on the weekly pittance he had earned. The constant need to pull strokes to earn a few extra quid for his extravagant lifestyle.

The need for more money was the reason he got in to the drugs business. But that brought its own headaches.

During that first week in Africa Johnny had experienced his first 'hubbly bubbly' pipe, smoking the pungent Kif which was abundant in the area. Johnny had smoked the odd joint with Chucky back in London but hadn't enjoyed it, making him lethargic and sleepy, a total anathema to his whole lifestyle.

The experience in a tiny tea shop in the local bazaar was totally different and altogether more enjoyable. A warm comforting shroud enveloping him added to the natural warmth of the African sunshine outside.

Sarah was obviously a more experienced smoker and watched over Johnny as he got steadily stoned.

The two young lovers purchased a small supply from the toothless, leathery old owner of the shop who seemed to find everything they did highly comical.

Once back in their hotel Johnny and Sarah shared a joint and spent the rest of the day and night having mind blowing, drug enhanced sex. The ceiling fan working overtime trying to cool the two sweat soaked, tanned bodies.

Waking up the next day well past twelve, Sarah rolled over and snuggled up to Johnny who slowly awoke from his slumber.

"Afternoon," she purred as Johnny opened his eyes hesitantly against the daylight.

"Afternoon babe," he replied with a smile.

"I've got a surprise for you today," she said with a mischievous smile.

"What?" Johnny said lazily.

"You'll see," she said with a giggle.

Johnny instantly sat up, rubbed his eyes and looked at her.

"What is it?" he said, slightly annoyed. Johnny wasn't one for surprises. The only ones he had experienced had been shitty ones. Like his dad fucking off, or his mum getting re-married to an arsehole.

"I want you to meet someone, that's all," she said.

"Nothing to worry about," she added quickly, recognizing his anxiety.

Two hours and a quick shag in the far from luxurious shower later and the two of them were walking along a jetty in the old port. Past a vast array of pleasure cruisers and yachts moored up by the rich tourists who had discovered the pleasures of the old North African town.

Johnny, still unsure why Sarah had brought him here, could not disguise his curiosity and apprehension as she jumped down onto the deck of a tasty looking 30ft cruiser, the sunlight reflecting blindingly off its whiteness.

Johnny frowned as a figure appeared from inside the boat and kissed Sarah on both cheeks.

Sarah turned around and beckoned Johnny to join them on the deck of the boat.

"Johnny, this is Giles," she said, "Giles, this is Johnny."

Giles Pilkington, first cousin to the Earl of somewhere or other smiled and stretched out his hand for Johnny to shake.

Johnny hesitated as he took in the man before him. Dressed in white linen trousers and pale blue cheesecloth shirt unbuttoned to the waist, sunglasses and a wide brimmed straw hat, the heavily tanned Giles waited for Johnny to take his hand. Eventually Johnny shook and Giles said.

"I've heard a lot about you old chap,"

Johnny looked at him and murmured, "Old chap, what a tosser."

"Come inside out of the sun I have a business proposition for you."

Giles Pilkington turned and headed back in to the coolness that the inside of the boat afforded.

Johnny looked at Sarah with raised eyebrows. Sarah smiled back and followed Giles.

Johnny stood in the blazing sun for a moment then walked inside.

Giles stood in front of the semi circular leather upholstered padded seat which took up three sides of the living quarters of the boat.

Bolted to the floor, a heavy wooden table sat in the middle, upon which lay a glass jug containing a pale red liquid and three wine glasses.

The toff poured out three glasses of the liquid unrecognizable to Johnny.

"Pimms?" he said extending a glass first to Sarah and then to Johnny.

Feeling intimidated by the man's wealth and confidence he looked to Sarah who gratefully accepted the refreshing drink.

Johnny took the drink, had a dubious sip and sat down, surprised at how nice the noncey looking drink was.

Giles irritated the young Londoner by waiting for Sarah to sit before doing the same, making him feel like an uncultured oaf.

"Sarah tells me you're involved in a big way in the supply of illegal pharmaceuticals back in our fair metropolis."

"Do what?" asked Johnny.

"You sell drugs old boy."

"That's right pal," answered Johnny irritated by Pilkingtons condescending attitude.

"Apparently you are the main supplier of speed in the West End."

Johnny cringed inwardly, having talked himself up to Sarah when they first met and having done nothing to dispel the image he had created about himself.

"What about it?" Johnny asked a bit too aggressively.

Sarah looked across at Johnny with shock at his rudeness but Giles didn't seem to notice or if he did he chose to ignore it.

"Well Johnny, I have the means at my disposal to transport large sums of the local produce from here along the coast through the straits of Gibraltar and onto a little place called Malaga on the Spanish coast. From there the produce can be put on a truck and driven up through Spain, into France loaded on a ferry at Calais, land at Dover and then onto London. The truck could then be unloaded in a warehouse I own on the outskirts."

Giles paused to see what effect his words were having on Johnny who sat listening in stony faced silence but was thinking,

Oh shit!

"Now I can handle everything from here to London but what I don't have is the contacts or the wherewithal to distribute the stuff."

Giles took another sip of his drink and as Johnny couldn't think of anything to say took one also and waited for him to continue.

"This is where you come in. I need someone to sell the stuff once it has been cut up. Someone who has all the right protection. I mean, we don't want to be upsetting any heavy duty people and from what Sarah tells me, you are under the protective wing of the aforementioned heavy people."

Me and my big mouth, thought Johnny, I knew my bullshit would get me in to trouble.

But the more Giles spoke, the more interested Johnny became.

"What with the large influx of Caribbean immigrants into the U.K. the demand will rise and the British people will soon discover the delights of a good smoke, so now is the time to get in on the action."

Sarah leant across and put her hand on Johnny's leg.

"What sort of dough are we talking about?" asked Johnny casually.

"On each load leaving here I calculate a conservative figure of..... ten thousand. Profit."

Johnny couldn't help but be impressed and started to get a bit carried away.

"What split you thinking about?" he said.

Giles crossed his legs and leant back in his seat.

"Well, as I have the large proportion of risk I suggest an 80-20 split. In my favour of course." He added the last bit with a wry smile.

"Fuck off, old boy," laughed Johnny sarcastically "What fucking risk? Sailing a boat then driving a truck. No one's interested in nicking a truck full of these sort of drugs on the continent. The risk is all in London where the Old Bill ain't as easy going. Plus we've got to sort out the "heavy people" as you call them. Nah mate you're having a laugh."

Giles rubbed his chin thoughtfully.

"Well what sort of figure do you suggest?" he asked pensively.

Johnny replied instantly "Fifty-fifty. Straight down the middle."

"Johnny?" Sarah said in surprise.

"Look Giles, me old mate. The way I look at it, you can bring as much stuff in to London as you want but without me you won't be able to sell fuck all. You need me and you need my connections. Simple as that."

The London Face was bullshitting through his front teeth but hey, if this upper class prick fell for it how difficult would it be to sort things out back in London?

Now his imagination started to run away with itself. Dreaming of making even more dosh selling cannabis, along with his speed operation.

He could carry on selling the speed on the Mod scene and sell the stuff from Giles to the blacks as well as Sarah's posh crowd who were into it. Some of the student lot he had come into contact were also into puffing.

Giles had stood up after a lot of thought.

"Okay old chap," he said, hiding any trace of annoyance at being outmanoeuvred by this ruffian, "You've got yourself a deal. Go back to London and I'll contact you when everything has been set up."

Sarah shrieked with joy and clapped her hands.

"Hurrah, let's celebrate," she said, grabbing hold of Johnny and giving him a big hug.

Johnny held her close, his head over her shoulder and looked directly into Giles' eyes.

The ex-public schoolboy held Johnny's stare and gave a weak smile in response to his beaming victorious one.

The last two days of their holiday was spent travelling up and down the coast in Giles' boat.

Stopping off to eat at out of the way little fishing villages, sunning themselves on the deck, drinking and getting stoned.

At night Johnny fucked Sarah like never before, making sure the two of them made plenty of noise. Johnny wanted to wind Giles up with the sound of their animal frenzy, certain that the toff had a thing for Sarah.

After one particularly energetic session, both young lovers having come, Sarah dozed, her head on Johnny's chest. He lay back with his arms behind his head and a huge smile on his face.

Things are just getting better and better, he thought.

CHAPTER 17

While Johnny was enjoying the sunshine and pleasures that North Africa and Sarah were providing, a meet took place at a Mile End lock up owned by Eddie Raven.

A lock up in the arches, under a railway line in the East End not dissimilar to the South London lock up used by Frank Saunders and the chaps.

A slight summer drizzle fell as Frank Saunders and Jimmy Sewell arrived outside in Sewell's black Daimler Sovereign.

Pulling up to the large sliding door two of Eddie Ravens goons approached the car and peered through the rain etched window. Recognizing the occupants of the car, the South London thieves were waved through into the arches.

Climbing warily from the beige leather upholstery Saunders and Sewell were directed to a flight of wooden stairs leading to an elevated office in the corner of the lock up.

The lock up felt damp and cold, matching the atmosphere of the occasion and the two outsiders unhurriedly climbed the wooden stairs and without knocking, opened the door at the top.

Eddie Raven was seated in his leather swivel chair behind a shabby looking desk on which sat just a telephone.

In front of the desk were two wooden chairs.

Saunders looked around the room. As well as Eddie Raven, three other men leant against the walls. Saunders made that eight, including the men downstairs and outside.

Not good odds if this was a set up. Frank cursed himself for not insisting the meet was held in a public place, but knew such a request would have been pointless if London's gang boss hadn't wanted to.

"Allo Frank," opened Raven. "Glad you could make it."

"Alright Jim?" he continued, nodding at Sewell, extending his hand to Saunders and Sewell in turn.

"Ave a seat lads," invited the gangster.

The two South London robbers sat and accepted the offer of a whisky.

Leaving the Scotch untouched, Frank, eager to get things sorted and get the fuck out of the place, quickly got down to business.

"Right, what's the S.P. then?" he asked.

"You're keen," laughed Raven, "Relax Frankie, take your time."

"Look, the sooner you give us the info, the sooner we can start planning. These things take time to sort out," answered Saunders.

"Course they do son," replied the gangster,

"This does need sorting a bit sharpish, time's running out," he added.

Another nagging doubt entered Frank Saunders head about this job.

"When exactly has this job gotta be done?" he asked.

Eddie Raven leant back into his chair, had a sip of whisky, savoured it and answered,

"Friday!"

"Friday?" questioned Saunders, "What, this Friday?"

"Yup," said Raven, with what Saunders detected as a slight smirk.

"You're taking the fucking piss," shouted Saunders, "There's no way we can plan any job in three days, it's impossible.

"We need to plan it, practise it, case it, time it," he paused, "We don't even know the fucking target."

"That, my old son is why you're here," said London's guvnor, "It ain't to socialise.

"I've got all the details here."

With that he leant forward, opened a drawer on the right hand side of his desk, retrieved a large brown envelope and nonchalantly tossed it across the desk.

Frank turned to face Jimmy. Both men had incredulous looks on their faces. Each checking the others reaction to see they were not over reacting to such startling information.

"Why Friday? What's so special about Friday for fucks' sake?" Asked Saunders.

Eddie Raven stood up, put his glass on the desk, placed his hands either side of it and leant forward.

"I will tell you exactly what is so special about Friday," said Raven.

"There is a place in Essex called Debden. In Debden there is a large, ordinary looking two storey building. From the outside it looks like any other sort of factory and office building. But it ain't no factory. They don't make things in there, they destroy things."

Eddie Raven paused and took another drop of Scotch. Frank and Jimmy's drinks remained untouched.

The gangster continued.

"The building is owned and run by the Royal Mint. In to that building every single week, huge amounts of one, five and ten pound notes are delivered from all over the country. These notes are sent there because they are not deemed suitable for circulation anymore. Old, worn, slightly torn notes are delivered from banks all over the country to be destroyed. Perfectly good money shoved in to incinerators and burnt to cinders.

"What the fuck is that all about?" he asked, "Burning perfectly good dosh. It's fucking criminal."

Eddie Raven chuckled to himself at his last comment.

"Anyway, the notes to be burnt are obviously all random numbers and totally, totally untraceable.

"They've got security up the arse there. All staff are thoroughly searched when they leave at the end of the day."

Total silence.

Raven continued, "I've got a man inside. Works in the maintenance department and according to him the old incinerator keeps packing up and he's always having to fix it.

"Well, the guvnors in there have decided to change the system completely. Update it like. New equipment installed. And that is happening this weekend."

Jimmy Sewell jumped in.

"So what are we supposed to do, raid the place? We ain't fucking commandoes you know. You said yourself they had tons of security."

Eddie Ravens jaw clenched and there was an audible intake of breath from his goons. The gangster slowly turned to Jimmy and gave him a look that could curdle milk.

Jimmy Sewell was a hard fucker, but under the withering, contemptuous gaze of Eddie Raven, he felt himself shrinking into his chair.

Without saying a word, the look was enough, Raven turned back to Saunders.

"All the dough, due to be fried this weekend now needs to be done elsewhere. They don't wanna leave all that money lying around the place over the weekend. It might be too much of a temptation for someone."

Once more, he laughed at his little joke and was joined by his underlings in the room. Frank and Jimmy just sat there, poker faced.

"The only other place that can deal with the job of burning the notes is over the river in Kent. A place called Crayford.

"Anyway, the dough is being taken by van from Essex to Crayford this Friday. My man on the inside managed to sneak into the boss's office and lift all the details of the transportation."

Raven paused for effect before continuing.

"A dark blue Austin J2 van will leave the compound at ten o'clock in the morning, with one driver and one drivers mate and a geezer in the back. The whole thing is very low profile. They don't feel it is much of a security risk. They don't think anyone would bother nicking such shitty old notes. They're more bothered about petty pilfering by the staff rather than a big hit."

Frank listened intently, every fibre of his body screaming to him that it was wrong. Here was one of those too good to be true jobs and they always ended tits up.

"All you and your boys have to do is intercept the van and nick the dough. Couldn't be simpler."

With that, the gangster sat back down, loosened his tie and poured himself another generous whisky.

"If it's so simple, why don't your bunch of genius's do it?" said Frank, looking over to the three heavies slouched against the office walls.

"Frankie, my motto has always been stick to what you know.

"You know about pulling off capers like this. My boys know how to cause pain and suffering. Something in which they are well capable," said Raven in a veiled threat sort of way.

"This is right up your boulevard," he finished.

Frank Saunders thought for a moment, then asked,

"How do we know there's no security back up?"

Eddie Raven leant across the desk and tapped the untouched envelope.

"My man inside broke into the guvnors office and lifted this memo. Like I said, it's all here."

Reluctantly, Saunders reached out and picked up the envelope, opened it, took out a sheet of paper and quickly scanned the information before him.

"What happens when they realise the memo is missing?" said Frank putting the piece of paper back in the envelope and returning it to its place on the desk.

The South London professional was just looking for excuses not to do the job and the East London gangster knew it.

"It's a copy," he answered.

"What about when we pull off the job? Old bill will be all over the place like a fucking rash. They'll question every worker in the place, suspecting an inside job. The 'inside man' always breaks under questioning. Civilians always do."

Eddie Raven smiled and replied, "My man is working under a moody name. He's got a moody national insurance number and a false address. I put him in there a year ago cos I thought it might be handy some day. That day has now arrived.

"Once the van has left the depot and "Mr Moody" has placed the call, letting us know everything is okay and there is no additional security he will disappear into thin air. He'll be flown out of the country under another false name. Old bill won't get a chance to question him."

"Flown out of the country my arse," muttered Frank, "He'll probably be propping up a flyover somewhere."

Frank Saunders kept his thoughts to himself but looked Eddie Raven directly in the eye to let him know he wasn't fooling him.

"Looks like you've thought of everything" Saunders chose to say, realising the job would have to be done.

The gangster leant back in his swivel chair, swung gently from side to side and said, "I like to think so," in a triumphant tone.

"Once we get his call, we'll give you the nod and the rest is up to you and your chaps."

"What's the route?" asked Frank.

Another piece of paper was produced out of another envelope, pulled from the desk drawer and once again slid across to Saunders.

Saunders read the details, which listed departure time, route, estimated time of arrival at points on route and arrival time at the Crayford depot.

"You've got two days," barked Raven.

Frank Saunders sat there in silence, mulling things over, reading the route, taking in the street names and timings. He didn't like it. Not one bit. Too simple.

"Well?" said Raven, "What d'ya fink? Piece of piss innit?"

"It's a bit short notice. Two days," said Saunders.

"Fuck me Frankie," said Raven, "It's a fucking cake walk. You could do it with your eyes closed."

Saunders looked dubious and Eddie Raven continued,

"The fucking coups you've pulled off in the past. This will be bish bosh, in like Flynn then out with the dough. You won't even break sweat."

Frank looked at Jimmy, then back at the formidable looking man across the desk.

"Frank. Look at it this way," Raven said, "You're fucking doing it. Whether you like it or not. Make the most of it. Earn yourself a few quid."

"We'd better get cracking then," replied Saunders with mock joviality and rose to his feet. Jimmy joined him in standing.

"Nice one," said the gangster. "See Mickey if you need any equipment, cars, anything. He'll sort out anything you want."

Saunders looked at Sewell, then back to Raven.

"No thanks," replied Frank. "We'll sort everything our end, keeps the security tighter."

Then looking over at Mickey Bristol added.

"No offence," but meaning plenty.

"Suit yourself," said the gangster cheerfully. "Memorise the route and I'll destroy it. No need to leave evidence about, is there?"

Frank spent the next half hour studying the paper with the route and timings. Going over it with Jimmy as if cribbing for an exam.

Saunders had a talent for reading and taking in information and soon was able to recite the complete route perfectly 100 times out of 100. When he was able to say it backwards a couple of times he was satisfied and handed the paper back to the boss of the London underworld, who had now removed his tie and rolled his shirt sleeves up.

"Alright?" said Raven, "Anything else?"

"Nope," answered Saunders. "Just the phone call once the van leaves. I'll contact you Thursday and give you a number you can call us on to give us the nod. If we don't get that call the jobs off. We ain't going in blind."

"No problem. We'll speak on Thursday then," replied Raven, walking round the table to shake hands with the two robbers.

The office door was held open and the two thieves started to make their way out.

"Oh Frankie, I almost forgot," said Raven shaking his head.

"When you call Thursday, I'll give you the address I want the dough taking to. You don't want all that dosh lying around now, do ya?"

Saunders smiled and replied, "Good thinking, I don't know what we'd do without you."

Eddie Raven didn't like the sarcasm in Saunders voice and said curtly, "Thursday. Don't fuck up."

As he walked back to his desk, almost as an afterthought, Raven turned and said.

"Oh, by the way. The guards will be carrying shooters." As casually as if he had just told them the guards would be having cheese sandwiches for lunch.

Frank and Jimmy turned back to the door and made their way out and down the wooden stairs once more.

As they climbed into the Daimler, the door to the arches was slid open and the car reversed out, stopped, then slipped into first gear and gunned off down the unmade road.

The rain had stopped and the sun now shone. Frankie hoped it was a good omen, but he doubted it.

CHAPTER 18

On the day of their departure Giles drove them to the airport having already sorted out a sample supply of local produce for Johnny to take back to London to get people interested.

The flight back to London airport had been fine, with Johnny sleeping most of the way, Sarah leaning on his shoulder.

Having collected their luggage, the two smugglers had a few hairy minutes walking through the "Nothing to Declare" channel but the couple weren't stopped and they were able to breathe a huge sigh of relief once outside the airport standing on the pavement trying to hail a taxi.

Sarah snuggled up to Johnny and slipped her arm through his and gave him a peck on the cheek.

He pulled himself away, embarrassed as he spotted a Mod sailing past on a Lambretta GT200. A cool machine.

It was an instant reaction for him. One he couldn't avoid.

All the time they had been abroad the two of them had strolled hand in hand or with their arms linked, the first time Johnny had ever done such a thing. They had kissed and cuddled, laying on the beach or standing on street corners, the first time he had ever shown such an overt display of affection to anyone in his life. The first time he had ever wanted to.

It had seemed an okay and natural thing to do. Very much in keeping with his feeling of relaxation. Away from the critical eyes of his peers where one slip in appearance or behaviour could bring about his downfall in the London style hierarchy.

Now back in London he self consciously slipped back in to cool mode something which didn't go un-noticed by Sarah who bristled at the rejection.

Deliberately moving up beside him again she tried to hold his arm again.

"Fuck off," he hissed involuntarily, "What's the matter with you?"

Sarah, never having been treated in this way, was angry and confused and spent the entire journey back to her flat in moody silence.

Johnny paid the taxi driver and retrieved the cases as Sarah flew up the marble steps to the main entrance door and was still making his way up the same steps when Sarah was already inside the flat making coffee.

He had the right hump having to carry all the cases like some sort of bell boy and threw them noisily onto the bedroom floor then went to find Sarah standing with her back to him in the kitchen.

The Chelsea girl didn't turn around when he walked into the room but carried on with her coffee making.

Despite the water reaching boiling point in the saucepan on the stove the room temperature dropped a couple of notches below zero, the atmosphere could be cut with a blunt razor.

"What's the matter with you, you moody cow?" He had never been able to cope with tantrums.

"Nothing," she replied tensely without facing him.

"Why the silent routine then?" countered Johnny stuffing his hands in to the back pockets of his Levis.

"You know," she sulked.

"Ah ha," he declared in flippant triumph, "So there is something up."

He stood there with a cocky smile on his face as Sarah spun round violently to face him.

"You think you're so fucking cool don't you? Mister know-it-all. Johnny the Face.

'Holding hands while we were away. Walking arm in arm. I really thought you had grown up. Started being a bit less insecure, not having to hide behind your image."

Johnny stood there flabbergasted.

Sarah was in full flow now.

"That's right. That's right. Using all the clothes you wear to stop people seeing the real you because you're ashamed of the real you. All that front you put up is because there is nothing of worth inside. If people are so impressed with the façade they won't need to go inside and find out you're a building full of empty rooms."

Sarah turned her back on him once more and stumbled her way through the coffee making process putting her hand to her mouth to stifle her gentle sobbing.

"You stupid cow," said Johnny eventually. "The whole reason you were attracted to me in the first place was 'cos of my image, how I looked and how I carried myself but now you want to change me. You love the whole scene around me, the fact that I'm considered a Face. The "Bit of Rough" in made to measure mohair."

"I thought there was more to you than clothes Johnny," Sarah responded quietly.

He was getting angry and frustrated now.

"I know exactly what you thought. A bit of working class rough to show off to your Sloane Street pals. Drug dealer. A bit of excitement for ya. Your way of rebelling against daddy."

"That's not true," screamed Sarah.

"Don't make me laugh. Probably the only reason you're going with me is to give your parents the hump. To shock them and their stuck up mates. But as soon as you want something it's "Oh daddy can you buy me a car? Oh daddy can I have a flat in Chelsea?""

"Why introduce me to your blue blood pal Giles and his drug smuggling idea? Your way of being a naughty girl. That's why you suggested going out there in the first place you sneaky bitch. It suits your purpose to be dating someone like me."

Johnny's attack on Sarah had been brutal.

"It's nothing to do with image. It doesn't matter what clothes you wear or the length of your lapels," she said sadly.

"But that's all part of me," he said softly, "Part of what I am."

Silence filled the space between them like the tide rushing in onto an empty beach.

Sarah just closed her eyes, forcing big, fat salty tears down her flushed freckled cheeks and took a few deep breaths.

After an eternity she said quietly.

"I fell in love with you not your clothes."

There was no response and Sarah eventually turned slowly to face him. The room was empty. Johnny had gone. Sarah broke down and really, really wept.

The youngster ran out of the flat confused as fuck. What the fuck does she want from me? he thought as he made his way out of the square and onto Sloane Street.

Looking up and down the street where the posh people shopped he saw a black cab with its orange "For Hire" sign, stuck the thumb and forefinger of his right hand into his mouth and let out an ear piercing whistle before shouting out.

"TAXI."

It was funny, he thought, how he used to hate taxi drivers but since he started making dough he used them all the time.

The cab pulled over and the driver slid his window down.

"Where to guv?" asked the cabbie in the time honoured manner.

Johnny leant forward and stated his destination. "Bar Italia, Frith Street" and pulled down the door handle and clambered into the back without waiting for a response.

The North London cabbie flung the window back up, settled himself back into his seat, flicked his sign off and executed a blind u turn heading in the right direction for Soho.

Leaning back in the rear of the cab he gazed out of the window in silence. Kensington and Knightsbridge were nothing but a blur as they drove past.

After a few minutes his silent contemplation was broken by the driver who, as was the case with most cabbies loved the sound of his own voice.

"This town's getting worse mate," he said looking up at his passenger in his rear view mirror.

"Yea mate," Johnny replied uninterestedly.

The cab driver changed lanes coming up to Marble Arch and didn't manage to take the hint.

"First that blackie, then a couple of days later them brothers," he continued.

Still Johnny didn't take any notice.

Unperturbed by his passenger's lack of interest in his conversation the cabbie ploughed on regardless.

"The Old Bill reckon it's all to do with drugs."

At the mention of drugs, the teenager was shaken from his reverie and his interest picked up.

"What's that?" he said, leaning forward to the glass partition that separated them.

"Drugs mate," said the driver looking up again. "They reckon that trumpeter was involved in dealing drugs. That's why he was topped. And them brothers too."

Johnny's stomach flipped and his failing love life was instantly forgotten as a cold fist of terror slammed into his gut.

"What trumpet player?" he managed to say in a strangled voice, the panic in him rising.

"What brothers?" he demanded.

"Where you been son?" said the driver once more looking at him in his mirror, noticing his passenger had gone very pale.

"It's been all over the papers and the telly."

"WHAT FUCKING TRUMPET PLAYER?" screamed Johnny.

"Oy, oy, oy," said the cab driver indignantly as if he had never heard the word "fuck" before.

"Sorry mate," apologised the young Face, a hot sweat draping his body, "but what are you talking about?"

The cabbie seemed satisfied with the boy's apology and reached over to the passenger seat without taking his eyes from the road and picked up that days newspaper.

"It's all in there son," he said sliding open the partition window and handing him the Daily Sketch.

"In black and white."

Johnny snatched the offered newspaper and scanned the front page devouring the printed information like a starving man in a restaurant. His head moving quickly from side to side reading the horrific details the journalist revelled in telling. How his friends had met their terrible fate.

Continued on pages 2, 3 and 4.

The boy read the sensational text frantically, hoping with all his soul that it was a different Negro trumpet player and two other brothers. A million to one shot but straws had to be clutched. Johnny collapsed back into his seat upon reading the names which leapt from the paper on page two.

The newspaper dropped to the floor from Johnny's shaking fingers as he raised his sweating palms to cover his face.

Fear, misery, guilt and anger were amongst the multitude of emotions that slammed in to his mind and body like a sledgehammer.

He felt stoned, his head in a total fog of despair. The cabbie prattled on but his voice sounded muffled and distorted as a million thoughts fought for space in his tortured mind.

The taxi approached Piccadilly Circus as Johnny's mind began to at least clear a little bit and he looked up to see where he was.Trying to get his bearings through tear blurred eyes.

Looking left and right it took a few seconds to recognize the location he knew like the back of his hand and in usual circumstances could make his way around blindfolded.

Now his survival instinct kicked in, and Sarah's image popped in to his head.

"STOP," he shouted banging the glass partition suddenly.

"Do what?" replied the startled driver.

"STOP THE FUCKING CAB," he roared smashing the partition violently with both fists.

The shocked cab driver slammed his foot on the brake as he entered Shaftesbury Avenue. Bringing the taxi to a screeching halt he got rear ended by a Triumph Bonneville motorcycle following too closely, spilling it's rider over the handlebars and across the road, a multitude of expletives coming from his mouth as he flew through the air.

"Think, think," muttered Johnny to himself oblivious to the suffering of the motorcycle rider.

"What you doing, you mad bastard?" shouted the cabbie as he climbed out of his means of earning a living and walked to the back of the cab to inspect the damage.

Johnny also jumped out of the taxi, grabbed its owner by his cardiganed sleeve and shoved a handful of fivers into the man's face.

"Forget the fucking damage," he shouted. "This'll cover it. Now get back in the cab and take me back to Sloane Street."

The taxi owner looked at the motorcyclist writhing in pain on the ground, then at the slight damage to the back of his cab and then at the money being held up to his face.

"Right you are guv," he said, doffing an imaginary cap.

The boy and the older man climbed back into the cab, another u turn was carried out and the car was heading back in the direction from where it had just come.

"Faster," the desperate passenger implored, "FASTER," and the taxi driver floored it.

Ten minutes later and the black cab pulled up outside Sarah's building in a cloud of diesel smoke.

Without looking at the sum on the meter, Johnny thrust a bundle of fivers through the window and on to the cabbies lap. More than enough for the fare and the damage done by the careless motor bike rider who at that very moment was being lifted in to an Ambulance.

The desperate youngster leapt up the steps to the main entrance, opened the door and darted up to Sarah's door where he stopped, took a deep breath, put the key into the lock and slowly turned.

Gently opening the door, Johnny thought he knew what would await him.

The flat smashed to pieces, the clothes and precious records he kept there destroyed and the sight he begged the god he didn't believe in he wouldn't see. Sarah lying dead with her throat mercilessly slashed.

Taking a hesitant step into the flat he stopped in the coolness of the tile floored hall.

"Sarah," he called. Nothing.

Johnny, step by careful step made his way into the living room. It was just as he had left it. Perfectly normal.

On into the bedroom and again the room lay undisturbed. None of the carnage his vivid imagination and speed induced paranoia had told him to expect.

The boy told himself not to get to hopeful and with his heart beating through his chest took deep, deep breaths and made his way to the kitchen.

"Please, please, please," he said over and over to himself.

Johnny stood with his back to the wall before swiftly forcing himself into the kitchen.

Again nothing. The room was in the same condition as he had left it with one exception. No Sarah.

As there was no sign of violence of any kind, he began to relax and dropped his guard as he put both hands on the worktop and hung his head in relief.

Pulling himself together he lifted his head, his eyes resting on a piece of paper taped to the wall unit in front of him.

What was this? A ransom note? thought Johnny. His drug confused imagination rising to number ten on the paranoia gauge, as he slowly peeled the paper from the cabinet.

"Dear Johnny," it read, "It was fun while it lasted but we are too different to be together. I thought you would be able to leave your immature world behind you but I can see it means more to you than I ever could. I just can't compete with Barbara Lynn, Barbara Lewis et al.

I am going to stay with my parents for a while. I would like you to get your stuff out of the flat and leave the keys.

I'm sorry you were not able to move on.

Love Sarah."

Johnny needed to take another deep breath as he read the note again, puffed out his cheeks and blew out slowly, his teenage mind going through yet another emotion. So many negative feelings in one short period was not right for one so young and he was struggling to come to terms with it all.

On one hand he was relieved Sarah was safe from the nutters who had done Chucky and who were now probably after him, but on the other he was heartbroken at losing her. His whole world had fallen apart within the space of an hour and he didn't know how to handle it. His head felt like it was going to explode, causing him to smash it violently and repeatedly against the wall unit, the demons gaining control again.

What am I going to do? he thought.

He was completely on his own. Girlfriend gone. Best mate dead. His protection, the Franklins were dead. No family to turn to.

Johnny the Face. Stylist. Cool as you like. Coolest dude in London felt like he was a ten year old boy again and for the first time in his life began to cry.

CHAPTER 19

Friday morning, 9.30. A lock up in Essex, East of London. Three men, boiler suits and gloves sat on packing cases, smoking, drinking tea and playing cards. A silent telephone sat on another packing case adjacent to the men, attracting constant, tense glances.

Over by the lock up doors sat a Jaguar 420, black, six months old, false plates. Stolen Wednesday night, tuned up.

This was the car to be used to follow the target. Another car, an Austin Westminster, stolen Tuesday and re-sprayed, new plates and with certain modifications had driven off earlier that morning.

The modifications carried out over the next couple of days after "lifting" the motor were done by Tommy Newman, who was going to be driving it.

The engine had been tuned and a seat belt had been fitted to the driver's seat. The belt was necessary because the car was intended to be a motorised battering ram.

Mechanic and ex racing driver Newman had also welded scaffold poles inside the two front wings, which ran from inside the headlights along the length of the wing. Poles had also been welded along the chassis from the front to the back. Unless someone looked very closely at the headlights, Tommy's handiwork could not be detected and to all intents and purpose was a bog standard Austin family car, not worth a second glance.

Due to the nature of the job, the fact that it was a one off and the target would never be transferred like this again, the gang of South London thieves were unable to carry out their normal meticulous planning. That planning would involve following a target vehicle if it was a security van job. Timing by stop watch, making note of all possible problems on route. Traffic lights, zebra crossings, roadwork's, schools and god forbid, Police stations.

All they could do was a few drive throughs of the journey, slowly driving the route which they hoped was the correct one as given to them by their nemesis Eddie Raven.

As the job had been presented to them only days previously and had to be done so quickly after, there wasn't time to go through everything as thoroughly as they usually would. They weren't even 100% sure what sort of vehicle would be used to carry the dough.

Due to all the imponderables surrounding the job, they decided the best approach would be maximum violence. From stopping the vehicle, to getting the doors open and incapacitating the armed guards they could take no chances. They had to get the vehicle stopped exactly where they wanted. No contact with guards would be made, just in case one of them wanted to be a hero and get arsey and not open the doors. Or worse, use their shooters.

That is why they had decided the best approach to their task would be the "battering ram" technique.

The follow car containing Frank Saunders, Alfie Booth and Jimmy Sewell would, upon receiving the "GO" call, leave the lock up in Essex and pick up the trail of the Royal Mint van.

Tommy Newman would be in car two, the Austin Westminster battering ram, waiting for Frank Saunders in the Jaguar 420 to contact him by way of walkie talkie radio to inform him if the route was as expected.

When contact was made, Tommy would head for the pre-planned collision point and wait half a mile or so down the street, facing the opposite direction that the target was headed with his engine running.

As soon as the van came into view Newman would slip on his crash helmet and goggles, engage first gear and pull away from the kerb. Keeping the car at a steady 30mph, Tommy Newman would wait until the van coming in the opposite direction was roughly one hundred yards away, before slamming his right foot down on the accelerator and swerving into the path of the target.

It would take skill and bravery but the intention was to smash the car head on into the van totally incapacitating the vehicle and the two men in the drivers' cab and the guard in the back.

The Jaguar by now directly behind the van, but not too close would be in the right position. Frank Saunders and Jimmy Sewell would jump from the Jag and quickly approach the now fucked van.

Alfie would also get out of the van but would be toting a sawn off to discourage interference.

Tommy Newman was to make his way from the smashed up Austin and take his place in the driver's position of the Jag, vacated by Alfie Booth.

As Tommy slipped behind the wheel of the getaway car and Alfie provided protection, Frank and Jimmy would place enough gelignite on the hinges and locks of the van doors to blow both sets off. When the twenty second fuses were lit they would retreat behind the open doors of the Jaguar for cover.

Once the doors were blown off, Saunders and Sewell would grab the sacks of dough and stick them in the boot of the Jag.

As soon as the van had been emptied and the car loaded Alfie and Jimmy would jump in the back and Tommy would pull up alongside the Austin at the other end of the stricken van, where Frank would be doing their usual trick of stuffing a burning rag in to the fuel tank. As usual burning the evidence.

Once Saunders had jumped into the front passenger seat of the getaway motor, Tommy Newman would floor the accelerator and make good their escape.

Changing cars, a couple of miles away, once more leaving another lovely car a burning wreak, the gang would high tail it through the Blackwall tunnel to the familiar streets of South London.

One more change of car and the boys would head for the safety of their Lewisham lock up.

Sanctuary.

That was the plan anyway.

And now, all the planning they were able to do had been done and Frank Saunders, Alfie Booth and Jimmy Sewell could only sit and wait.

The Essex lock up had been rented under a moody name. The phone had been connected by a fella they knew who worked in the G.P.O.

The members of the gang had arrived there the previous night under cover of darkness and had bedded down on camp beds and sleeping bags that had been delivered there that day.

A camping stove, kettle, food supplies, cards and fags were delivered at the same time.

The men awoke at six a.m. had breakfast and the first of endless cups of tea. Once they had wished Tommy good luck and he left to prepare for his solo part of the heist, they waited. And waited.

The team were used to playing the waiting game, it was in their job description, but no matter how often they did it, it never got any easier.

Seconds seemed like minutes, minutes seemed like hours. Watches were constantly checked. Smoking and playing cards did nothing to speed the passage of time.

Tension hung in the air like nuclear fallout.

The information given to them by Eddie Raven had stated that the van would be leaving the Mint building at 10.a.m.

It was now 10.25 as Frank Saunders checked his watch for the umpteenth time.

"Where the fuck is this call?" he muttered to himself. A question all the gang members were silently asking.

Suddenly, in the large silent room the phone rang, echoing loudly around the lock up causing all the men to jump in their seats.

Saunders snatched the hand piece as his team leapt to their feet watching him with bated breath.

"Allo," growled Saunders in to the mouthpiece.

"Hello, is Dolly there?" enquired an old women's voice at the other end of the phone.

"DO WHAT?" shouted Saunders almost snapping the handset in half with the grip he had on it.

"I'm sorry my dear, I'm after my friend Dolly, I think I've got the wrong number," the voice replied.

"To fucking right you have love," bellowed the thief. "Now get off the line there's a train coming."

"Charming!" exclaimed the shocked voice as Saunders slammed the phone down and looked over to the chaps who slowly sat down in disappointment.

Saunders shook his head in disbelief.

"Some old dear looking for her mate Dolly," he explained.

Jimmy looked at Frank with a wry smile on his face, "Get off the line there's a train coming?" he questioned.

The team burst out laughing, "I couldn't think of anything else to say," replied Saunders joining in with the laughter as the tension eased instantly.

Frank joined his mates and was dealt in for the next hand. Although the mood had lifted, the gang still kept checking their timepieces.

It was strange. Although the team hadn't wanted to do the job when it was put up by Raven, now they had got this far, none of them wished the phone call wouldn't come, allowing them to back out gracefully. It wasn't the fact that the gangster would still be on their backs it was a question of getting so psyched up for a coup that the anti climax would be a bastard.

Once a thief had set his mind on doing a job and had got this far, it had to be done. After doing the planning, all be it as limited as it was in this case, had got all the necessary gear- the shooters, supplies, motors- and were actually sat waiting for the call the adrenaline was at such a level that they simply had to do the job or they would explode.

Occasionally a job would have to be called off at the last minute due to some unforeseen cock up and the chaps would have to let off steam in a big way. This would involve hitting the West End, drinking huge amounts of booze, maybe a bout of fisticuffs with some other rival team and pulling a dolly bird and giving her a right good seeing to in some swanky hotel.

Despite the pressure being eased by the old girl looking for her mate Dolly the minutes still ticked by slowly. Tick-tock, tick-tock. Agonising.

Tommy Newman was also constantly checking his watch which he wore with the face on the inside of his wrist so he could see it without moving his hand off the wheel whilst driving. He sat behind the wheel of the lethal Austin Westminster in the car park of the Red Lion pub in Basildon and waited to hear from Frank. Tommy had spent the night at the lock up with the other chaps and had woken, splashed his face with cold water from a standpipe tap in the corner of the empty hide out and had breakfast, a quick brew and a fag before shaking hands with the others and driving the Austin off to get in position for action.

The phone rang. Saunders leapt across to it, knocking over his packing case seat in his haste, not giving it a second chance to ring.

Pay phone. Beeps. All eyes on Frank. The whirring noise as a coin was inserted. Everyone held their breath.

The voice on the end of the phone said the word. "Bingo."

Saunders slammed the phone down. "We're on," proclaimed the thief.

He hadn't reached the n of on before the team were on the move, swooping up all traces of them having been there.

The wooden camp beds and sleeping bags had already been burnt to cinders in the night watchman's brazier and they were joined by the supplies, cards and anything else which would burn. The camp stove and kettle were slung in the boot of the Jag as well as the telephone which Saunders had ripped out of the wall. Once the car had fulfilled its purpose it would be torched in the usual manner along with the contents.

Jimmy Sewell ran over to the lock up doors and slid them open as Alfie Booth jumped in to the driver's seat and was joined by Saunders next to him in the passenger seat. Alfie gunned the car into life and the deafening roar of the exhausts echoed around the empty lock up as he eased the car out into the light.

Jimmy shut the large wooden doors behind them and climbed into the back of the car, sliding over the black leather upholstery.

"Right," said Saunders. "Lets do it."

The Jaguar 420 eased off towards their target. Down the alley where the lock up sat. Left at the end, two minutes up the road and third left. Follow the road for ten minutes before coming to a junction of a main road.

The phone call that had been received and the word "Bingo" had confirmed that the route chosen by the security van was as predicted. The team were now sat at their pre-planned pick up point.

The place where they would join up with the van to follow it closely but not too close until it reached the spot of the intended hit.

Alfie pulled the car up to the kerb some ten yards from the junction and left the engine running.

The team only had to wait six minutes before the dark blue van from the Mint came in to view.

Saunders lifted his walkie talkie to his mouth and attempted to contact Tommy Newman in the other car.

"Car two, this is car one. Come in car two over."

Static, crackling.

Frank tried again, "Car two, this is car one. Do you read me? Over." Again there was just a load of static and crackling noise. Nothing. Frank looked at Alfie who wasn't very good at hiding the worry he was feeling.

Again Saunders tried as he checked the position of the van. It was getting too close.

"Car two, this is car one, Do you read me? Where the fuck are you? Over."

As Frank lifted his finger once more from the button on the walkie talkie, he heard the faint voice of Tommy responding.

"This is car two. Receiving you. Not very loud and not very clear but I am receiving you. Over."

Frank grinned at Alfie and replied, "Target is on route. ETA you in ten minutes. Repeat. Target with you in ten. Over."

"Message received and understood. Over and out."

Tommy in the battering ram Austin placed the walkie talkie on to the passenger seat, started the engine and revved it up a couple of times then just sat there letting the engine tick over.

The blue van slowly cruised past the side street where the rest of the gang sat.

Alfie Booth eased the 420 out onto the main road, allowing two other vehicles to get in between them and the van and at a steady 30mph stalked its prey.

"Don't get too close," instructed Frank as Alfie concentrated on his task.

"They're getting too far," he said a minute later. This was just Frank being Frank and Alfie ignored his promptings. Alfie Booth knew what he was doing. Before Tommy Newman had joined the team, he had been the driver and although he wasn't in Tommy's class he still knew what he was doing behind the wheel.

The van sedately made its way through the streets of the county of Essex, through non descript suburbs and high streets unaware that all the time it was accompanied by the long, sleek, black predator, carrying a gang of South London villains two cars back.

Saunders constantly scanned the area for Old Bill and security but his experienced eyes detected nothing untoward.

Tommy's handset once more crackled into life as Saunders made contact again.

"Car two. This is car one. Are you receiving? Over."

"Car two to car one. Receiving you. Over," replied Newman.

Saunders clicked his radio again. "ETA you in two minutes. No company. Over."

Once again Tommy replied, "Understood. Over and out."

That was it for radio contact, unless there was some last second problem, so Tommy placed the handset in the footwell of the passenger seat and gripped the steering wheel tightly.

After having given up his motor racing career he had done a bit of banger racing at places like Catford and Walthamstow just to make a few bob and to still be involved with cars. That was before Frank had given him a job.

Tommy was sweating with apprehension but told himself that this would be no different to banger racing only the prize money would be better. A lot better. The Austin slowly exited the car park and headed for the spot where he would get the maximum view of the van, thus giving him as much time as he needed to set himself and reach the necessary speed required to make it impossible for the van to avoid him.

Tommy Newman pulled in to the side of a long stretch of road, flanked by shops in the distance, the pavements edged with trees. Friday afternoon shoppers bustled up and down the street but in their hurry were oblivious to the man just sitting in the Austin family car, just as that man was oblivious to them. The former racing driver's eyes were firmly fixed on the road ahead. Concentrating on the horizon he could feel the excitement rising in his body like lava in a soon to erupt volcano. The same excitement he used to feel when waiting for the green "GO" flag to be dropped at the start of a race.

The two minutes had passed when as predicted by the voice on the walkie talkie the dark blue van came in to view and Tommy readied himself for action. This was the most important part of the blag. Timing was everything. If he fucked this up, the job wouldn't be a success.

Tommy slipped his balaclava on his head and down over his face, covering everything except his eyes and mouth. He then reached over to the passenger seat and grabbed a black crash helmet and put that on as well. Finally buckling up his safety belt which he had fitted to the car himself, he was ready.

The wheelman flicked on the right indicator to show he was pulling away from the kerb. He didn't want an accident did he?

Tommy proceeded through the gears and was doing a steady 30 mph as the van got closer. Sweat dripped down his back and his forehead was soaking under the crash helmet and woollen headgear.

It wasn't the clothing he wore or the boiler suit over that clothing. It wasn't the heavy wool garment and crash helmet on his head or the black leather gloves he wore which was the cause of his perspiration. He could have been stark bollock naked in the middle of winter and he would have still been sweating like a pig as the target got nearer. It was always the same with him just before a race or just before a bit of business.

The van was now 200 yards away. Take it easy. 140 yards, nice and steady. 100, here it comes. 80, this is it. Clutch down, drop the gear from third to second, boot the fucking accelerator. COME ON!

The tyres on the Austin Westminster screeched as second gear bit and the car shot forward like a bullet. The noise of the tyres on the road drew worried looks from pedestrians who anticipated the excitement of an everyday shunt.

Tommy Newman swung the car across from the left hand lane into the opposite one and grabbed the wheel tightly as he reached 80 on the speedo.

The driver of the van took a second to realise that there was a car headed towards him and it wasn't intending to move out of his way. But that second delay ensured he was unable to take evasive action.

The attacking car tore towards them and the occupants of the van could only scream in impotent horror as it ploughed into them, totally demolishing the front of the Royal Mint vehicle.

The thieves had anticipated the guards wearing their seat belts. They were wrong.

The force of impact threw the van driver violently forward, smashing his chest against the steering wheel crushing him to death.

The driver's partner was also propelled forward at great speed. He flew head first through the windscreen which disintegrated on impact slashing his face to ribbons.

The man went through the glass screen at the combined speed of the van and the car which had hit it. A total of 120 mph.

The plan, at that split second started to go terribly wrong. The impact of the collision shot the van passenger through the windscreen and straight through the windscreen of the car which had hit it, smashing into the crash helmeted figure of Tommy Newman, snapping the thief's body back hideously half way up his chest. Both men were killed on impact.

The hooter of the van blared incessantly with the weight of the driver pinned against it. Smoke and steam billowed into the sky from the collision as the villains in the Jag which had overtaken the cars between them and their target moved onto the next stage of their plan, oblivious to the disaster which had taken place at the front of the van.

The three robbers leapt from the Jag. Alfie Booth stood beside the car toting a sawn off as covering protection for Frank and Jimmy. They didn't want any heroes interfering. Frank and Jimmy ran to the van and placed the explosives on the hinges and locks before retreating behind the protection of the open doors of their car. The three of them just had time to duck below the doors before the 20 second fuses they had fitted ran down ripping both sets of van doors clean off, rendering the guard in the back unconscious.

The three thieves rose as one. Alfie scanned the area once more. Frank and Jimmy headed for the smoke engulfed van. The former jumped in to the back and the latter waited on the road to retrieve the bags of money thrown out. Out they flew, three in all. Canvas bags waist high stuffed with £100,000 of used notes. Jimmy carried two, leaving the last one for Frank who jumped back through the smoke on to the road and dragged his bag to the boot of the Jag and threw it in before slamming the lid down.

In all the noise and confusion, it was a short time before the gang who were just about to get back into the Jag realised that Tommy hadn't taken his place at the wheel of the getaway car.

Alfie Booth, shotgun in hand, whistled over to Saunders, gestured to the empty driver's seat and shrugged his shoulders in bewilderment indicating that there was a problem.

Saunders breathing heavily cursed under his breath and ran to the front of the van but was stopped in his tracks with the sight before him.

The Austin Westminster had been wrapped in a cloud of smoke which was impenetrable to Frank's eyes until a gust of wind blew and the horrific scene was exposed. There before him lay his friend crushed and twisted. His shattered body lay limp and lifeless covered in blood with smashed bones protruding through his flesh.

"FUCK," shouted Saunders, knowing there was nothing he could do as another silent gust of wind once more covered the hideous carnage with smoke. With the smoke belching out of the crash sight it was as though a heavenly hand had drawn a grey blanket over the deceased men.

The stunned thief ran back to the getaway car but before he got there the plan took another turn for the worse.

Out of nowhere the tinny sound of a loud hailer echoed across the street.

"STOP. You are surrounded by armed police. Put down your weapons and lay on the ground with your hands on your heads."

The villains froze like rabbits in the headlights of an oncoming truck. Noise exploded all around them. Police sirens. Shouting. The loudhailer. Screams from the public and the constant blaring of the vans hooter allied to disgruntled drivers of cars further down the road beeping their hooters at the hold up, unaware of the drama unfolding.

The trapped robbers frantically looked around in all directions for the forces of law and order who apparently had them surrounded.

It was Jimmy Sewell who spotted the Old Bill first. Three of them. Guns drawn aimed at the thieves, shielding themselves behind a parked Rover.

"IT'S ON TOP," he shouted to no one in particular and for a split second thought about going for his revolver but upon seeing more coppers aiming weapons at him decided that discretion was the better part of valour and threw his arms up in surrender. It did him no good. Jimmy Sewell collapsed to the floor in a hail of bullets. The volley of small arms and shotgun fire rang out to the accompaniment of screams from the onlooking public. The screams were drowned out by the eighteen rounds which hit his body, ripping it to pieces, splattering blood and flesh all over the pavement as he was knocked back by the force of bullets hitting him.

Alfie Booth saw the carnage inflicted on his mate, and threw his shooter down to the ground his hands flying up in surrender and called out in desperation. "Don't shoot. I give up. I'm unarmed."

The loud hailer instructed the trembling thief to get on his knees with his hands on his head which he did immediately.

Saunders was stood against the side of the van, stuck like a rat in a trap.

He cursed again. More at himself for agreeing to do the job than anything else. Too good to be true eh? Bollocks, he thought.

The whole street was in utter confusion. The noise, the gunfire, the smoke and the steam from the busted radiators gave Saunders the opportunity which he needed. It was only a slim chance and he only had a split second to act upon it. If he delayed he would be nicked or shot dead.

A heavy cloud of acrid smoke was propelled by another gust of wind, enveloping Saunders and the van completely as well as covering the 420. It was this act of nature which gave him his exit card and he made his move, his bid for freedom.

The robber sprinted to the Jag and dived into the driver's seat as the Police let rip with another round of fire power. Saunders returned fire with four shots from his handgun that had been tucked inside his waistband. Not aiming at anyone or anything in particular, more to keep heads down. The engine of the getaway car was still running and Saunders only had to engage reverse and whack down the accelerator keeping his own head well down.

As the car moved backwards, he glanced down to his mate Alfie kneeling in the road with his hands on his head. Booth looked up to him with a pleading look in his eyes but there was nothing Frank could do. A shot rang out from the right; Frank looked up to see a copper running at him through the smoke and flinched as the policeman raised his gun to shoot again. Three shots rang out and as he didn't appear to be hit, he just thought the copper, who was a scruffy looking bastard, was a shit aim. But as the car moved away he looked down again at Alfie who was laying face down on the ground, the blood from three bullet holes in his head and back seeped out of him onto the road. The copper had shot Alfie in cold blood, deliberate. Saunders knew he had to get away or he wouldn't just be arrested and banged up, he would be killed. The Old Bill wanted to kill them all. Fucking hell this was a bit extreme.

The car shot backwards and to the shock of the cautiously approaching coppers appeared out of the smoke like a bat out of hell, scattering them to all sides. One constable wasn't quite as fleet of foot as his colleagues and the chrome bumper of the car smashed into his legs across the shins snapping both of them and knocking him to the ground several feet away. The impact did nothing to stop the momentum of the Jaguar which carried on reversing over the unfortunate Policeman, crushing him to death.

The car sped up the street in reverse until Saunders completed a perfect handbrake turn and got the car facing in the direction he wanted it to point. Gun fire rang out as Frank, his head sunk down between his shoulders engaged first gear and booted the gas. The next problem he faced was the build up of traffic which now blocked his path. Yanking the steering wheel to the right the powerful car mounted the kerb, scattering pedestrians in all directions and tearing along the pavement, just about squeezing the car between the shop fronts and the lampposts, scraping the shit out of both sides of the Jaguar and ripping off the wing mirrors.

Once past the obstacles on the road Saunders bumped the car heavily down the kerb and back onto the road, the back swinging violently from side to side as he tore off up the road, momentarily out of danger.

Sweating like a bastard he anxiously glanced in the rear view mirror, the vehicles that had been in his way were now providing protection from any pursuing Police and for that he was truly grateful.

As he made good his escape in the bashed up Jaguar he knew that in this car he was a sitting target. A dead duck.

He had to change motors and he had to do it fast. Tearing through the streets, the clanging sound of the Police cars in hot pursuit he momentarily tried to work out what had happened.

It was a total fuck up that's what had happened and the only possible explanation was a tip off. Someone had grassed. But who?

Saunders couldn't think straight as he needed all his powers of concentration to feed the heavy car through the busy streets, all the while looking for an opportunity to ditch the motor.

There. On the left. Saunders spotted his chance.

A petrol station and garage with a solitary car at the pumps. Saunders slammed on the anchors but was going so fast he passed the petrol station before his tyres complainingly brought the car to a halt.

The Jaguar had left thirty foot skid marks on the road but no one seemed to notice as Frank completed a slow u turn and the throbbing car eased on to the forecourt.

The thief had witnessed the owner of the car, a red MGB Roadster, pay the attendant who then pointed out a building beside the main part of the petrol station. The small building had two doors. On which one said Ladies, the other Gents. The attendant made his way back to the office, the customer headed for the bogs.

Frank drove the battered getaway car to the back of the office where the car repair department was housed.

As the fugitive climbed from the car, a voice called out from an inspection pit under an Austin A40.

"Be with you in a jiffy," called the grease monkey.

"Not if I can fucking help it you won't," muttered Saunders with a wry smile as he opened the boot to the 420.

Suddenly the clanging of police sirens disturbed the quiet scene and Saunders instinctively pressed himself against the wall and watched his pursuers hurtling past the petrol station totally unaware of his enforced pit stop.

The sirens faded in to the distance and Frank leant into the boot and winced as he lifted one of the heavy bags out. Reaching inside his boiler suit, he pulled out his gloved hand and saw it was covered in blood. He had obviously taken a Police bullet, but with all the excitement and the huge rush of adrenaline he hadn't noticed until he reached for the money bag.

The bullet had entered his side and was still lodged there but wasn't causing too much pain, a little discomfort maybe, but it wasn't going to stop him.

Quickly removing his boiler suit and throwing it in to a nearby bin he grabbed the other bags from the boot and slammed down the lid. It went against the grain not to torch the car in their usual manner but he knew that a fire in a petrol station was probably not a great idea. It might draw a bit of attention and he needed to create as much time as possible for himself to get away.

Saunders ran to the corner of the repair centre and breathed a sigh of relief to see the MG owner had not returned to his car.

Hopefully he's having a shit, thought Frank smiling to himself again.

Dragging the money bags across the concrete forecourt, he turned his head away from the office, hoping the attendant wasn't looking out. Luckily for Frank the overall clad attendant had just settled into a chair in the storeroom at the back of the office, with a dirty book and a large supply of tissues.

Heaving the bags into the roofless convertible Frank climbed in and was just about set to hotwire the sports car when he had his first bit of luck all day. There stuck in the ignition, shining in the sunlight was the key.

"Tut-tut," said Frank, "Don't you know you could get your car nicked like that? Silly boy."

The thief turned the ignition key and the sports car fired in to life as Saunders checked the rear view mirror for the hapless owner. No sign. He must have had a curry last night.

Saunders screeched away from the petrol pumps, off the forecourt and away to what he hoped would be his freedom and a life in the sun.

As he drove, Saunders started to relax for the first time in what seemed ages. The sun warmed his face and he began to formulate his thoughts, trying to unravel the chaos in his head.

It couldn't have been any of the chaps who had set them up. Alfie and Jimmy had been shot dead and poor Tommy had been splattered all over the upholstery of the Austin.

Thinking of his dead pals caused a black cloud of sadness to descend over him. They'd been through so much together, going back a long way and because of this fucking Eddie Raven caper his team were now brown bread.

And what was that all about? The way the lads had been nailed. Unarmed. In cold blood. There was something odd about the Old Bill he had seen there. They weren't like West End or South London coppers. A right scruffy looking bunch. Essex country bumpkins, Frank supposed.

Think, think, screamed Franks mind. Who had betrayed them? It couldn't have been Eddie Raven or any of his mob. The gangster wouldn't have double crossed them without getting his hands on the dough.

That just wouldn't make sense. Or did it?

All Frank could think of was Ravens voice. "It'll be a piece of piss." Bastard. "It's a cakewalk." Bastard. "Easy." BASTARD!!! screamed Frank as he jammed his foot on to the brake, bringing the stolen MG to a violent, sudden stop at the side of the road. Panting. Sweat pouring from his head. It had been a set up all along.

"CUNT," screamed Frank, punching the steering wheel with both fists.

That was it. Raven wasn't bothered about the money. It was him and his team he wanted. Jealous of their success. Nose out of joint because all the faces in the criminal underworld showed them too much respect for his liking. Respect given because he and the boys were top class thieves. Grafters who earned their money, rather than parasites, pimps or pushers like Eddie fucking Raven and his mob.

Saunders leant back in his seat and looked up at the clear blue sky then closed his eyes against the ever increasing pain. Not just the pain in his side from the police bullet but also the pain of being set up by that bastard Raven. Pain that he had persuaded his three mates to do the job and now they lay dead. Because of him.

The torment he now felt was much, much more painful than any bullet in him. He had been shot before, stabbed, hit with iron bars but nothing compared to what he was feeling now.

Saunders leant over to the glove box, hoping the car owner was a smoker. God he needed a fag.

Opening the flap in the dashboard he was relieved to see a pack of Players and a box of matches. Another piece of luck, albeit a small piece, but Frankie was clutching at straws at the moment.

Removing a cigarette, he placed it in his mouth, struck a match, inhaled and blew a long stream of smoke in to the air as he leant his head back once more.

Think, think, repeated his mind, going over and over. It could only have been Eddie Raven, but how did he know to tell the Old Bill where to ambush them? The only people who knew that detail was him and the members of his team.

He was certain that the Police hadn't tailed them, he could spot a Police tail a mile off. But what about Tommy? Had he led them to the robbery sight unwittingly?

Frank finished his fag and instantly lit another and forced himself to think. The trouble with making yourself think is you have to think something no matter how far fetched. This is what happened now in Franks head.

Perhaps it wasn't unwitting. Perhaps Tommy was the grass. Saunders thought back to the evening after he had had his meet with Eddie Raven and reluctantly agreed to do the job.

Tommy had changed the habit of a lifetime and come for a drink. In fact he got quite pissed. Something he had never witnessed in all the years he had known him. Was it out of guilt? Was that evening spent in the Kings Head, the Casino and the nightclub their last supper? Was Tommy Newman the Judas?

Shut up you prick, Frank said to himself. You're getting totally paranoid.

He was disgusted with himself for thinking along those lines.

Saunders was giving himself a headache trying to work out what had occurred and ran into dead ends with every thought. He decided he would never get to the bottom of it sitting in a stolen car at the side of the road. In fact, he realised grimly, he knew he would never get to the answer where he was going. But he had the money and hopefully his future life in the sun would gradually erase the need to know.

The thief looked down at the bulging bags on the seat beside him and patted them lovingly. As he caressed the bag he was overcome with another thought which grabbed his insides and twisted them into knots. It must have been Eddie Raven who had set them up but it didn't make sense for the gangster to sacrifice that amount of money just out of jealousy. Looking at the bags a thought grabbed him and slapped him in the face. There *was* no money. The authorities, if they had been tipped off would not dare take a chance and let the van carry real money, just in case the robbery had been a success. Even if there had only been a one per cent chance of success the law would not let £100,000 in used notes go on offer to professional criminals.

Eddie Raven was so eaten up with jealousy he just wanted to get Saunders and his team nicked and locked up for a very long time.

What a sick fucker! Frank grabbed the draw string to one of the bags, ripped it open frantically and looked inside. Saunders, expecting bundles of worthless packing paper was stunned and surprised to see bundles of beautiful cash. Reaching inside he grabbed a handful of dough and peered at it. Dropping the notes into his lap he picked them up one by one and held them up to the sky. Watermarks. Real notes.

The thief was really confused. What the fuck was going on?

Saunders couldn't come up with an answer. He was certain Eddie Raven had set them up to get nicked and the Old Bill had got carried away leaving his three mates dead.

Eddie Raven was a cunt and no mistake but Frank had got away and had got the dough as well. Now he had to get as far away as possible.

As Saunders sat parked up at the side of the road, the engine ticking over with cars and lorries speeding past, fate dealt him another card. Lighting another cigarette, he leant his head back once more and blew grey smoke into the air then lowered his tired gaze from the sky. Giving up on receiving any sort of divine inspiration his eyes fixed on a road sign barely twenty yards away. A big metal sign at the side of the road proclaiming DOVER SOUTH and a white arrow pointing in the direction that he should take to freedom.

*

For what seemed like an age Saunders stared at the sign. The ash from the burnt down cigarette dropped on to his lap. He knew 100% with all his mind and body he had to drive off and take the sensible option. South and to Dover. Disappear in sunny Spain with his bags of cash. He could live there like a king. Sun, sea and senioritas. Forget Eddie Raven. Forget any thoughts of revenge. Forget shitty grey old London and all its aggravation.

Frank threw the hardly touched, burnt down cigarette onto the road and put the car into first, let out the clutch and screeched away. Half a mile down the road he came to the junction signposted for Dover and Frank eased into the exit lane.

The rider of a BSA motorcycle positioned close to the rear driver's side wing of the red MG swerved violently and swore at its driver as the car, at the last second veered suddenly and unexpectedly away from the junction and back on the road which was signposted LONDON.

Frank Saunders, his face set in stone, knew he couldn't just forget about it. He owed it to his mates. His dead mates and to himself. There was no way Frank could let it go and live in peace in Spain.

Frank Saunders had to head for London, the West End and Eddie Raven.

CHAPTER 20

Saunders, now bleeding heavily from the bullet wound in his side, slowed the MG down as he left the Essex countryside and started to hit the gradually more populated areas which got heavier and heavier with traffic the further he got into London's East End. The back to back housing took on a stifling and claustrophobic feel.

Driving along through East Ham, Bow and Mile End, Saunders was careful to keep his head down; fully aware he was travelling through Eddie Ravens manor. On through Stepney, Whitechapel and Aldgate where he couldn't stop himself looking up to see one of his favourite cafes, a regular meeting place for him and the chaps far away from the Old Bill south of the river who knew them only too well.

Scooters stood parked outside the café same as usual. Some things never change even when everything else seems to be doing exactly that.

As Saunders approached the City of London his senses were on high alert, aware that the car he was driving would probably have been reported missing by now and the last thing he wanted was to get nicked over a stolen car full of stolen cash.

With this in mind Frank knew he needed to dump the car he was in and find another as reports on the car radio had named him as someone the police would like "to help with their enquiries."

A change of car was top on Frank's list of priorities as he could hardly dump the MG and catch the fucking tube. Not with three bags of stolen cash. A bit suspect especially with a bullet in his side and covered in claret.

As the wounded thief drove on looking for his opportunity, the imposing building that was the Tower of London loomed up in the distance and for some reason he glanced up to check the name of the road he was in. Saunders burst out laughing despite the pain he was experiencing. The laughter was due to the irony that had led them to drive along Royal Mint Street and he looked down at the bags of cash beside him which belonged in the big building he was now passing.

The Tower of London got bigger in front of him, bringing his merriment to an end as he thought of the many poor souls imprisoned, tortured and beheaded there throughout history. Frank was big on history.

Instead of heading around Tower Hill and further on in to the city as he had intended, his criminals sixth sense which had served him so well throughout his career until recently, caused him to suddenly swerve left and onto Tower Bridge Approach, heading over the bridge and across the water. Southside.

The sudden change of direction threw the money bags about in the passenger seat and a bundle of notes spilt out on to the seat.

Straightening up the car once more, Saunders looked down and saw the bundle of banknotes laying on the leather upholstery with the Queens face on the notes looking up at him reproachfully.

Driving across the bridge with the water of the Thames rushing beneath him, the combination of Her Majesty looking up at him to his left and Traitors Gate passing on his right made him feel a touch uncomfortable. He scooped up the spilt money in his gloved hand and shoved it back into the canvas bag.

"Sorry Ma'am," he said respectfully, tightening the drawstring.

Once over the other side of the river, *his* side, Frank did a right into Queen Elizabeth Street, then on into Tooley Street before slowing to a cruising pace and chose to turn left into a grubby little road called Shand Street which ran under one of the many railway bridges that littered the area of South London close to the river. South London seemed to be full of these dingy roads under the railway system which took commuters to and from their daily toil.

Dark, foreboding little places that stank of piss. Rusty water dripped from above. Sometimes a scrawny stray sniffed about or quite bizarrely a single shoe discarded in the middle of the road.

Office workers cars were parked up under the Victorian arches, covered in pigeon shit full of acid spoiling the paintwork.

A train thundered overhead as Saunders sat, despite the increasing pain he felt, watching the street for danger. No sign of human life, the only noise that of the receding rumble of the 5.15 to Sevenoaks.

Saunders winced as he made his move. Gingerly climbing out of the MGB Roadster he left a bright pool of blood on the magnolia leather upholstery.

As quick as his bullet wound injury would allow, he grabbed the money bags, opened the boot and slung them in. It might take a few minutes to find another motor and he didn't want some thieving bastard helping himself to his loot, even though he had nicked it himself.

The street was dark and damp and cold. The early evening sun never reached its long fingers into the inner recesses of this arch and the hundreds of similar arches around London's ageing railway system.

That was one of the reasons Frank Saunders had pulled up there.

The inhospitable side street was a place people only ventured into if it was absolutely unavoidable. Once there, they would hurry through, heads down paying no mind to anything but the echoes of their footsteps and the sudden clatter of the wheels on tracks above, scared the whole thing was about to come tumbling down on them. Scared also that danger lurking in the shadows would pounce on them.

The street was completely uninhabited apart from the thief who now made his way along the line of cars parked against the kerb, casually trying each door handle to see if any were unlocked, not looking down at the cars, keeping ever vigilante.

Finally a handle succumbed under the weight of Frank's hand who breathed a "Yes" to himself. However his elation was tempered by a feeling of disappointment as he looked down to see his getaway car. A white Morris Minor 1100. Top speed of 80 mph. 0 to 60 in about two and a half weeks.

If necessary he wouldn't be able to out run a copper on a push bike with a flat tyre.

Hardly what a top notch villain was used to as a mode of transport but he didn't have much time and shot robbers can't be choosers.

The hole in his side was becoming increasingly more painful and he needed to get inside. Somewhere safe where he could rest and get patched up.

Saunders climbed into the modest little car and leant forward, ducking under the big steering wheel. Ten seconds later and the car coughed into life. Some things stay with you forever and for any thief, hot wiring cars was one of them.

Leaving the car running, Frank shuffled painfully back to the MG, opened the boot and retrieved the money bags, which seemed to him to get heavier each time he lifted them and slammed the boot shut as a pigeon emptied it's arse onto the open topped cars drivers seat. Frank looked up and raised his eyebrows; the corners of his mouth turned down and nodded.

"That's lucky," he murmured to himself.

Saunders lugged the bags back to the Morris Minor, threw them into the boot, eased himself behind the steering wheel and pulled sedately away from the kerb.

Five minutes later, Frank, starting to feel faint from his injury, saw what he needed and pulled up beside the bright red telephone box.

The now desperate robber pulled open the heavy door and virtually fell inside the G.P.O owned telephone box, grabbing hold of the phone to stop himself collapsing on to the floor.

"Number?" he said to himself trying to think "What's the fucking number?"

A telephone number popped in to his thumping brain and he hoped it was the right one as he knew it would be his only attempt. Dialling it with shaking hands was made more awkward as the gloves he still wore were now soaked through with his blood.

"Answer, answer," he implored and eventually the receiver at the other end was picked up.

Quickly shoving in some change, he began talking immediately, without identifying himself.

"Listen, it's me. Don't say anything. Don't say my name. I need help. I need to rest up somewhere and I need fixing up. I'm hurt bad. I've got nowhere else to go. You're my only chance."

The female voice at the end of the line gasped and quickly replied "Of course I'll help you. Come over. Stay as long as you need to."

"Thanks darling, I knew I could count on you," wheezed the robber, "I'll be there in ten minutes," and dropped the phone on to the hook as his fingers started to stiffen.

It did indeed take the expected ten minutes to make his way along the Embankment back over the Thames via Waterloo Bridge and to park up in the street where he sought sanctuary albeit a short distance from the actual flat he needed.

Despite the pain, his blood soaked clothing and his near exhaustion Saunders still had enough about him not to park outside his final destination but thirty yards away and on the opposite side of the street. Frank turned off the engine and waited. And watched. Still the consummate professional he checked the street for any signs of a trap.

After a few minutes of watching, interspersed with the occasional drift out of consciousness he knew he had to compromise his usual diligence or he'd pass out completely. He slowly, tortuously climbed out of the car, shuffled across the road and slipped into the sheltered doorway, leant against the wall and pressed the buzzer to flat 4.

The girl's voice crackled over the intercom warily, "Hello?"

Franks head joined his shoulder pressed against the wall above the mouthpiece and said in a hoarse whisper.

"It's me. Open up,"

"I'll be right down," said the disembodied voice.

Saunders, his head now in a permanent haze heard a door open inside the building, followed by gentle footsteps pit patting down the stairs towards the front door and then the sound of the locks being undone.

The solid wooden street door was pulled open and the girl screamed in horror as Saunders collapsed into her arms covering her simple dress in blood, nearly causing her knees to buckle under his weight. She had to lean against the wall to prop the two of them up.

"Frankie, Frankie," she whispered in her accented English, stroking his neck with her long fingers, trying to sum up the strength to get him inside to safety.

The slight girl struggled to get the much taller and heavier man up the single flight of stairs. Pausing several times to rest she finally staggered through the open door to her flat, where she eventually managed to reach the bedroom and literally drop him on to the large double bed. Breathing heavily from her efforts she collapsed on top of him.

Saunders slept for a solid 24 hours watched over by the concerned girl.

Slowly waking from his slumber he found himself laying in the bed, his blood stained clothing having been removed and the cuts and bruises which covered his body having been treated.

His body was raked with aches and pains and the bullet wound in his side still hurt but realised as he gingerly touched it with his fingers it too had been treated and bandaged.

Although still in some pain he felt a hundred per cent better than when he had arrived thanks to the girl's tender nursing and the much needed sleep.

As his eyes focused he realised there was a female figure sitting at the foot of the bed.

"Hello sleepy head," she said, getting up to move closer to him.

Leaning over, she gave Frank a gentle kiss on the lips making Saunders smile.

"Hello Miss Nightingale," he replied, "How long have I been out?"

"Twenty three, twenty four hours, something like that."

Saunders blinked heavily a couple of times and shook his head before a look of grave concern appeared on his face as he struggled awkwardly to get out of the bed.

"What are you trying to do?" the girl shrieked trying to hold him down.

"The car. The car I drove here in," he growled, "It's got something I need in it."

The thought that the Police might have found the stolen car and its contents struck a feeling of desperation into the robber. That, or some petty car thief might have nicked it and found out he had hit the jackpot upon opening the boot.

Saunders heaved himself off of the bed and brushed past the girl, slid open the sash window and craned his neck out to the left.

The car was gone.

The thief pulled his head back inside, leant back and screamed in anguish. The sound of pain and frustration reverberated around the room and travelled out of the window to the street below where despite the heavy early evening traffic was heard by several passers by who likened it to the cry of a wounded, tortured animal. Frank Saunders was that animal.

Franks hands rested on the window sill and he dropped his head forward in despair.

From behind him he heard movement and the girl's voice.

"Is this what you're looking for?" she said as she opened the wardrobe door with a soft smile of achievement, revealing the three canvas money sacks.

"How the fuck did you know?" questioned Frank as he checked the bags over.

"While I was cleaning you up and tending to your wounds you became quite crazy, rambling on about guns and killing and set ups. Most of the time I couldn't understand but you did manage to tell me about the car and the money. So once I'd made sure you were okay I went down to the car and managed to get them up here one by one. They were bloody heavy though."

Frank loved to hear her swear in her accented English.

"And awkward," she continued. "Anyway, I had to wait until no one was passing by, so it took some time on a busy street like this, what with everyone on their way to restaurants and to the theatre."

She paused and smiled at Saunders, who had sat down on the bed listening in amazement, but knowing he should not have been surprised at her resourcefulness and bravery.

"Then I phoned a friend of mine and got him to come over and steal the car. I gave him twenty pounds and he took it and dumped it somewhere miles away."

Franks expression changed again to one of concern.

"What is it honey?" she said, worried at the look on his face.

"You didn't tell him why the car was there did you?"

She jumped up from the bed and put her hands firmly on her hips in mock indignation.

"What do you take me for? Of course I bloody didn't. I just told him someone owed me money and I wanted to teach him a lesson. Bloody cheek."

Again the accented swearing and Frank smiled and relaxed, seemingly satisfied with her explanation.

"It's from the robbery in Essex isn't it?" She said, her soft voice purring with excitement.

"The one on the radio." Her eyes widening with a sexual thrill at the criminal act.

"Yea," he said casually. "Got a smoke?"

"In the drawer," she replied nodding at the cabinet beside the bed.

Frank slid the drawer open, rummaged around amongst the condoms and make up and found the pack of Dunhill and a lighter at the back.

The girl accepted the offered cigarette, her bright red lips wrapping around the Dunhill and pursing as Frank lit her.

Saunders coughed violently as he lit his own cigarette and inhaled.

Each cough shot pain through his damaged body, his spluttering uncontrollable as the smoke filled his lungs. In his delicate condition the nicotine hitting his brain made him feel unusually light headed but it soon settled down and he began to enjoy his smoke.

His guardian angel stood and walked over to a record player on the sideboard, her backside catching Frank's attention as it swayed appealingly from side to side.

Switching on the record player she lifted the arm and placed it on to the 45 already on the turntable.

The sound of Barbara Lynn beautifully singing "You'll lose a good thing" crackled out of the built in speaker and drifted into the room, causing the girl to close her eyes. With her arms crossed, she took a drag on her cigarette and slowly swayed in time to the music her soul drifting up to heaven.

"This is nice," said Saunders listening carefully to the song and who as a Sinatra fan appreciated a good singer when he heard one.

The girl shimmied over to Frank and still with her eyes closed, floating on a cloud, she told him what the song was and who sang it.

"A friend of mine recommended it to me. He's in to all this kind of stuff. Lovely isn't it?"

Frank listened to the lyrics, trying to work out if the barefoot girl dancing in front of him was trying to give him a message.

A thought popped into his head, which at first seemed ridiculous but as the record turned at 45 revolutions per minute the idea didn't seem to be so crazy.

Looking at her gently swaying her hips and shuffling her bare feet through the deep pile of the carpet, her eyes closed and with a slight smile turning up the corners of her mouth he thought, "Fuck it, why not?"

She may be 20 years his junior and from totally different backgrounds, but they always got on great. They enjoyed each others company immensely and the sex was always fantastic, even if he did have to pay for it. And what with his injury he might need some help fleeing the country.

Frank let the record finish and as she opened her beautiful eyes he just came out with it.

"Listen darling," he said. "I've gotta get out of the country. After this latest bit of work there's no going back. The Old Bill know I was involved and they'll leave no stone unturned to find me.

"I've got about a hundred thousand quid in those bags," he continued, nodding in the direction of the wardrobe.

"I'm heading for the sun and the good life. A mate of mine has got a boat down on the coast and for a few quid he'll get me down to Spain or the South of France."

The girl listened; her head cocked to one side making her look younger than she was.

"Fancy coming with me?" he said.

The girl put down the record she had selected to put on next and straightened her head, her eyes fixed on the armed robber laying on her bed.

"Are you serious?"

Frank stood up and walked over to her.

"Deadly. Look, we can have a great life. We can both give up grafting. We won't need to work. Let's get out of this suffering city. What d'ya say?"

"Oh Frank," she said and leapt into his arms wrapping her shapely legs around his waist causing him to cry out in pain as she bashed his wound.

The girl held his face in her hands and kissed him wildly, their tongues dancing frantically together.

"Of course I will." She smiled as he carried her to the bed where they made love slowly and gently, mindful of his injuries but more so because neither of them wanted it to be just another lust driven fuck.

Once their needs had been satiated they lay back naked in the bed, her head on his manly chest, both smoking as he stroked her hair lovingly.

"We gotta go tonight," he said suddenly. "The longer I stay here the more chance there is of getting my collar felt."

"Whatever you say Frank," she said running her fingers through the hairs on his chest, humming to herself.

Frank was now starting to get switched on again. Professionally not sexually, although he was getting a lazy on.

"There's something I've got to sort out first," he said looking at his watch. 11.00pm.

As he raised himself from the bed, lifting her up as he did so, she looked in to his eyes, concern written all over her young face.

Seeing this worried look, Saunders kissed her gently on the lips and told her not to worry.

"It's okay I just gotta sort out a motor and settle a debt," he said and gave her his most disarming smile which instantly reassured her.

Frank Saunders got dressed quickly in a plain white cotton button down shirt and a pair of silver grey slacks the girl gave him from an array of men's clothing stored in the wardrobe where the money bags lay.

Frank felt a twinge of jealousy at seeing the other men's clothes but shrugged it off. Jealousy was a destructive emotion and he had no time for it. Besides he knew the score.

Tucking the shirt into the grey trousers he gave the girl her instructions.

"Get yourself ready. Transfer the dough from the sacks into suitcases. Only pack what personal stuff is absolutely necessary. Once we've got abroad we can buy anything we need."

"Okay Frank," she said obediently.

Frank crossed the room to the door with the girl in close attendance. He kissed her again as he opened it and as if a thought had just occurred to him, although in reality it had been in his head for a while, said seriously.

"You will behave yourself won't you darling?" Looking across at the bags of cash, then back to her, locking her gaze with a steely hardness in his eyes. His grip around her waist tightening.

"Off course I will, silly," she said not realising how serious Frank was. "Don't worry, I'll be here when you get back," she said smiling.

Frank wasn't smiling.

"You better be. Cos if you ain't, I'll find you. You know that don't you?"

"How dare you?" she screamed wriggling free from his grasp. "If I was going to run off with your bloody money I could have done it when you were out cold, you fucking bastard."

Frank smiled again at her swearing and held his hands up in mock surrender.

"Okay, okay," he said laughing, "I had to say it though," realising what she said made perfect sense and wondering why she hadn't fucked off.

"No you didn't," she said in a sulk.

Saunders put his finger under her dropped chin and lifted it up until their eyes met.

"I won't be long," he said, kissed her once more, turned and headed down the stairs to settle that debt.

CHAPTER 21

Not a million miles away, Johnny too had been sleeping since the previous day.

After finding the "Dear John" or in this case "Dear Johnny" letter he grabbed a bottle of Scotch and drank himself into a stupor to the accompaniment of some of the soul ballads he kept in the flat. Waking the next evening, with a fucker of a headache he shovelled a handful of pills into his mouth, rifled through the kitchen draws and found the keys to Sarah's brand new bright red Mini Cooper. A present from Daddy. She had obviously gone to her parent's house in Hampshire by train. Sarah didn't like to drive alone for that distance.

Johnny ran from the flat down to the square and quickly found the car parked by Sarah at the usual crazy angle.

The car as ever was unlocked, something that irritated him immensely, knowing that if it got nicked, her parents would just buy her another. Spoilt brat!

Teaching him to drive was another thing Sarah had shown him and he had picked it up pretty quickly, although he had insisted all lessons take place well out of the way. Away from any witnesses to his kangarooing and stalling. Very uncool.

Not letting a little thing like having no licence or insurance bother him, he jumped into the little car and with tyres squelling and a slight suggestion of an antipodean marsupial, tore away out of the square and on to Sloane Street.

Around Sloane Square and heading south. South, across Albert Bridge and away from the riches north of the river.

Fifteen minutes of close calls and near scrapes of an inexperienced driver driving too fast and he was pulling up outside his gaff in the Elephant.

Despite moving in with Sarah just a few days after meeting her, he still kept his bed-sit on, even though he could have afforded something better and he spent most of his time at Sarah's.

He kept the place because no one knew about it. No one had ever been there. Not even Sarah. Especially Sarah. No, it made sense to keep it as it might provide him with a bolt-hole should he need it someday and it was also an ideal place to stash his supply of drugs and cash, nicely tucked away under the floorboard beneath his bed.

Despite his constant spending spree since coming into money Johnny had still managed to save quite a bundle and now his life was in danger he intended to retrieve the cash and pills he had stored and do a runner.

There was enough money under the floorboard and enough drugs to sell to enable him to start a new life somewhere.

Anywhere out of London, as far away as possible because whoever had killed Chucky and the Franklin boys would have him next on the list and he wasn't about to give up breathing just yet.

London had nothing for him anymore. His dreams were in tatters.

Johnny pulled up across the road from his building and ducked in through the alley into the back yard where he stopped suddenly.

What lay before him caused his knees to buckle. The once gleaming and cherished Lambretta, which had carried him around London in style, was now just a burnt and twisted skeleton. The tyres had melted and burst. The body, a black gnarled wreck. The cover and sponge which had been the seat had disappeared, exposing its' naked springs.

Johnny's anguish suddenly turned to fear as the smoke still rising from the wreckage signified that it had been torched recently.

They knew where he lived! And they had been here recently. Or were they in his flat? SHIT!

The young Mod stood frozen like a rabbit in the headlights. His feet refused to turn him around and run the hell out of there. Anyway, where would his size nine's take him without any money?

The teenager took a deep breath. Decision time he thought as the feeling started to return to his bottom half.

Time to make one of several choices.

One. He still had his health, which if he backed out now, jumped in the Mini and fucked off to god knows where, he would keep.

However he would be skint, with just the clothes he stood up in. Backing out would mean starting from scratch. Fully limbed, but with nothing else.

Two. He could hope his scooter had spontaneously combusted, go up to his room, retrieve his cash and pills, grab his clothes and make good his escape. Set himself up in some other town.

Three. Go to his room. Get grabbed by whoever did Chucky and suffer a similar ghastly fate.

Four. "Oh for fucks sake," whispered Johnny, "life is getting very complicated" and headed purposefully for the back door to the building.

The doors ageing hinges complained as he eased it open and suddenly he didn't feel so purposeful.

Biting the bullet he peered inside, looked carefully up the stairwell and carried on into the building.

The stairs creaked painfully causing Johnny to cringe with each carefully placed foot. His hand trembling on the rickety banister.

Step by tortuous step, he made his way up to his floor, taking about a hundred times longer than he normally would.

Finally reaching his door, Johnny realised he had been holding his breath since walking in to the building, so it was hardly surprising he felt like he was going to pass out. Lack of oxygen does that to a person.

Finally letting a breath out through pursed lips, he wiped the sweat from his young forehead and was terrified to see that the door to his room was ajar.

The young Mod pressed his ear to the slab of wood that stood between him and possible death or at the least a considerable amount of discomfort.

Hearing nothing, Johnny watched his own hand move in slow motion to grasp the handle and slowly, oh so slowly, inch by painful inch opened the door, ready to get the fuck out of there if confronted with big blokes' hell bent on disturbing his good looks.

The Face, the super cool prince of London wanted to squeeze his blue eyes shut as the door continued its way on its journey but he didn't dare blink let alone shut them. A blink might waste valuable running away time.

Once the door was fully open he surveyed the scene of devastation that was his room. No nasties but his insides crumbled and he hit rock bottom when he saw what had been done to his life, his history.

Every single item of clothing had been slashed to ribbons. Suits, shirts, jackets, tops all destroyed. The bastards had even cut up his shoes. His gaze panned around the room. Each piece of clothing his eyes rested on he remembered where he had bought it, who he was with, what the weather was like. What style his hair had been in at that period. It was though his life was flashing before him like a drowning man.

Looking further around the room, the boy let out an anguished cry as he saw that his past had been completely erased.

The records. All three hundred or so of them had been smashed to smithereens. Shattered into a million pieces of jagged black vinyl.

The pain was as though his insides had been ripped out and Barbara Lynn, Smokey Robinson, Martha Reeves and all the rest had been massacred and lay there dead before him.

Johnny was as shattered as the 45 r.p.m discs and sank to his knees scattering pieces of broken records across the room. Putting his hands up to his face he covered his eyes and sobbed.

With the build up of tension involved in entering the room and what he had encountered there he had forgotten that he might still be in danger. Quickly coming to his senses he remembered what he was doing there. To rescue what he had stashed under the floorboard beneath the bed he was kneeling beside.

Johnny spread his fingers and peered through them, his eyes flicking from side to side. Thinking. He still might be able to salvage something from the wreck his life had become.

Twisting his head, his brain started to work again as he peered beneath his sleeping place.

Suddenly, as if he had been hooked up to the mains, he threw himself onto his stomach, lifted the old worn bedspread hanging over the edge of the bed and peered in to the dusty darkness. Johnny's spirits soared like the strings on a Sam Cooke ballad upon seeing the floorboard undisturbed. Turning quickly he looked around the carnage of his room and grabbed a sliced up suede jacket still clinging to its hanger. Discarding the once beautifully soft jacket, he kept the hanger and sliding under the bed once more he inserted the hook into the empty nail hole in the wooden floorboard and prised up the two foot length of timber.

The wood was flung behind him across the room and he plunged his hand into the void, scraping his arm as he did so but ignoring the pain. Nothing.

Johnny's hand desperately searched around the void beneath the floor, stretching his arm in further, patting his hand around in every possible direction until finally his little finger came in to contact with canvas. Moving his hand across, he grabbed the canvas bag, breathed a huge sigh of relief, closed his eyes and muttered "Yes. Thank you god."

Johnny shuffled backwards out from under the bed dragging his future from its dusty resting place. Money! Diving back under the bed he located the other bag containing his other bag of treasure. Pills!

The dust and spiders webs covering his sleeve didn't register in his brain like it would have done twenty four hours ago. Twenty four hours ago he would have had a heart attack if his clothes had got in such a state, but it didn't seem to matter now. Now he just slung the bags on top of the bed and kneeling over them dared to look inside.

Johnny once again thanked a god he didn't believe in upon seeing the contents of the two bags. In the first bag nestled 10,000 amphetamines. Lovely.

In the other, nearly a grand in cash which he lifted up to his lips and kissed with his eyes shut. Beautiful. The grand he had saved for a rainy day and today had been a fucking monsoon.

Shoving one bag into the other, Johnny's temporary elation was curtailed upon hearing a car pull up in the street outside and he rose sharply to his feet.

Scuttling to the window he pressed himself flat against the wall and with one finger eased the curtain back just a fraction.

A fraction was all he needed to feel his walls come tumbling down again. They had returned. Shit.

A huge black finned Cadillac oozed slimily up to the kerb like some great mechanical shark and disgorged four very large, very nasty looking individuals.

Oh fuck, thought the boy. Just as he felt his luck was taking a turn for the better another punch to the solar plexus. He was still in big, big trouble.

For the first time that day he suddenly stopped feeling sorry for himself and assessed the situation in a second.

Going out the front or back door was a no no. Impossible. The only way was to go up, somehow get to the roof and take his chances from there. Shoving his hand into the bag of uppers he grabbed half a dozen and threw them to the back of his throat and despite the dryness managed to swallow them. Johnny felt like he needed a lift.

With the speed and agility of youth he leapt across his bed and tore out of the room and up the three flights of stairs to the top floor. No windows. Fuck! Just two doors leading to two more flats. Flats which stretched from the front of the building to the back.

They must have windows leading to the fire escape, Johnny thought, a luxury his one room at the front of the building did not have.

Which door would provide his salvation? Left or right? He started with the "eeny meeny miney mo's" but gave up due to lack of time and plumped for the door to the left. Gently tapping on the tired looking door he held his breath again hoping the occupant, who he rarely saw, would be able to hear. And praying the owners of the heavy footsteps and growling voices starting to climb the stairs below couldn't.

"Come on, come on," he pleaded silently to himself taking nervous glances over his shoulder as the sound of large brogues got ever louder.

Johnny knocked on the door again, his breathing getting heavier, sweat popping out on his forehead.

"Pleeeeese answer the fucking door you silly old bast…"

The door slowly opened, just a couple of inches and the bloodshot eye of a suspicious old man looked through the crack.

"Yes what do you want?" the old man asked cautiously.

Johnny let out a sigh, quickly glanced over his shoulder again then turned back to face the man, leaning in closer to the door so as not to be overheard by the men below.

"Mr. Williams," started the youngster. Thankful he remembered the old war hero's name. "It's alright it's me. From the first floor, flat 2. Could I have a word please?"

The door opened further as the old mans dodgy eyes recognised his normally ever so smart young neighbour.

"Oh hello there," he said in the sort of loud voice that hard of hearing old folk tended to use. "I've seen you coming and going on your motor bike."

Johnny cringed and hunched his shoulders at the volume of the mans voice. Why not use a megaphone? he thought and despite the gravity of the situation Johnny felt he needed to correct him about his mistake in the description of his two wheeled form of transport.

"Scooter," he whispered through clenched teeth.

"Pardon?" shouted the old man.

Johnny raised his eyes to the heavens, his heart missing another beat.

"It's a scooter," he repeated. "Can I come in? I need your help."

Not waiting for a reply he eased his way through the door, like an insurance salesman eager to do his pitch.

The old man stepped back to let the young man into his time warp flat.

"Would you like a cup of tea?" said the pensioner, his initial and natural suspiciousness giving way to hospitality, glad for a bit of company.

"No thanks," replied the boy as the old fella started to prepare a cuppa.

"How many sugars?"

As was the case with many lonely old people Mr. Williams completely ignored what was being said to him. So unusual was it for him to have anyone to talk to and to hear his own voice, he wanted to use it as much as possible and started rabbiting on about anything which popped into his under used brain.

Johnny started to get frantic at the old mans ignorance of his situation and gently but firmly took hold of the stained, cracked mug in his claw like hand and placed it back on the draining board.

The seventy nine year old man turned to face his visitor with a look of disappointment and sadness in his bloodshot eyes.

"Look, I'm really sorry but I really haven't got the time," urged Johnny, "I need help."

The cardigan clad old chap looked into the youngsters desperate, pleading eyes and totally surprised him with his next words.

"So you're visitors weren't here for a social call then?"

"Not exactly," replied Johnny in the understatement of the year.

"I thought they were a bit noisy," said the old fella, who had heard the commotion three floors below despite his failing hearing.

His old neighbour with nothing else to do with his lonely life would stand at his front window and watch all the comings and goings in the street below from the moment he got up to the moment he went to bed. It was his real life television set.

"What have you done to upset Eddie Raven then?" Mr Williams asked the boy sixty years his junior.

"What?"

"Eddie Raven," stated the old man pleased his knowledge was obviously of interest.

"Who is he?" said Johnny not certain he wanted to hear the reply.

"Eddie Raven. The man sitting outside in that big yankee motor car. A right nasty piece of work. Fingers in all sorts of illegal pies."

The old boy spoke in hushed tones as though if he were overheard it might summon up the devil himself into the grotty little flat.

"Run's all the rackets in the West End. Prostitutes, clip joints, gambling, drugs, everything," he continued.

At the mention of the last on the list of illegalities the penny dropped for Johnny and he turned away from the old man with his head leant back, eyes closed, his hands on his hips.

"Oh no!" he said, shaking his head, biting his bottom lip, the tears welling up in his eyes. The fear and panic rising inside him again like a volcano about to erupt.

He turned and ran to the sink, brushing the man aside and erupt he did, not with laver but acidic vomit which gushed from his enflamed mouth, snot dripping from his flaring nostrils.

As he leant over the sink the old man looked on, seemingly unperturbed by his new friend yakking up over the dirty crockery waiting in the sink to be washed up.

Through the pain thumping in his head and the smell of his puke he could hear the man talking again.

"Oh yes, Eddie Raven a wrong 'un and no mistake," he said. "I used to have a newspaper stand on Shaftesbury Avenue, up the West End and the stories I used to hear about that man would make your hair fall out."

The Face instinctively put his hand to his hair. Still there, he thought.

Johnny turned to face the ex-newspaper vendor and wiped the moisture from his eyes and the mess from his face with the sleeve of his jacket, his standards dropping still further.

"Mr Williams, you've got to help me. Those men sitting in my flat are Eddie Ravens boys and they mean to do me unimaginable amounts of harm. They're just waiting for me to return."

"What have you been up to young fella?"

Sheepishly looking down at the floor, for the first time ashamed of his drug dealing he replied. "Just a misunderstanding that's all."

The old man, unconvinced, beckoned his guest with a gnarled, liver spotted finger and made his way into the bedroom.

Johnny followed and looked over to the peeling sash window the man was pointing at, hoping it hadn't been painted shut.

Instead of going over to the window the old boy opened an ancient looking wooden wardrobe and rifled about for a moment as the young boy tried to prise the sash open.

"Ere you are son," the old timer said, turning back to his young neighbour with a conspiratorial look on his wizened old face, holding up a moth bitten raincoat and a battered old checked flat cap.

"You can use these as a disguise."

Johnny turned and studied the unstylish apparel being offered to him and nearly baulked at the idea but decided it might seem churlish to turn it down on style grounds. Besides, it wasn't such a bad idea. An idea which might help save his life.

"Cheers pop," he said, taking the clothes from the man and at the same time catching a glimpse inside the wardrobe. He felt a bit guilty about taking the man's coat considering the lack of garments hanging there and ashamed that he nearly refused such a kind act on the grounds of it not being cool enough.

His guilt was somewhat assuaged when remembering the contents of the bag he was carrying, shoved his hand inside and being careful not to give the old man a handful of speed, located some notes and shoved twenty quid into the mans hand. The money was more than the kind old man had seen in a long time and took him a moment to digest the value of the currency in his palm.

"Thank you son," he said simply as Johnny struggled into his newly acquired coat and pulled the cap on low over his eyes.

"How do I look?" he said catching his reflection in the mirror on the inside of the wardrobe door, thinking he looked like an escaped lunatic, rather than a hip young dude. A perfect disguise.

The old man, obviously with the right knack, slid open the sash window with an ease which embarrassed the younger and much stronger boy and wished him good luck.

Johnny climbed halfway out of the window, turned, looked the old man in the eyes and stuck out his hand.

"Cheers mate," he said. "I won't forget this."

The man took his hand. The boy was surprised at how frail it felt and was careful not to shake too hard for fear it might snap off.

"You're welcome son. And if they come up here I'll fight the fuckers off for as long as I can."

The teenager laughed at the old boys joke and climbed out on to the metal landing of the fire escape and down the rusting stairway.

Johnny was surprised and relieved to see that darkness had fallen. Another aid to his escape.

The dark blanket that had descended on London gave him a huge shot of confidence and his natural optimism coupled with his earlier intake of speed gave an extra spring to his step and almost a return to his cocky old self. He smiled as he got to the bottom of the staircase and into the overgrown garden.

Over the fence into the neighbouring garden and quickly down the enclosed alley way between the buildings that led to the street.

Edging closer to the brightness thrown off by the street light, Johnny peered around the corner of the building to suss out the situation.

The Cadillac was still there. The silhouette of the man in the rear seat seemed enormous, now he was that much closer to it.

Sarah's Mini stood where he had left it. Directly opposite the archway which framed him.

The distance between where he stood and the bright red car was about twenty five feet but it might as well have been twenty five miles to his nervous eyes.

The youngster's thoughts drifted to Steve McQueen looking through the prison camp wire to the woods and freedom in "The Great Escape."

The thought of the super cool McQueen, one of his heroes, gave him the confidence and strength to attempt his way across no mans land.

Realising that to copy McQueen's cocky persona and swagger across the street would not be prudent he took a deep breath and adopting a posture more in keeping with the disguise he was wearing he bent over and slowly shuffled his way across the road.

With every step he wanted to abandon caution and burst into a run but knew he couldn't afford to, so each second seemed like an hour. He also avoided the considerable temptation to turn his head to look in the direction of the American car to see if he was being watched and kept his eyes fixed firmly to the ground, old man style. He felt like a right prick.

Finally reaching his objective he unlocked the door and climbed in. Sweating like a bastard he managed to drop the keys on to the floor of the car, his hands were shaking so much.

"Get a grip," he chastised himself, bending over to retrieve the keys before inserting them in to the ignition.

"Nice and cool Johnny boy," he said to himself repeating it like a mantra.

Key turned, engine started, first gear engaged and the rookie driver pulled away from the kerb, repeating his "keep cool" chant before kangarooing down the road past the Cadillac whose occupant looked over, muttering at the flat capped driver. "Silly old fart," growled Eddie Raven before returning his attention to the first floor window of the building opposite.

"Well that was really cool," said Johnny to himself with lashings of sarcasm.

Turning left at the end of the road, he drove without thinking, not knowing where he was headed, just as long as he got as far away from his street as quickly as possible or as quickly as his inexperienced driving would allow.

Before very long he found himself approaching Waterloo Bridge, though why he was heading back into town was a mystery to him as he really needed to get as far away from London as possible.

As he drove onto the bridge Johnny pulled over to the kerb and stopped, turned off the engine and sat in silent relief at having escaped his pursuers, albeit temporarily.

After sitting quietly for several minutes, he climbed out of the car removed the old mans raincoat and cap and rolled it into a tight bundle. Smiling as he did so and thanking him in his head.

Walking over to the parapet wall, Johnny looked over into the oily blackness of the Thames, the water racing under the bridge.

Extending the bundle to arms length he dropped his disguise into the unforgiving water below and watched it swirl around in the current.

"Cheers pop," said Johnny as the coat and hat disappeared out of sight under the bridge.

171

No one noticed the lone figure standing in the darkness thinking a thousand thoughts, re-living a million memories as he gazed at the lights of London, twinkling like jewels. A beautiful sight to the young Mod who suddenly realised why his subconscious had led him to drive here.

This London child, this West End dandy, this Soho peacock realised he didn't know when he would see his town again and had come to say goodbye to her: regardless of the danger he was placing himself in again.

Putting his hands on the low wall Johnny started to hyper ventilate as he tried to come to terms not only with having to say goodbye to his physical and spiritual home but also with the fact he had only just escaped serious maiming or worse back at his flat.

Once again he felt beads of sweat pop out of his forehead, his stomach churned and his mouth constricted, as for the second time that evening Johnny spewed his guts up. This time into the already polluted river.

Several times the burning fluid poured out of his throat along with strings of snot from his nostrils and water from his eyes.

Panting and out of breath from the violent effort involved in his vomiting Johnny had to spit several times to get rid of the last dregs and the taste in his mouth and wiped his nose and mouth on his sleeve.

He wished he'd kept the old mans coat on when he saw the shiny silver snot glistening on his jacket sleeve but knew it didn't matter anymore.

Bending forward once more to rest his head on the cold stone on the top of the parapet wall gave him some relief, cooling his flushed face and easing his thumping head.

The now former stylist took another deep breath, blew his cheeks out and turned his back to the river, leaning against the wall deep in thought.

What was the time? he wondered, looking down at his watch only to see the expensive timepiece, a gift from Sarah was broken. The glass was cracked, the hands frozen at six o'clock. He didn't realize he had damaged it.

Turning around he peered up river to the ever reliable time piece that was Big Ben. The giant hands told him the evening had raced on to eleven o'clock. Time flies when you're having fun!

Johnny knew what he had to do. Get the fuck out of London. Head south, perhaps to the coast. Margate or Brighton, somewhere he could blend in and be anonymous.

The thought depressed him. No more being a Face. He'd have to tone down his style considerably. The love of the clothes and of course Soul music was in his veins, that would never change, but he wouldn't be able to stand out in a crowd any more.

Johnny sighed. Yep, that was it.

Out of London.

Head south.

After one last Soho night!

Who was he trying to kid? He couldn't just drive away. Turn his back on five years of his life. Johnny worked it out quickly in his head.

Banking on the fact that the murderers after him didn't know what he looked like and wouldn't expect him to turn up on his old stamping ground, he calculated he could spend a couple of hours trawling his favourite old haunts.

A couple of dances at The Scene, on to the Flamingo for a groove there. Say goodbye to a few fellow Faces (they'd probably be glad to see the competition leaving town).

Although the speed was rushing through his blood stream and exaggerating his desire for a symbolic goodbye he wasn't stupid enough to realise that the Soho grapevine wouldn't get word to Eddie Raven who would send his goons into the darkened alleyways and backstreets of Club Land in search of him.

Knowing this, Johnny knew he would have to keep on the move, not staying in one place too long. Not letting anyone know his next move. Keep to the shadows.

Toying with the idea of going back to Sarah's flat to change into something smarter to really cut a dash on his last appearance in the West End he decided such a move would be trying his luck a bit too far. If Eddie Raven had found his South London shithole he more than likely had been able to find Sarah's Chelsea palace. He was just relieved she was out of town.

Using a combination of the Mini's windows, wing mirrors and reflection from the shiny red paintwork, Johnny made himself as presentable as he could considering the situation he found himself in.

After all, someone had described their lifestyle as "clean living under difficult circumstances." And you couldn't get a much more difficult circumstance than the one he was in now!

Topping up on his earlier speed intake and looking at his reflection when he had finished, he felt a surge of confidence just like the old Johnny. The Johnny of twenty four hours ago.

Was it only one day since everything had been rosy in his garden?

Only a few short hours since that fucking big dog of life had shit all over his perfect garden.

Climbing back into Sarah's car he took a deep breath and turned the key.

The Mini roared into life and in a blaze of smoke and burning rubber, Johnny headed "Up West."

Down The Strand, around Trafalgar Square and up Haymarket. Twice around Piccadilly Circus for old times sakes, then prowling up into Shaftesbury Avenue. Left into Berwick Street and his first stop of the evening. Parking up in Berwick Street, he got out of the Mini Cooper and bowled into Ham Yard, home of The Scene. Cool Central.

Walking through Ham Yard and up to the entrance Johnny felt all eyes were on him, although tonight it felt different. Tonight it didn't feel as though the looks he was getting were looks of admiration or respect. Tonight the looks were malevolent; there were no friendly greetings, just whispers and words spoken in hushed tones.

Words not spoken to him but about him. The looks he received were a mixture of distaste and fear as though he carried an aura of trouble after the recent spate of killings. Chucky Wilson was a popular Face on the scene and Johnny was sure he heard his dead friends name spoken a couple of times.

Floating out of the entrance, the Face heard the sound of "You can't sit down" by The Phil Upchurch Combo, a storming record, a record so fucking cool it could give you frostbite and guaranteed a packed dance floor. It was one of Johnny's all time faves.

As he was about to enter the club he nodded hello to a group of Faces he knew standing to one side but instead of acknowledging his greeting the group turned their backs on him muttering amongst themselves.

Shaken and a little bit stirred by this reception he paid his entrance fee and mustering as much bravado as he could swaggered inside.

If Johnny thought the reaction to his appearance outside was a one off he was very much mistaken. As if omitting a smell of death, to his fragile mind the entire population of the club seemed to turn to witness his entrance. A wall of blank faces looked back at him, parting like the Red Sea as he made his now faltering way to the dance floor.

The disc jockey had changed the 45 to Martha Reeves and the Vandellas singing "Heatwave" another up tempo dance track which ordinarily would have had him instantly grooving around the floor.

Not tonight. The other clubbers were not dancing but watching. Waiting. Just shuffling from side to side. Waiting and watching.

Johnny's feet stayed rooted to the floor. Unable to move. Unable to feel the music which normally would so easily seep in to him and carry him off on a magic carpet ride.

Johnny's whole recent life had been about showing off. About people looking at him and being noticed. Now with the whole rooms' attention on him he felt intimidated and self conscious and without dancing a step, stormed out, in desperate need of air, away from the claustrophobic atmosphere of The Scene.

Rushing out of Ham Yard without looking at the stony faces following his rapid exit and into Berwick Street he turned the corner, leant panting against a wall and stared up at the night sky. The night was black as the vinyl on a 45 with just a few stars twinkling like diamonds.

He calmed down as he gazed up to the never ending universe. The sky seemed as peaceful as it always did and he wished he could be up there instead of down where he was amongst the hate and pain and disappointment.

The youngster was shocked by the reaction of what he thought were his soul mates but managed to shrug off the feeling of rejection and headed off to the Flamingo, determined to have one last big night in Soho.

Five minutes later and if he thought the people at the Flamingo would give him a better reception he was very much mistaken. If anything, the feelings he felt directed at him were even stronger and he stumbled out into the night, shell shocked, confused and totally dejected. His day was going from shit to even shittier. He only wanted to have a last dance and say a few goodbyes for fuck sake but even that small pleasure was seemingly going to be denied.

As he had done on many happier, more carefree occasions he began to wander the streets, but this time his head was bowed, causing him to crash in to other Soho pedestrians, ignoring their protests as he forced his way through the West End crowds.

Stepping into a doorway he slipped his hand into his pocket and necked another handful of pills, concerned that he didn't seem to be feeling the right effect from his previous intake.

Johnny turned and looked up and down the street full of people on their way to having a good time or on their way *from* having a good time. It seemed to the youngster that everybody but him was having a whale of a time in the world's most exciting city.

He wiped the moisture from his forehead. Fuck, it was hot.

Hard to breathe.

Where to now? All thoughts of having a fond farewell on the dance floor somewhere were bitterly abandoned although he was still reluctant to do the sensible thing and get out of Dodge!

Across the road from where he stood, the intermittent flash of the neon sign above La Bastille café caught his eye, the windows heavily steamed up.

Checking right and left for traffic he darted over, pushed open the door and peered nervously in. Pleased that the place was virtually deserted, Johnny walked in.

The only customers, sitting at a table nearest the counter looked up to see who was entering at the clang of the bell sounding out as the door opened.

He didn't recognize the two older blokes and as they didn't know him they went back to their conversation and their hot tea.

Ordering an espresso from the Italian behind the counter Johnny sat down at a table nearest the window and slowly wiped away a circle of condensation from the glass with the palm of his hand and peered mournfully out. Lost in his own world of confusion and self pity.

The coffee arrived as Johnny lit up a cigarette he had removed from the dented cigarette case he used to think was so cool and classy but which now looked as tired and worn out as himself.

The street outside was alive as usual. Clubbers and restaurant goers intermingling with the Show people who had finished entertaining for the evening and were off looking for someone to entertain them.

Theatre goers and hookers, lovers arm in arm, people he knew and a million faces he had never seen before and would never see again.

Johnny's gloom deepened as his thoughts turned to his departure from this magical world of hipsters and freaks and was unaware that the bell to the door had rang again signifying another potential espresso customer.

Deep in thought and staring through the hole in the condensation, he hadn't heard the footsteps signalling the approach of a familiar face.

"Hello Johnny," said the soft voice.

Johnny jumped in his seat, registering surprise for once, no longer pre-occupied with being cool.

Standing in front of him in a plain black slip dress covered by a white plastic mac was Julie.

"Oh," he said not disguising his disappointment that it was old conquest Julie and not his beloved Sarah standing there.

Unable to hide his irritation he turned away from her sad face and carried on studying the comings and goings outside. He didn't need any more shit.

"Can I sit down?" the young girl asked nervously.

"Do what you want," he replied.

After taking a seat there was a lengthy silence as she tried to find the words she wanted and needed to say.

"What are you going to do?" was all she could come out with.

No response. More staring.

Another awkward silence eventually produced another question.

"Why?" she said.

Johnny turned his head slowly to face the girl whose eyes were moist with emotion.

"Why what?" he replied caustically.

"Why did you get involved in drugs? It's alright taking them. We all take them, but selling them is somehow wrong."

The floodgates had opened up now and the words poured out in a torrent.

"We always despised the pushers," she continued. "Parasites, that's what we always called them. That's what you called them. I heard you say it."

There was no stopping her now.

As she speed talked, he looked at her properly for the first time. Not just the first time since she had walked in but properly for the first time since he had known her, even though they had shared a bed together.

The pretty youngsters eyes were full to the brim with salty water and was on the verge of breaking down into floods of tears but just managed to keep her shit together. Her whole body seemed to be pleading with Johnny for an explanation.

"Oh Johnny. Why? You're.....You had it all."

Slowing her outpouring down, she fumbled for words again as Johnny just stared blankly back at her.

Coming to a halt she took one of the cigarettes from the pack buried deep in her BOAC shoulder bag, and lit it herself as Johnny didn't offer. Johnny just lit his own.

Both young groovers sat in silence drawing deeply on their cigarettes and filling the table area with exhaled smoke.

"Everyone looked up to you Johnny. You were a real Face. And now you've ruined it."

He noticed her use of the past tense in referring to him and it really pissed him off.

The words she then chose really finished him off.

"Chucky's dead because of you."

Johnny knew what she said was true and responded in the only way he could. Looking directly in her flushed, tearful face he said.

"Go away."

"What?"

"Go away Julie," he repeated with harsh bitterness.

With tears rolling down her face, she dropped her head to her chest as huge sobs racked her body, her shoulders heaving up and down with involuntary spasms.

The young girls crying got louder, drawing the indifferent attention of the two men at the other table and the owner drying a coffee cup behind his counter.

Johnny slowly got to his feet scraping his chair backwards across the tiled floor and looked down at the sobbing teenager who hadn't moved.

"Fuck off Julie," he said with contempt.

Contempt not for the girl but for himself. She was one hundred per cent right in everything she had said to him and although he could admit to himself that he had fucked his whole life up, his stubborn pride would not let another realize he knew it.

Still Julie had not moved, unwilling or unable through total and complete misery.

"FUCK OFF!" Johnny roared, his words finally forcing the young girl to jump to her feet in shock, knocking over her chair as she did so, before turning and running, wailing out of the café.

Breathing heavily from his outburst, with palpitations in his chest and the vein on the side of his head throbbing painfully he turned to look at the three other people in the café.

Hearing their tutting and clocking their reproachful looks he inhaled deeply, drew himself up to his full height, pulled his shoulders back and expanded his chest.

Johnny had known he would have to leave his fantasy life sometime but thought it would be later rather than sooner and on his terms, no one else's.

Drawing on all the inner strength his harsh life had given him and accepting the situation he was in, he looked directly at the men and addressed them as if he were speaking to the whole world.

"And you can fuck off as well!" he said and walked out.

CHAPTER 22

Outside the café Johnny gulped in the air he so desperately needed to stop himself from passing out. He felt as though he were suffocating, everything was closing in on him and he needed to break free and breathe again.

Sarah, he thought in delusion, I've got to speak to Sarah. If I can get her to change her mind then everything will be OK.

For someone who had spent most of his life on his own and living on his wits, the thought of now having to be on his own suddenly filled him with dread.

A telephone, Johnny's scrambled brain told him, I've got to find a phone.

A minute later and the desperate youngster was stood outside a bright red G.P.O telephone box on the corner of Leicester Square and Wardour Street fishing about in his pockets for the necessary change to make the call he hoped would be his salvation.

Opening the heavy metal and glass door he selected the right coin, picked up the receiver and racking his brains came up with the number to Sarah's family phone number.

The telephone in Hampshire rang and rang until Sarah's father picked it up and sleepily, with not a little irritation said.

"Hello, who is it?"

"Hello," said Johnny awkwardly, "Can I speak to Sarah please?"

"Do you know what the time is?" Blustered the voice on the other end, "Who the devil is this?"

"Er… I'm sorry to be calling so late….. this is Johnny. I'm a friend of Sarah's. Can I speak to her please?"

"No you bloody well can't," said the ex army officer. The owner of the voice looked at the grandfather clock in the hallway in which the telephone stood.

"It's two o'clock in the morning and Sarah is asleep. Now bugger off."

And with that the phone in Johnny's hand went dead.

The desperate teenager erupted and smashed the receiver against the phone box window.

"FUCKER," he screamed in frustrated fury, drawing startled looks from a couple of passers by.

Muttering filthy oaths to himself he once again rooted around in his pockets for some more change.

Producing another coin, his last, he placed it in to the money slot and re-dialled the number.

Again the phone in the impressive country house rang for a long time and again the same voice answered and its owner wasn't best pleased.

"Look young man, I don't know what you're up to but if you don't stop this I will contact the police and."

Johnny interrupted the indignant flow at the other end of the phone, "Please, I must speak to Sarah" he pleaded desperately, "It's a matter of life and death."

Silence reigned in Hampshire while the old fart mulled things over in his tired mind.

After what seemed like an eternity the voice spoke.

"Wait a moment. I'll just get her"

Johnny breathed a huge sigh of relief and thanked the man who had already put the phone gently on to the telephone table and started up the wide oak staircase.

Johnny nervously nodded his head as he waited for his angel to pick up the phone.

"Hello?" said Sarah's sleepy voice quietly.

His heart flipped, he loved her voice.

"Hi Sarah, it's me. Johnny"

"Johnny?" replied Sarah groggily, "it's two o'clock. What do you want?"

He leant his forehead against the glass of the telephone box and drew pictures in the condensation his earlier outburst had produced.

Lost for words eventually he said weakly.

"Say something nice to me baby."

There was the briefest of pauses and then the phone went dead once more. And so did Johnny's soul.

Closing his eyes, he let the receiver slip from his trembling fingers and dangle lazily by his side.

Johnny felt like a drowning man and his life flashed before him once more. From his earliest unhappy memories of a troubled childhood, up to and including the last six glorious weeks where he had lived the fantasy lifestyle of his dreams.

Six fantastic weeks when he had attained his dreams of Style nirvana and lived the good life.

Until yesterday. Was it only yesterday?

Or the day before? He had lost track of the hours and days, everything was beginning to blur in to one.

So near he thought dejectedly.

So close to being Someone and having it all. The money, the clothes the records. The classy bird who was introducing him to a life of sophistication that a working class boy from a shitty backstreet in South London could never dare to dream of.

Johnny had had a taste of honey. He had got to the end of the rainbow but still couldn't dig up the pot of gold.

It was as if the gods had allowed him a bit of the world he yearned for and now out of pure sadism or spite or maybe even for a laugh they had said "times up!" Too much of a good thing my old son now fuck off to the shitty little world you come from and ripped it all out from underneath him.

What a bastard! he thought.

A hammering on the phone box made him jump out of his skin and bring him back to reality.

Looking around, fearing the worst, Johnny breathed a sigh of relief and a comforting feeling, when he saw the smiling, speeding, friendly face of Steady Eddie.

Pushing open the door he greeted his old friend with unconcealed pleasure.

"Hey Steady howzit going man?"

"Cool man cool," replied Eddie. "But you look like shit baby."

"I *feel* like shit," Johnny replied grinning at his friend's honesty and at his own dishevelled state. Cool was no longer on the menu and he was surprised how good it felt, as though a monkey had been lifted from his weary shoulders.

"I've been looking for you all over," said the Soho entrepreneur, looking over his shoulders, worry invading his young features.

"Well, now you've found me," answered Johnny flippantly, trying to disguise the feeling of desperation seeping through his veins.

"Some heavy dudes been looking for you," said Eddie, again casting concerned eyes all around, "First at The Scene, then at The Flamingo. All your usual haunts. People I been speaking to reckon it's the same cats who done Chucky."

"Yeah, I know," said Johnny quietly looking up at the mention of his dead pal's name.

Steady Eddie put his hand on his friends shoulder and asked. "Do you need anything Johnny? Money? Somewhere to stay?"

Johnny smiled, realising it was the first time he could remember Eddie using his name, rather than "man" or "baby" or some other groovy word.

"No thanks Steady Eddie," he replied. "I've got dough. Thanks anyway. I'm blowing this town. It's getting a bit on the warm side for my liking."

"Understatement of the fucking year man," said Eddie and the two friends laughed together on the Soho pavement for the last time.

"Well good luck baby," Eddie finally said stretching out his hand which Johnny looked at before grasping and shaking it warmly.

"Thanks, I'll look you up some day. That is if you're not too rich and famous for me."

Eddie smiled, "I've got plans man."

Johnny nodded and said, "I know man, I know."

The two friends stood in silence for a few moments before Steady Eddie turned and was gone, swallowed up by West End nightlifers.

Once more he was on his own and despite the warmth of the summer night felt a shiver run through his body as he worked out his next move.

Nothing left for him here. The net was closing in on him. He must get back to the Mini and leave.

CHAPTER 23

Saunders put on the jacket the girl had given him and checked left and right before stepping out of the doorway. Head down, hands thrust deep into his borrowed trouser pockets. With his jacket collar turned up to shield his face from recognition, he walked briskly down the street.

Soho was a small village and he was well aware that the jungle drums would soon signal the fugitive robbers' presence on the street.

It would not be beyond certain slimy individuals if they happened to catch sight of him to quickly run to inform the police or even Eddie Raven hoping to pick up a nice little reward for their information.

Even certain individuals who were on friendly terms, acquaintances rather than friends, with Frank Saunders wouldn't think twice about such treacherous behaviour if it benefited them. Such was the world Frank Saunders lived in.

The time was coming up to three o'clock and the streets of Soho were starting to get quieter. The theatre and restaurant crowd were all safely tucked up in their suburban beds. The night clubbers were happily pilled up and dancing away in the various clubs which would provide their musical fix until daybreak. No pass outs after 3 a.m. so once an entrance fee was handed over the payee tended to stay put until chucking out time.

A few taxi cabs chugged up and down looking for fares or heading home after a night of stitching up the tourists and the drunks.

A hooker tottering home on her six inch heels, despite being knackered from a night of selling her body to fat, sweaty businessman tried to entice Frank in to a "bit of fun."

Her invitation didn't even register in Frank's brain as he brushed past her and neither did her volley of verbal abuse questioning his sexual orientation.

A dustcart and a road sweeper tried to carry out the impossible task of cleaning the filth from the streets in the few hours when the night people were mostly gone and the start of another early morning business day in Soho.

Paper, cigarette butts and used condoms could be cleared up. Rubbish from the restaurants and pubs could be got rid of but it would take more than a broom and a bin to get rid of the real filth. The low life inhabitants of the back streets and darkened doorways. The cut throats, users and abusers.

Saunders felt the heavy revolver he still had from the robbery, which was now tucked into the waistband of his trousers covered by his buttoned up jacket. The gun only had two bullets left in it so he knew he couldn't afford to be wasteful. Frank Saunders rarely wasted anything, so he was grimly confident he would be able to carry out his bloody plan.

As the robber, hell bent on revenge, got closer to his target the streets became totally deserted. The only sound now was that of his footsteps echoing around the narrow back streets and the occasional sound of a rat scavenging through the yet to be collected rubbish behind one of the many restaurants that filled this part of London.

The click-clicking of his footsteps slowed as their owner became acutely aware that there was no other sound to drown them out. Keeping to the shadows even more Saunders senses were on high alert, tensed and ready for action.

Slowly and deliberately unbuttoning his jacket, Saunders slipped his hand inside and pulled out the heavy Smith and Wesson revolver with no suggestion of even the slightest tremor in his experienced hand.

Reaching the end of the street, the buildings protecting him ended and he felt a blast of cold air blowing off the river Thames. All was quiet as he observed the scene before him.

The famous London landmark that was Big Ben stood imperiously, stretching into the night, informing anyone awake at this ungodly hour that it was now ten past three.

Below the famous old time piece stood Westminster Bridge under which the Thames raced. Swirling and bubbling. A death sentence for anyone who entered her and many did. Accidentally and sometimes deliberately. Jumped or pushed. If they didn't drown the pollution would be sure to do them in.

Beside the bridge was a set of stone steps which led down to a jetty. Beside the opening to the steps, parked up illegally and arrogantly on the wide expanse of pavement was the huge black Cadillac owned by one Eddie Raven, looking evil, sitting there at rest bathed in the pale moonlight.

Saunders peered across to the car and confident there was no one in it, started to make his way cautiously across the road, scanning up and down the Embankment to see if there was anything that may threaten him.

Once across the road Saunders placed his hands on the stone parapet wall and peered carefully over.

There she was.

"THE SHOWBOAT."

Eddie Raven's pride and joy. The small waves the Thames always produced slapping gently against her sides.

Of all his business interests, the boat restaurant done up to look like a Mississippi paddle steamer was Eddie Ravens favourite.

Frank Saunders looked down at the boat and observed the two decked vessel for a moment. The upper deck contained a lounge area and the lower deck the restaurant, bar and dance floor.

Dinner and dance. Very popular.

The top deck was in complete darkness but the lower deck was bathed in a red light coming from the red tasselled lamp shades which sat on every table, giving the whole area a Faustian air.

The robber's heart was starting to pound as he felt himself within touching distance of his prey.

Squinting hard through the darkness Saunders could see a figure sitting grandly at one of the tables and although it was too far to distinguish the man's features he just knew it was Eddie Raven.

The phone call had worked. The girl had, on Franks instructions contacted the gang boss to inform him that she knew the whereabouts of a certain Frank Saunders and a certain large sum of money. Putting on her sexiest voice she told Raven that she wanted to meet him there at 3 a.m.

She would tell him where to find what he was looking for in exchange for £5000 and almost as an afterthought she told him to come alone as she was very nervous and would only deal with him.

The sound of Big Ben striking caused Frank to jump, breaking his concentration on the picture below.

The chiming of the bell did Saunders a massive favour. As he returned his gaze to the boat he saw the sudden glimmer of a match being struck at the far end of the vessel. The flame travelled in the dark the short distance to the end of a cigarette held in the mouth of one of Ravens bodyguards. A puff of smoke followed, further revealing the presence of someone not invited to this particular party.

Frank knew he was fucked if there was more than one guard on the boat, and he mentally crossed his fingers as he made his way down the moss covered stone steps which led to the jetty.

Eyes fixed like radars on the glow coming from the end of the cigarette, Frank reached the boat and keeping low, checked the scene inside.

He was right. There he was. Eddie Raven.

Cunt.

Sitting at a table at the far end of the restaurant with his back to the wall smoking a huge cigar. A silver ice bucket stood beside the table containing a bottle of the most expensive champagne and on the table sat two crystal glasses.

The sound of Frank Sinatra on the tape deck drifted out down the river.

'Fly me to the moon' thought Saunders who caught himself humming along. He loved this one.

Turning his attention back to the cigarette smoker, Frank stepped carefully onto the boats narrow gangway and made his way along the slippery deck to the front of the boat.

The silhouette of the man smoking in the darkness provided a large and inviting target but Saunders knew he couldn't use the gun as it would instantly alert his main target inside the boat.

Creeping towards the bodyguard Frank put his hand against the wall to the wheelhouse to steady himself as the wake from a passing dredger bobbed "The Showboat" gently up and down. As he stopped and leant against the wall for balance his hand came to rest against a fire bucket full of sand. Beside the shiny red bucket was the solution to his immediate problem. A beautiful red handled fire axe. Perfect.

This should do nicely, thought Frank tucking the gun inside his jacket and removing the axe from the wall and weighing it in his hand.

Saunders knew his movements from here would have to be quick and quiet. Any noise or struggle would alert Raven and his whole plan would go tits up.

The man standing with one foot perched on the deck rail had finished his cigarette and began to turn causing Frank to cover the last few yards with one giant leap. As he reached his unaware foe he brought down the axe from high above his head and smashed it with ferocious power straight into the mans unprotected skull. The shiny blade catching the moonlight with a flash before disappearing into the man's head in a mass of mangled bone, blood and brains.

The bodyguards head cracked like an egg as the axe buried itself deep inside showering Saunders in a sticky, gooey, mess.

The man's body collapsed to the deck, the axe still in the place Saunders had left it, blood on the handle causing it to slip from his grasp.

Breathing heavily from his efforts and with the adrenaline coursing through his body Frank Saunders bent over the stricken mess of a man at his feet and slipped his hands under his armpits. Struggling, he hoisted the lifeless rag doll up, until the man's stomach leant on the rail.

The blood splattered thief grasped hold of the fire axe and with a real effort pulled it out of the man's head. It might be needed later.

Saunders peered through the darkness at his victims face to see whose head he had just crushed.

Charlie Fletcher. Good. Frank had never liked him.

Satisfied with a job well done, Saunders grabbed Fletchers ankles and tipped the thug into the murky river making a soft splash as it hit the water.

Nothing to worry about.

Now, thought Frank turning to make his way to the main event of the evening, wiping copious amounts of blood and brains from his face and neck.

Time to sort out Eddie Raven.

Heading back to the restaurant section of the boat Frank glanced up at the illuminated clock face of Big Ben. Three thirty five. Time was running out as Frank removed the gun from his waistband.

He located the entrance to where Raven sat and winced as the flimsy door creaked angrily as if it was trying to alert its owner.

The sound of Sinatra got louder with his rendition of "Mack the Knife" oozing coolly out of the speakers. Saunders eyes settled on the man sitting at the table at the end of the room bathed in the glow of the red lights.

Saunders stood silently in the darkness watching his enemy. The sight of the man filled him with hate and his breathing became laboured. He knew he should just shoot the fucker and get the hell out of there but he needed the bastard to know who was sending him to meet his maker.

Frank Saunders took three paces forward bringing him into the red light, his arm extended, the pistol pointing directly at Ravens head.

"Hello Eddie," Frank said calmly.

The gangster looked up, a momentary flash of fear mixed with shock invaded his eyes but he kept his composure.

"Evening Frankie," he said looking at his blood splattered enemy and with a heavy dose of irony continued, "You're looking well."

Saunders had to admire his balls even though he hated the man.

"Popped in to say goodbye," said Frank keeping the mood convivial,

"Just wanted you to know I've got the dough from the blag. Every penny of it. I'm off abroad. Early retirement. Know what I mean?"

Eddie Raven nodded slowly in mock approval.

Saunders had the gang bosses undivided attention. Training a gun on someone's head normally manages to do the trick.

"But before I go, I just came down here to kill you."

Very matter of fact. Very business like.

Raven didn't bat an eyelid and referring to the phone call he had received to set him up, said.

"Who's the bird?"

"Never mind who the bird is, but she'll be coming with me to help spend all that lovely dough."

"Yea, I heard about the robbery on the radio. Got a bit messy eh?" continued Raven.

"Apparently Old Bill got a bit trigger happy. Killed all your boys didn't they?"

Saunders wiped his hand across his mouth feeling the bristles of a few days beard growth scrape across his palm.

"That's right. I was lucky though......."

Frank stopped in mid sentence.

"How did you know about the Old Bill killing 'em? No specific information has been given out. The authorities ain't gonna broadcast that sort of information. Killing men in cold blood."

Raven nodded in agreement.

"Yea Frank. Especially as they had given themselves up and had their hands in the air."

This last sentence was said with a smirk creeping across his face.

Franks brain was trying to work out what was being said to him but with the pain he was feeling from his bullet wound and the fatigue starting to seep through his body he knew something was wrong but he couldn't put his finger on just what.

Eddie Raven helped him out.

"Frankie, Frankie," he said slowly shaking his head. Smiling.

"You don't get it do ya? It weren't Old Bill. It was my firm. Dressed up like the filth.

"The whole thing was a set up. You were getting too big, Frank. You and your boys. Taking the piss. Not paying me my share of your blags. Steps had to be taken. You were getting too flash. Rubbing my nose in it."

Frank was trying to comprehend what was being said to him as Eddie Raven continued, clearly enjoying himself despite the gun pointing at him.

"And moving in on my drugs operation was the last straw. So you had to go."

Franks head was swirling. Ravens words were becoming a blur, something about drugs was said as Saunders started to sway from side to side, blinking repeatedly and shaking his head in an effort to clear it.

Raven continued his taunting.

"I knew the only way to get rid of the lot of you would be in one fell swoop. If I did ya one at a time you'd be alerted so the only way was getting you all together at the same time and as the only time that happens is when you're on a job I set one up. With the added bonus of making a tidy little sum at the end of it."

Eddie Raven stopped and there was silence. Until Raven broke it.

"The only problem was you got away."

Frank's mind was racing. No it can't be true. Outfoxed by this cunt.

"You see Frank," said Raven,

"The idea was for you to carry out the job. My boys dressed up as plod would intercept you. Kill you all and make off with the dough. Unfortunately you were a bit tasty as usual and you had it away on your toes and most of my boys ended up getting nicked, the doughnuts"

There was another pause in the story before Raven finished off.

"I had you lot followed around all week. Oh, not by my idiots. I used ex army special forces guys. I know how careful you are. I knew none of your team would let anything slip regarding the plan for the raid so they just followed you lot about and we just moved in at the right time. Simple."

Franks outstretched gun hand trembled. His tired brain felt like it was going to explode as it tried to make sense of the information he was being given.

As he tried to digest Raven's words, the shame of doubting his comrades, even though it was only fleetingly, engulfed him and his concentration level hit the floor.

With Frank's thoughts momentarily elsewhere, there was a blur of movement from beneath Eddie Ravens table and his hand leapt up brandishing a gun of his own. A flash of light, an explosion and Frank was violently and shockingly flung back against the wall, a searing pain ripped through his shoulder. The gun he was holding flew out of his grasp and clattered impotently to the floor and bounced under a table. The axe arced through the air as the force of the bullet entering his body threw his arms up.

The sound of the gun firing in such a confined area was deafening and the following silence was absolute.

A smell of cordite filled the air as the revolver in Eddie Ravens hand omitted a wisp of smoke rising slowly to the low ceiling.

Sinatra sang "Moon River."

Frank lay on the floor and groaned in pain but also in frustration. Through the mist descending over his eyes he could just about make out

Eddie Raven standing and pushing the table in front of him noisily to one side. The champagne glasses smashed onto the dance floor.

"D'ya think you could outwit me Frank?" A voice was saying somewhere in the distance.

"I mean, you're good, but not that good. I've been on top for a long time and I ain't about to let people start taking liberties."

Frank squirmed on the floor, the blood from the bullet hole in his shoulder mixing with the blood of his axe victim.

"Who the fuck d'ya think you are?" said the gang boss who had made his way across the dance floor and was now towering over the stricken thief.

"You should have stuck to blags my son," sneered Raven.

"But you had to be clever didn't ya? Not giving me a little sweetener from your action was bad enough but trying to move in on my pill racket. Trying to mug me up!"

Again the reference to drugs.

"What you fucking talking about?" said Frank, the initial shock and pain subsiding ever so slightly.

"Don't take me for a fucking idiot Frank. I know about your mate in the factory. I know about you getting those young kids to knock 'em out in my clubs.

"IN MY FUCKING CLUBS YOU CHEEKY CUNT."

Raven knelt down at Frank's side.

"Well, thanks to you, all those kids are dead now. Apart from one and he shouldn't be too hard to find."

Placing the revolver against Frank's forehead and easing back the hammer he spoke again.

"Now, where's my fucking money? And who's the bird helping you?"

"Go fuck yourself," spat Saunders clasping his shoulder.

"Charming," replied Raven with the confident air of a man in control of the situation.

Franks screams filled the room as the man leaning over him knocked the hand covering his wound to one side and plunged his forefinger into the gaping wound pushing the metal bullet further inside.

The pain was incredible. Sheering and shooting like electricity through his whole body as Raven twisted and turned his finger in the bloody hole.

Frank involuntarily flung his head from side to side arching his back as the psychotic's finger went even deeper.

"Where's my money Frank?" persisted Raven.

Saunders nearly passed out, the pain was so intense. Sweat poured out of every part of his body as Raven moved his finger about inside him.

The wound in his shoulder slurped noisily as the finger was finally removed. Franks head rested limply on his shoulder, his chest heaving up and down. Adrenaline ran through his body trying to act like a natural pain killer but failed miserably.

Frank finally opened his eyes which had been slammed shut trying to block out the pain of his ordeal.

Once the focus returned, he realised he was looking at the blood covered axe which had dropped from his hand when the bullet slammed into him and bounced under a chair close to him. Just out of reach.

Eddie Raven had walked behind the bar confident that his enemy was in no fit state to mount a counter attack, and poured himself a large whisky from the optics.

"Cheers," he said to Frank and raised the glass in piss taking salute before emptying the contents.

From a wooden box on the bar Raven produced a huge cigar. Cuban. The best.

Rolling the cigar in his fingers he smelt the aroma and nodded with approval.

Snipping the end with his solid silver cutter he put it into his mouth and started the lighting process.

Several sucks, a burst of flame and Raven inhaled. Leaning his head back before blowing the expensive smoke up to the low ceiling, thoroughly enjoying himself.

Frank took this break in proceedings to try to edge closer to the hidden axe.

Feigning a pain spasm, although he didn't have to feign too hard, he rolled over onto his side clasping his shoulder and adopted the foetal position. In doing so he covered the distance required to be just an arms length away from his only chance of survival.

"Frank," said the cigar smoking gangster as he walked nonchalantly back to Saunders.

"You in pain son?" he asked, not giving a fuck as he knelt down beside Frank once again and rolled him on to his back.

Saunders groaned, both in pain and frustration as he was rolled out of reach of the axe before he could retrieve it.

"It's gonna get a lot worse if you don't tell me where my money is," continued Raven ominously.

Frank shook his head defiantly which was the signal for Eddie Raven to clench his teeth and pin Frank's shoulder to the floor with his left hand.

With his right he plunged the red hot tip of the cigar straight into the open bullet wound.

Pain like he had never experienced before hit Saunders like a runaway train.

Explosions went off in his head and a million volts of pain shot through his body as the cigar burnt the flesh under Frank's skin.

The smell was nauseating and the crackling and popping sound his burning flesh made was sickening.

Franks head thrashed from side to side like a shark on the end of a hook. His body automatically tried to heave himself up but the weight of Eddie Ravens knee stuck on his chest kept him from moving.

The blood in Franks wound doused the cigar and Raven eventually removed it with a disappointed air, casting it to one side.

Raven quickly lit another and repeated the torture, interrogating his victim once more.

The incredible pain acted like a truth serum and try as he might he was unable give Raven a moody girls name and address. The only name popping into his head was her real one and to his utter shame he gave the girl up.

"Well, well Frankie," responded the gangster, clearly amused at the name he had been given, a name he recognised.

'You dirty old git."

With all the pain, frustration and shame in his mind and driven by hate and a rush of adrenaline the injured robber seized his chance.

With Eddie Raven momentarily relaxed, Frank rolled suddenly onto his side flinging his tormentor backwards onto the floor and in the same movement flung out his arm and grabbed the handle of the axe.

With one huge, pain filled effort, using every fibre in his body he forced himself up on to his knees and with a desperate swing brought the axe high above his head and down towards the shocked gangsters head.

A combination of Frank's battered body affecting his timing and Eddie Ravens survival instinct caused him to miss the gangsters head by a fraction. Instead of the axe landing in his head it smashed its way through his collar bone.

The scream was heard on the other side of the river as Raven grabbed his mangled bone which now stuck out through his flesh.

"AAAAAARGH......... YOU CUUUUNT!" screamed Raven as he writhed on the floor like a hyper-active Anaconda.

Frank was unable to move. He just knelt there, breathing heavily, the axe still in his hand. Watching his enemy, listening to his animal screams in a trance like state.

Blood poured from Ravens body and strange gargling noises came from the back of his throat.

The light from the full moon caught the whiteness of the two pieces of broken bone sticking through his flesh, illuminating them in the darkness of the room.

Frank knew the job wasn't finished. A wounded animal is even more dangerous and he began to summon up the strength to deliver the final fatal blow.

The axe felt like a ton weight as Frank, still on his knees beside Raven straightened himself and held it above his head with both hands.

Frank Saunders had clearly underestimated the London gangsters desire to survive and a little thing like a shattered collar bone wasn't about to make him throw in the towel.

As Saunders brought down the axe towards Ravens face his intended victim snatched up a champagne flute which had fallen to the floor and drove the glass into his face, slicing open Saunders cheek as he twisted it in.

Once more the axe fell from Franks grasp as he tumbled backwards. This power struggle was far from over.

Both battered and bleeding, the two powerful men fought desperately, each knowing there could only be one winner and that there would be no consolation prize for the loser.

Tables were turned over, bottles and glasses were smashed. Teeth and more blood was spilt as the two men punched, kicked, bit and gouged until eventually one man stood victorious over the other. The loser lay dead with a broken champagne bottle stuck in his throat. The victor breathing heavily, in immense pain but still alive. Just.

Certain his foe was vanquished he slowly turned and staggered out of the door and onto the slippery gangway.

With his chest crackling with every intake of breath he placed both hands on the guard rail and gulped in the night air.

The cool breeze blew across the water and caressed his face. The fresh air seemed to have a slightly rejuvenating effect upon him and despite the agony he felt, his inner determination was bolstered and he forced himself on.

Across the gangplank and up the stone steps to the embankment he staggered, not bothering or unconscious of the need to check that the coast was clear. Each step was murder and as he finally reached the Cadillac he clambered across the bench seat and sat behind the big steering wheel.

The key was, as usual left in the ignition. Who would dare nick Eddie Ravens car? The man smiled grimly.

The yank motor fired up, first gear was engaged and the big car bumped down the kerb and was away.

Each gear change slammed a shock wave through his fast failing body but with eyes fixed on the road ahead like a radar he drove steadily to his objective.

The money.

CHAPTER 24

Johnny quickly walked back to the car. Climbing in to the red Mini Cooper he started the engine, grasped the steering wheel and said quietly to himself,

"I'm on my way."

What was the point in hanging around? The longer he delayed his escape, the more chance there was of getting grabbed. He had been stupid to return to Soho. What had he been thinking of?

Returning to the heart of Eddie Ravens criminal empire just to get out on the floor one last time.

Sarah's "borrowed" car pulled away and threaded through the backstreets that he knew like the back of his young hand, keeping his head down and hunching his shoulders to avoid recognition.

The busy West End traffic had all but disappeared and Johnny quickly found himself heading down Regent Street towards the traffic lights at Piccadilly Circus.

Numbness had descended over him like an anaesthetic as he pulled up at the red traffic light. The stop signal made up a fraction of the kaleidoscope of neon brightness which illuminated the area, lighting the night time darkness that surrounded it.

Johnny looked up at the statue of Eros, the god of love. The flashing lights projecting onto the stone statues face made it look like it was winking at him causing him to smile at the irony of it.

His dreamlike state was shattered as something passed across his line of vision. Johnny couldn't believe his eyes and he had to rub them and blink a couple of times. Was it the light playing tricks on him again or had all the drugs he had taken finally fucked his mind?

Or a combination of the two?

Heading slowly across the Circus and up Shaftesbury Avenue was a big black American Cadillac.

The red signal changed to green and instead of heading straight on down Haymarket something inside him made him turn the wheel left into Shaftesbury Avenue.

Driving slowly he kept his distance behind the huge tail fins of the car he had recognised, his curiosity having got the better of his need to escape.

The car was the same one that he had seen outside his bed-sit when he had got his unwelcome guests. There couldn't be another one about like that. American cars in London were as rare as rocking horse shit.

Up ahead the Cadillac turned left with Johnny copying the movement moments later.

Turning into the street he jammed on the brakes as he saw the car he was following had pulled up a hundred yards or so, on the right.

He turned off the engine, killed the lights and watched.

As the driver of the car stumbled out and shuffled his way to a street door, the teenager peered through the windscreen at the dishevelled figure.

"Bastard," he hissed through gritted teeth. "Eddie Raven."

The figures clothing seemed to be ripped, he was covered in blood and was holding his shoulder as he quickly disappeared inside the building.

A moment later there was a scream from inside the first floor flat where a solitary light shone brightly, then a lot of banging about followed by a deathly silence.

A couple of minutes later and the man appeared again. This time he was carrying two heavy looking suitcases.

Studying the shuffling figure opening up the car boot and uncomfortably heaving the cases in, Johnny could see the man was in a hell of a lot of pain.

Once more the man entered the building.

Johnny's breathing became laboured, the vein in the side of his head starting to throb painfully again.

Shoving his hand into the bag on the seat beside him he grabbed another load of uppers and threw them into his mouth. How many was that?

Fuck knows.

A lot. That was for sure. That's the trouble with speed. You take some and then a while later you forgot how much you had taken, so you take some more. And then some more. That's how some people he knew had ended up overdosing. They had simply forgotten what their intake had been.

Clenching his teeth, Johnny grabbed the steering wheel so hard his knuckles turned white almost bending it in half.

The man inside the building had destroyed his life, had taken everything away from him.

With his temperature beginning to rise and sweat popping out all along his forehead, his body stiffened with rage, his stomach gripped by an icy fist.

The shuffling figure emerged again from the building and made his way to the back of the car carrying another case.

The thermostat in Johnny's head exploded and without thinking turned on the ignition, crunched the car noisily into first gear and with tyres screeching and leaving a trail of burnt rubber on the road tore off up the street.

The man turned his head as he heard the noise of the Mini roaring up the street.

"What the fuck?" he said as the car tore towards him.

The injured man tried to run but he reacted too late and his battered body was too slow.

The Mini Cooper covered the distance to the man in rapid time and slammed into him with a sickening crunch of breaking bones, headlights and metal.

The man's body was thrown across the back of the Cadillac and rolled limply out on to the road.

Steam rose from the Minis busted radiator as it came to an abrupt halt buried in the back of the Cadillac flinging its driver forward causing his head to come into contact with the steering wheel.

Johnny climbed from the car holding his damaged head and made his way unsteadily to the crumpled body laying in the middle of the road.

The figure on the street groaned with the added pain of a broken leg and shattered ankle to accompany the various wounds and injuries already inflicted upon him.

Johnny stood over the fallen criminal breathing heavily.

"That's for Chucky you cunt," he spat victoriously.

The man turned slowly and looked up.

"Who the fuck are you?" he moaned.

"I'm the one you've been looking for," replied the boy angrily, delivering a hateful kick to the man's ribs.

"JOHNNY!" screamed a girl's voice. A voice he recognised.

Looking up from the man at his feet he saw Misty running towards him.

Looking all around, he suddenly saw where he was. In the state he was in he hadn't realised he was standing outside Misty's place.

The girl grabbed his arm and pulled him away from the groaning man.

"What do you think you are doing?" she demanded.

Pointing to the mess of a man on the floor, Johnny replied.

"This… This bastard, this piece of shit is the one who killed Chucky. And he has been trying to get me as well."

"What?" she replied incredulously.

"Eddie fucking Raven," said Johnny grabbing her by the shoulders and leaning towards her lovely face.

"He found out that me and Chucky were selling pills and he killed Chucky and a couple of other lads and he was gonna kill me next."

The body on the floor groaned as Misty shook her head slowly.

"That isn't Eddie Raven you idiot," she said in her heavy accent.

"This is Frank Saunders," she continued. "He's a friend of mine."

Misty knelt down beside Frank in an effort to comfort him.

Johnny scratched his head and looked around at the Cadillac.

"But the car? That's his car. And he looks like Eddie Raven."

"Well he's fucking well not," shouted Misty.

The boy was really confused. More confused than he had ever been in his young, confusing life.

"Well, what you doing with him then? Why is he in such a state?" he asked lamely.

Misty stood and faced him, her hands on her hips.

"Well apart from you running him over, he's in trouble and I was helping him get away."

Johnny bowed his head in embarrassment like a naughty schoolboy as the young girl continued,

"Eddie Raven was trying to kill him. Now it looks as though you have done the job for him."

"Oh shit," he said as he knelt down beside Saunders who was really struggling with the pain which was getting worse.

"Sorry mate," said Johnny eventually, unable to think of anything more helpful to say.

Saunders opened his bloodshot eyes.

"That's alright mate," he replied with as much sarcasm as he could manage.

"I thought you were a bloke called Eddie Raven.

"You see, he killed some of my friends and he was after me. I saw you in this car and thought……"

Johnny's voice tailed off. The bloke didn't look that interested.

Saunders beckoned him to come closer. An act he was a bit reluctant to do seeing as he had just knocked him flying with his car and might get a clump. But seeing the state he was in and realising he wouldn't be able to clump the skin of a rice pudding he did as he was instructed.

"Eddie Raven is dead," croaked Saunders.

"What?"

"Raven is dead. I done him tonight."

Johnny's head dropped to his chest and prickles of tears moistened his eyes. Tears of relief.

Breathing a huge sigh he sat down in the road next to Saunders and pulled his knees up to his chest, wrapping his arms around them as he shook uncontrollably.

Wiping the salty water from his eyes and looking slightly embarrassed to have displayed such weakness in front of Misty, he eventually said.

"We'd better get you an ambulance mate."

"That would be handy," murmured Saunders whose body may have been broken but his sarcastic wit was still intact.

Johnny looked up at hearing Misty hissing his name and saw her beckoning him to join her at the back of Eddie Ravens Cadillac.

Standing up, he joined her at the boot, the lid of which had sprung open upon impact from the Mini.

"Look," she said flipping open one of the cases.

Johnny peered inside.

"Blimey," he said with admirable understatement.

"This night just gets weirder and weirder."

"There's nearly a hundred thousand pounds in these cases," said the husky voiced temptress, looking directly at her young friends face, trying to gauge his reaction.

"Blimey," Johnny repeated.

Misty's business brain was already thinking ahead.

"Look," she said conspiratorially and a little unsympathetically.

"Franks fucked. He needs medical help. He'll die if he doesn't get it and get it quick. This money is from a robbery he pulled off but there is no way he'll be able to get away and use it."

Johnny was staring at the cash but still taking in the implications of what Saunders had told him.

Eddie Raven was dead. Everything would be okay. There was no need to go on the run. For a moment his hopes rose but then he caught sight of his reflection in the car window and reality kicked in.

What was there left for him in London? His mates were dead. The whole scene had turned against him and Sarah didn't want to know. And beside that he had just put the boot into the ribs of a dodgy looking geezer who he had run over with a stolen car.

Things were not looking that much better.

"So what do you say?"

Misty grabbing him by the arm as she asked the question snapped him out of his contemplation.

"Eh?" responded Johnny with a blank look on his face.

Misty sighed with exasperation.

"We call an ambulance for Frank then you and me take the money and go away together."

"Are you serious?"

"Look Johnny," she said holding his face in her soft hands.

"As soon we call an ambulance the Police will be informed. They will know that Frank has not just had an accident."

"They might."

Misty raised her eyes to the heavens.

"Oh right, they will just think he is the unluckiest man alive. Not only has he been run over but the person jumped out of the car, shot him, stuck a glass in his face then kicked him in the ribs for good measure."

Johnny studied the floor trying to hide the spread of red embarrassment creeping across his face.

"Listen to me Johnny," said Misty trying to convince him she made sense.

"Frank has arranged to get out of the country by boat. There is this guy he knows called Little Barry who has a boat moored down at Ramsgate harbour.

"Instead of me and Frank meeting him, me and you can go there. Give him some cash and he'll get us out of the country."

Johnny thought for a moment before replying.

"What if he won't take you and me? What if he would only take you and Frank?"

"According to Frankie if he is given enough money he would take the Queen out of the country."

Johnny stood there looking at Misty's earnest face, biting on his bottom lip as he mulled it over.

Fucking hell, he thought, she really is beautiful.

"Johnny," Misty said again. "It's either that or Frank gets arrested, they take all the money and probably arrest you and me as well."

Johnny's deliberations were interrupted by a loud groan from Saunders who was fading fast.

"You're on," he decided as his trademark, bird pulling smile spread across his handsome face for the first time in ages.

Misty jumped into the air, clapped her hands and gave a whoop of joy before running over to bend down beside Frank to whisper soothingly to him that they were getting help. She told him that an ambulance would soon be on its way but omitted to tell him they were fucking off with all his money.

Returning to Johnny, she took control of the situation.

"Okay baby," she said. "You grab the cases and I'll go inside and phone for help."

Giving him a big kiss on the lips, she turned and ran back inside her building as Johnny manhandled the cases out of the Cadillac's boot.

Once inside, she closed the street door and leant back against it breathing deeply with excitement.

She had no intention of phoning an ambulance. She knew what Frank Saunders was capable of and if by some miracle he did pull through and live he would make it his life's mission to find them and exact his revenge.

Allowing enough time to convince Johnny and Frank that the phone call had been made, she swung open the door once more and ran out onto the street.

Misty ran to Saunders and knelt beside him.

"An ambulance is on its way Frankie darling," she whispered. "Hold on."

Misty didn't know if Frank had understood or even heard her as she stood and turned to face Johnny and grabbed one of the cases.

Grabbing him by the arm she hurried him down the street, casting an anxious look behind her at the still figure of Frank Saunders lying on the ground.

The two youngsters exited the road at the Shafesbury Avenue end and looked up and down.

The two of them heard the chug of the diesel engine before the black taxi came into view around the bend. When it did they saw the orange "For Hire" sign blaze brightly as if it said "To the Rescue."

Johnny dropped the cases and raised his arm to signal the taxi to stop.

Inside the cab the driver, on his way home after a long night cursed himself for forgetting to turn off the light and was about to pretend he hadn't seen the young man's signal.

However, Johnny was wise to the habits of London taxi drivers and simply jumped into the middle of the road and put both his arms up to signal to the driver his services were required.

"Bloody hell mate," the driver said as his prospective passenger leant in to the open window.

"I could have killed you."

"Join the queue pal," the boy said with a grin as he opened the rear door and ushered Misty inside before slinging the cases in after her.

Resigning himself to the fact that he had one more fare for the evening the cabbie sighed, turned off his light and said.

"Where to guv?"

"Ramsgate please mate," replied Johnny with the casual air of someone asking to be taken to Buckingham Palace, ten minutes away.

"RAMSGATE?" exploded the cabbie who looked as though he would do a shit.

"That'll cost you a bloody fortune mate!"

Johnny leant into the back of the cab, grabbed a handful of cash from a case and held it up to the man's face and grinned.

"I've *got* a bloody fortune mate."

This seemed to satisfy the driver and caused Misty to burst out laughing.

Clambering into the cab, he shut the door and slumped back into his seat.

The driver pulled slowly away as Misty snuggled into Johnny's chest, his arm draped over her shoulder.

The Soho Face gazed out of the window staring into space.

Well, he thought, with the West End hurrying past, that was close, as he contemplated the previous forty eight hours.

He smiled as a scooter glided past in the opposite direction.

"I thought I was a gonna there for a while," he said quietly to himself.

The cab lurched lazily around a bend forcing Misty up even closer to him.

Well, he thought as Sarah popped into his head, I've lost one girl, but I seem to have found myself another and I've got myself more dough than I ever dreamed of, as he looked down at the cases.

The taxi chugged its way past Big Ben and across Westminster Bridge as the sun started to rise down the other end of The Thames coming up behind St Paul's Cathedral.

The taxi crossed the river, leaving his past well and truly behind.

Johnny was definitely moving on. Whether he was Moving On Up, only time would tell.

THE END.

SOME OF THE AUTHORS FAVE 45'S

Barbara Lynn	'Until Then I'll Suffer'
Barbara Lynn	'You'll Lose A Good Thing'
Barbara Lynn	'This Is The Thanks I Get'
Barbara Lewis	'Hello Stranger'
Barbara Lewis	'I Remember The Feeling'
Bettye Swann	'Make Me Yours'
Frank Wilson	'Do I Love You'
Martha Reeves	'My Baby Loves Me'
Martha Reeves	'Heatwave'
Martha Reeves	'Dancing In The Street'
Jack Montgomery	'Dearly Beloved'
Brenda Holloway	'Every Little Bit Hurts'
Brenda Holloway	'When I'm Gone'
Jimmy McGriff	'All About My Girl'
David and Rubin	'I Love Her So Much It Hurts Me'
Deon Jackson	'Ooh Baby'
The Yum Yums	'Gonna Be a Big Thing'
Bobby Kline	'Say Something Nice To Me'
Darrell Banks	'Open the door to your heart'
Fascinations	'Girls are out to get you'
Jimmy Radcliffe	'Long after the night is all over'
Curtis Mayfield	'Move on up'
Jackie Wilson	'Sweetest feeling'
Gene Chandler	'Nothing can stop me'
The Invitations	'What's wrong with me baby'
Mary Wells	'You beat me to the punch'
Mary Wells	'What's easy for two is hard for one'
Otis Redding	'Try a little tenderness'
The Temptations	'Girl(Why you wanna make me blue)'
Etta James	'The wallflower(roll with me Henry)'
Tommy Ridgley	'Jam up twist'
Booker T and the M.Gs	'Green onions'
Smokey Robinson	'Ooo baby baby'
Moody and the Deltas	"Everybody come clap your hands"
Willie Tee	"My friend John"
And many, many more.	

About the Author

Born in London in 1962, Nick has always been fascinated by the 60's. This fascination led to him becoming something of a Face on the second wave of the Mod scene of the late 70's, early 80's. Nick has performed at the National Theatre and was lead singer and songwriter in London band "Moocher." Nick is a qualified football coach and has lived in America and Tenerife and travelled extensively around South America. Twice married, Nick has two daughters, Charlotte and Holly, from his first marriage and a step son, Shaid, with his second wife, Rebecca. Visits to Cuba, and to his house in Turkey, are how he likes to spend his time when not renovating old properties.

Lightning Source UK Ltd.
Milton Keynes UK
UKOW050632220812

197892UK00001B/133/A